The Beauty an

Certain the "smart" Steffington twin is the person who can help her recover her late husband's nearly priceless stolen Chaucer manuscript, Catherine Bexley tearfully persuades the scholar to assist her. A deal is struck. She's particularly pleased that the Doctor of Letters is not interested in seducing her because she's finished with men (owing to her late husband's multitude of unfortunate alliances with. . .doxies). Regaining the manuscript and its subsequent sale will give her independence to ensure she never has to marry again.

Once he learns the poor, delicate widow is in danger of losing her heavily mortgaged home if they cannot find the valuable hologram, Dr. Melvin Steffington vows to do everything in his power to restore the rare Canterbury Tales to her. It's obvious the pretty little thing needs a man to help her. Not normally the twin to take note of pretty little things, Melvin can't help but to observe that Mrs. Bexley's physical appearance is much like the beauties so admired by his twin brother.

He hadn't counted on the fact he would have to pose as her husband as they race against the banker's ticking clock. He hadn't counted on the mysterious thief attempting to kill him. Most of all, he hadn't counted on how close he would become to the lovely widow or how the kissing of said widow would become the most pleasant experience in his entire seven and twenty years...

My Lord Wicked
Winner, International Digital Award for Best Historical Novel of 2011.

With His Lady's Assistance (Regent Mysteries, Book 1)
"A delightful Regency romance with a clever and personable heroine matched with a humble, but intelligent hero. The mystery is nicely done, the romance is enchanting and the secondary characters are enjoyable." – *RT Book Reviews*

Finalist for International Digital Award for Best Historical Novel of 2011.

A Duke Deceived
"A Duke Deceived is a gem. If you're a Georgette Heyer fan, if you enjoy the Regency period, if you like a genuinely sensuous love story, pick up this first novel by Cheryl Bolen." – *Happily Ever After*

One Golden Ring
"*One Golden Ring*...has got to be the most PERFECT Regency Romance I've read this year." – *Huntress Reviews*

Holt Medallion winner for Best Historical, 2006

The Counterfeit Countess
Daphne du Maurier award finalist for Best Historical Mystery

"This story is full of romance and suspense. . . No one can resist a novel written by Cheryl Bolen. Her writing talents charm all readers. Highly recommended reading! 5 stars!" – *Huntress Reviews*

"Bolen pens a sparkling tale, and readers will adore her feisty heroine, the arrogant, honorable Warwick and a wonderful cast of supporting characters." – *RT Book Reviews*

Also by Cheryl Bolen

Regency Romance

The Brides of Bath Series:
The Bride Wore Blue
With His Ring
The Bride's Secret
To Take This Lord
The Regent Mysteries Series:
With His Lady's Assistance *(*Book 1*)*
*A Most Discreet Inquiry (*Book 2*)*
The Theft Before Christmas (Book 3)
The Earl's Bargain
My Lord Wicked
A Lady by Chance
His Lordship's Vow
A Duke Deceived
One Golden Ring
Counterfeit Countess

Novellas:
Lady Sophia's Rescue
Christmas Brides (3 Regency Novellas)

Romantic Suspense

Texas Heroines in Peril Series:
Protecting Britannia
Capitol Offense
A Cry in the Night
Murder at Veranda House
Falling for Frederick

American Historical Romance

A Summer to Remember (3 American Historical Romances)

World War II Romance

It Had to be You

Inspirational Regency Romance

Marriage of Inconvenience

Love in the

Library

(The Brides of Bath)

Cheryl Bolen

$\mathcal{C}$hapter 1

Catherine Bexley had been removed from Society—and these sweltering Upper Assembly Rooms—for too long. Her good manners had eroded most deplorably, but she simply could not force herself to listen to Maxwell Longford's incessant prattle when other, more interesting topics were being discussed so close at hand.

She was far more interested in Felicity Moreland's conversation. (Though Catherine was quite certain anyone else's words would be more interesting than Mr. Longford's yawn-worthy accounts of his brother's betrothed—a sixth cousin, twice removed, to a viscount.)

While nodding at and faintly smiling at Mr. Longford as if she had actually been listening to him, Catherine inched across the settee that faced the dancers in order to be closer to Felicity. Now less than a foot separated the two ladies—the same distance that now separated Catherine from the stricken-looking Mr. Longford. It was a gap the determined man soon closed—without the least lapse in his monologue.

Felicity was telling her companion about one of the Steffington twins. "Melvin is nothing like his rakish brother," Felicity had said. "He's quite the bookish one. Can you credit it? One of my brother's friends actually taking a doctorate at

Oxford in classical literature? There's nothing Mr. Steffington doesn't know about old books and manuscripts."

At the mention of old books, Catherine's interest spiked.

"That's why I brought up this topic," Felicity continued, lifting her gaze toward the crush of couples dancing in front of them while continuing to speak to the matron beside her. "He's seeking a position at a private library, and I immediately thought of your brother's."

"Oh, dear me." Felicity's rotund companion twisted at the string of huge pearls which dangled from her flabby neck. "Wharton's already got the most able man you can imagine running the library at Havenworth." The older woman shook her head sadly. "Such a pity *that* Steffington twin shall have to *earn* his living." She could not have sounded more sympathetic were the unfortunate twin lying upon his deathbed. "And to think, the one who shared the womb with him is a baronet!"

The beautiful Felicity offered her companion a devilish smile. "You must know, Lady Ann, that I find much to admire in men who make their own way in life."

Lady Ann's hand flew to her mouth, and crimson rose to her cheeks. "I had quite forgotten your dear husband was a nabob."

Catherine herself had difficulty remembering Thomas Moreland's humble origins. Not that she gave a whit about maintaining the separation of classes. She'd read too much Thomas Paine. (So much, in fact, that her late husband had thrown out her copy of *Common Sense* when Catherine had suggested their footman be permitted to vote, and her *Rights of Man* was pitched into the fire when Mr. Bexley learned she had sat down to tea with their cook.)

Soon the two other women began remarking on the young beauties in Bath this Season, and Catherine's interest wilted.

"I say, Mrs. Bexley," Catherine's male companion droned on as she fanned herself, "I know you don't fancy standing up with men so soon after throwing off your widow's weeds, but surely you don't find a daytime ride in Sydney Gardens too frivolous."

This was the first time Catherine had actually listened to the poor bore since taking her seat on the scarlet damask settee that fringed the ballroom. Now she availed herself of the opportunity to peer at the man. He was possessed of an aquiline nose and strong chin and a very fine face that was framed with fashionably styled hair the color of bark. His starchy cravat was expertly tied in the waterfall fashion. There was nothing in his appearance that did not please. Unless he was standing. His height was considerably shorter than the average man.

"I don't think riding is at all frivolous, Mr. Longford. I know ever so many serious-minded persons who do so daily."

"Then it will be my pleasure to collect you tomorrow afternoon." His watery blue eyes flashed, and his brows lifted cockily. "Now that you have so singularly honored me."

She was rather relieved that her rude disinterest had gone unnoticed by Mr. Longford. What a fine actress she must be. (Or did he believe his words so fascinating that everyone to whom he spoke listened rapturously?)

The man actually felt himself honored! Now if

he would just leave her. She was most anxious to question Felicity about the scholarly twin. Perhaps if she were overtly rude to the man beside her, he would take his leave.

It did not come to that. Mr. Longford soon caught a glimpse of his brother—no doubt standing up with the sixth cousin, twice removed, of the much-respected Viscount Someone Important—and asked permission to take his leave. "I must make myself agreeable to Miss Turner-Fortenbury, who you will remember is the cousin of Lord Finchton."

"Sixth cousin, is she not?" Catherine said, offering him a coy smile.

"Indeed she is. It will be just one more connection between my family and the nobility— once she weds my brother."

As he walked around the perimeter of the ballroom, his brows perfectly level with most of the lady's bosoms, it occurred to Catherine that one of the reasons Mr. Longford persisted in sitting beside her could be that he was pleased to find a lady who did not dance. It must be embarrassing when a man's dance partners all exceeded him in height.

Another of her attractions to him, though, could be her connection to the Earl of Mountback. That sort of thing seemed to hold great appeal for Mr. Longford.

Flicking her hand-painted fan against the chamber's stuffy air, Catherine immediately faced her old friend, the fair and lovely Felicity. "Pray, my lady, can you tell which Steffington twin is which?"

The lady shook her head. "Blanks is the only one who's ever been able to tell them apart, though I do seem to recall that Glee indicated she thought she was growing proficient at how to detect which was which—or who was who."

"I've never been able to understand how one does tell one identical twin from the other," Catherine said.

As Catherine spoke, Felicity's older companion stood. Light from the five massive chandeliers which trailed along the ballroom ceiling far above illuminated her face as her glance fanned over the assembled dancers. "I seem to have lost sight of my Maryann. I shall just have to assure myself the delicate girl hasn't fainted. It is so terribly hot in here."

Catherine did not understand how anyone could lose sight of Maryann St. Clare for the lady was exceedingly large. Catherine had easily witnessed the violet mass that was the lady's dress amble through the generous doorway to the tea room, where an assortment of cakes was no doubt currently passing through that young lady's lips.

Once Lady Ann made her way toward the tea room, Felicity turned her full attention upon Catherine. "I am so happy to see you back in Society, as are many of the gentlemen here tonight. You are being much too severe in not standing up with them. It's been over a year since Bexley died."

"I know you're right. It's not just that I find dancing frivolous after a death. I also do not like to encourage any men because I have no desire to remarry." Catherine suppressed a yawn, thankful that the evening's festivities would soon draw to a close. She had made the curious discovery that sitting and watching dancers was far more tiring than actually dancing.

Felicity remained quiet, but her sapphire eyes softened. Now Catherine understood why Felicity's husband always preferred her in blue as she wore this night, no doubt to please him.

Catherine shrugged. "Of course, I may be forced to marry if I can't reclaim Mr. Bexley's legacy."

Because they were good friends, Felicity was one of the few persons who knew about Catherine's precarious financial situation. "It's quite beastly that Bexley's only thing of value was stolen. I think you should let it be known far and wide that Bexley's rare treasure was stolen. That should keep an unsuspecting collector from buying it."

"I wish I could, but to honor Bexley's memory, I refused to let it be known that one single item was his only valuable possession, though I will own, it was *extremely* valuable. Poor Mr. Bexley was such a proud man. He wanted all his friends to think him wealthy." Honoring the image her late husband tried to project was her peculiar way of atoning to him for being a merry widow.

"He was far too proud, and I wish you wouldn't canonize the man. He was a most insensitive husband, and well you know it."

"Oh, I do. That's why I must see that memories associated with Mr. Bexley are pleasant ones, for I'm afraid his final resting place is anything but pleasant."

Felicity giggled. Then apologized. Then gripped her friend's arm with her gloved hand. "Look, Catherine! There's one of the twins. I declare, I haven't seen them in an age, and as soon as we speak of them, one of them materializes."

The widow Bexley spun around to gaze at the door to the card room. There stood one of the dark haired, well dressed, taller-than-average twins. His black jacket fit perfectly. In fact from head to toe, his dress was impeccable. She studied him. Any sense of weakness implied by his slim build was quickly offset by the power of his countenance and the solidity conveyed by his patrician nose. From the man's haughty demeanor, Catherine was almost certain this twin must be the baronet. Is that how Blanks told them apart?

She remembered Glee telling her the smart twin was a bit of an introvert.

Introvert or not, Catherine knew that the smart, introverted twin was precisely what she needed. But how could she enlist him to help her? She had no money, and she refused to use her feminine charms even if that particular twin would be susceptible to such a ploy—which she was convinced he would *not* be.

Catherine turned back to Felicity. "Since your brother's one of his best friends, I beg that you beckon him to join us."

Felicity raised a quizzical brow. "If you like, dearest."

As the solitary twin's gaze connected with Felicity's, a smile crossed his face, and he began to cross the lofty chamber toward them.

He bowed before the beautiful blonde, kissing her proffered hand, then nodded at Catherine.

"You remember my friend, Mrs. Bexley?" Felicity inquired, coyly refraining from addressing him so as not to mistake him for his brother.

"Indeed I do." He smiled upon Catherine. "I trust your period of mourning is up?"

"It has been up these two months past,"
Catherine replied.

"Then you must do me the goodness of
standing up with me."

"Alas, I have not yet returned to dancing."

"Speaking of dancing," Felicity said to the twin,
"it has been an age since I've seen you at the
Assembly Rooms, though my brother keeps me
informed about all his friends—including you and
your brother."

He frowned. "I daresay the reason you haven't
seen me in an age is that Bath has lost its lure
since your brother and Blanks have wed and gone
to their estates. Even my brother don't hang
around anymore."

So this twin definitely was not the scholar.

"You must be very proud of your brother,"
Catherine said. "I understand he's obtained a
Doctor of Letters—a most impressive
accomplishment."

"I've always been proud of him, but I do wish
he were a bit more fun loving."

"I'm going to sound like an older sister," Felicity
said, "and tell you that it's time you settle down
and marry like George and Blanks have done."

Catherine's gaze flicked to him, and she
nodded. "You must own, those two men appear to
be deliriously happy."

"Pray, don't think I'm not vastly pleased that
my old friends are happy." He looked at the space
on the settee beside Felicity. "Would you permit
me to sit beside you, my lady?"

"Please do."

He lowered himself onto the settee and
commenced to talking almost as if he were
thinking aloud. "Sedgewick certainly deserves the

happiness he's found after his grievous loss."

Felicity nodded solemnly. "I know you miss him."

"The fun we used to have before Blanks and Sedgewick were married!"

Though Catherine had never spoken more than fifteen words to either twin, she felt compelled to interject her opinion. "It's my belief, Sir Elvin, that you're simply blue-deviled because you're about to lose your brother's companionship."

His brows squeezed together. "Don't know why he thinks he's got to make his living. I've told him he can live with me always."

Felicity's voice gentled. "I daresay he's exerting his independence. How old are you now?"

"Seven and twenty."

The same as Catherine. "I think he sounds like a most admirable man."

"Oh, that he is," his twin said.

"Where is your brother?" Catherine prayed he was in Bath.

"Oh, he's with me now. . .well, not actually now. What I mean is, he's here in Bath, but he don't like assemblies. He's one who prefers his books to the ladies—which is just another way in which we're different." He gave a little chuckle as his appreciative glance raked over Catherine.

Felicity nodded. "Everyone knows the two of you are vastly different."

"Even if you do look the same," Catherine added.

He gazed at her. "You wouldn't know it if you didn't see us side by side, but Melvin's a full inch taller than me."

"Actually, I once commented on that at an assembly," Felicity said with a little giggle, "but I didn't know which of you was the tall one!"

The dancing had now ended, the musicians were packing away their instruments, and the thousand or so who had filled the chamber moments before were now leaving. Catherine had to act before the baronet left. "I beg that you give me your direction for I should like to send a note around to your brother in the morning."

He gave her a querying look. "We have a house on Green Park Road. Number 4."

From that house on Green Park Road the following day, Melvin Steffington set off in his brother's tilbury to the Royal Crescent, where Mrs. Bexley resided. Why in the devil did the woman wish to see him? Her short missive had been particularly vague.

Try as he might, he could not remember a Catherine Bexley. He could not even remember Catherine Hamilton—the name Elvin told him she was known as before her marriage.

A pity he could remember every single character in *Plutarch's Lives*, but he couldn't remember a single female. Except for Pixie. Who wasn't really Pixie. She was Glee Blankenship now that she'd married Blanks. But Pix wasn't like other females. She was one of the bloods.

He tethered his horse in front of Number 17, the address of this Mrs. Bexley. The forty or so houses of the Royal Crescent were some of the finest in Bath—if not the finest. Melvin supposed the vast parkland in front of the semicircle of stately residences contributed to the homes' desirability, but for his taste, he appreciated most the clean classical lines employed by the architect. He was enamored of all things that originated with the Greeks and Romans.

He mounted the steps. Before he even knocked, the door swung open. "Mr. Steffington?" asked a man in lime green livery.

Melvin nodded.

"Please follow me upstairs to the drawing room. Mrs. Bexley's expecting you."

He wasn't particularly interested in furnishings and such, but he could not help but to notice how lovely was the Bexley home. The stairway was constructed of fine marble, and the iron banisters were gilded. Turkey carpets lay below, and a glittering chandelier hung above.

In the pale yellow drawing room he was shown to, light from tall windows illuminated the woman who sat on a silken cream-colored settee in the center of the room. It seemed almost as if the chamber's light framed her face rather like those hooded halos in Renaissance paintings of the Madonna.

He supposed Elvin would find her pretty, but all Melvin could notice was that she was on the smallish size, was not unattractive, and she was of a similar age to him. Possessed of light brown (or was it dark gold?) hair, this woman looked vaguely familiar.

It suddenly occurred to him that in his seven and twenty years he had never been alone with a woman. Other than his mother. And possibly his nurse when he was in leading strings. He could converse for hours with his dons at Oxford, but he was moronically inept when it came to speaking with a women.

She sprang to her feet and moved to greet him, a smile on her face, her hands outstretched to him. What in the bloody hell was he supposed to do with her hands? Though Melvin was unaccustomed to noticing women, he found himself thinking of how lovely was her smooth, creamy skin. And exceptionally large bluish-greenish eyes. At so close a distance he was able to determine that her hair was golden. Yes, indeed, Elvin would find her lovely.

The woman was remarkably friendly. She took both his hands in hers as if they were lifelong friends and proceeded to gush her gratitude. "It is so very kind of you, Mr. Steffington, to come to me today. Please do sit by me so I can tell you why I so desperately need you."

Of what use could he possibly be to this self-possessed woman? Bereft of words, he dropped onto the settee.

Mrs. Bexley had no problem speaking to men she scarcely knew. "When I heard your name mentioned last night at the Upper Assembly Rooms, I knew you would be the very one to answer my prayers."

Good lord! Did the woman have designs on him? He'd heard of women like that before—women who thought like a man, acted like a man, and—at least Mrs. Bexley didn't look like a man. He cleared his throat. "I fear you have me confused with someone else."

She shook her head vigorously. "Not at all! Are you not the gentleman who's looking for a post at a private library?"

His experiences with private libraries convinced him that this townhouse was far too small to hold the kind of library to offer him employment, and he did not think her late husband was in possession of a country home, either. He raised his brows hopefully. "You have such a position to offer?"

Her shoulders sagged. "Not actually."

Their eyes locked and held. He noticed hers were green, or perhaps blue, or perhaps a blending of the two colors. That particular shade reminded him of the Adriatic, which he had greatly admired on his tour of Italy.

"I have a dire problem that I believe a man possessed of your knowledge can help me solve."

"Are you saying you wish to employ me to help solve this problem, madam?"

"Not actually."

Then what? Had this unfortunate woman been dropped on her head as a babe? "I confess that you've roused my curiosity."

"My dear Mr. Steffington, you must think me the silliest scatterbrain. Allow me to explain. I need your help in tracking an extremely valuable book that was stolen from my late husband's library."

"May I know the title of the book?"

"Chaucer's *Canterbury Tales.* It's one of the earliest—hand lettered on vellum with lovely coloring as well as drawings."

His eyes widened. "That manuscript's 400 years old!"

She nodded. "Yes, I know."

"Such a book would be worth a fortune." A sudden desire to see the rest of the late Mr. Bexley's library seized Melvin. "Are there not only three such manuscripts in existence?"

Her brows lowered as if she were in deep contemplation. "I believe Mr. Bexley, my late husband, may have mentioned something to that effect."

He met her gaze and nodded. "Gutenberg came

along in the same century that Chaucer died, and those lovely old holographs went the way of chain mail."

"Pray, Mr. Steffington, what is a holograph?"

"Forgive me. My brother says I have a deplorable habit of not communicating in a readily understood manner. A holograph is merely a document or manuscript that's written entirely by hand."

A radiant smile brightened her face, giving her a child-like quality. "I knew it!"

"Then why, madam, did you ask me what a holograph was?"

"Oh, I didn't know what a holograph was, but I knew last night at the Assembly Rooms when Felicity spoke of you that you were the very one to help restore the manuscript to me!"

In what way did this woman think he could be of assistance? Did she think he cavorted with criminals? "I am truly sorry for your loss, but I fail to understand why you believe I might be able to aid in the recovery of your late husband's book."

"Oh, I understand that you have no expertise in recovering stolen goods, but you, Mr. Steffington, are extremely knowledgeable about old books. Only a person with such knowledge would be interested in a position at a private library. And are you not interested in such a post?"

"I am. But- - -"

She raised a dainty hand, palm facing him. "Please, hear me out. I believe you possess the skills to research all the private libraries in England."

That was true. "But some of these libraries

already have manuscripts of *Canterbury Tales*. I believe Lord Spencer's library has one in its possession, and so does Lord Oxford's library, which I've had the honor of visiting. You do realize, Mrs. Bexley, you can't just waltz into someone's library and claim their works as yours?"

"You see, you are the very one for this commission!" The crazed woman sat there smiling at him. "You already have knowledge of some of the finest private libraries in the British Isles."

Had she not understood anything he said? His brows lowered. "I am humbled by your confidence in my abilities, but I assure you I am not the man for this assignment."

"That is simply not true. You are the perfect person." Her voice lowered. "I mean to sell the book when I recover it, and I shall give you fifteen percent of whatever amount I receive from the sale."

He calculated what that fee would be based on the recent sale of a Shakespeare first folio and adding fifty percent. Since Chaucer predated Shakespeare, his works were considerably more valuable. Melvin had not heard of anything as valuable as a Chaucer holograph coming on the market in the decade he'd been a serious student, but his knowledge of books told him it should be worth half again as much as a Shakespeare first edition. Perhaps double. After all, Shakespeare wrote a great many plays, but Chaucer had just one major work.

With his cut from the *Canterbury Tales* sale, Melvin would have enough money to buy a cozy home in Oxford—which held all the attractions he could want: namely, libraries.

He would never have to be a financial burden to his twin, of whom Melvin was exceedingly fond.

Mrs. Bexley's proposal was enticing.

But he had no idea how to track stolen literary works. Melvin Steffington did not like to do anything he could not do well. In fact, he not only liked to do things well, he liked to do things *better* than anyone else could do them. He detested failure, and Mrs. Bexley's proposal was primed for failure.

"I assure you, Mrs. Bexley, I am ignorant of the process by which one would trace such a stolen item."

The look she gave him was part pout, part smile, and it displayed ample dimples. Yes, he thought, Elvin would most definitely find this woman attractive.

"Silly man! Of course, I know you have no knowledge of thievery. You're a scholar. That's why I selected you. I simply won't have anyone else."

He stiffened. "I regret, madam, that you have misunderstood what I said. I am attempting to convey to you how ill equipped I am to conduct an investigation of this nature."

She put hands to hips and glared at him in a rather formidable manner. "I won't have anyone else."

Would that he could avoid being rude to the lady, but what was a fellow to do? This search she proposed was out of his realm of expertise. Why could she not merely be seeking an educated man to oversee her library—if she'd had one, that is? "I'm sorry to disappoint, but it is out of the question."

Those aquamarine eyes of hers regarded him

most solemnly. Then they brimmed with tears. Dear God, had he made her cry? This was really too shabby of him. "Please, madam, I beg that you not cry."

With that comment, she burst into sobs, burying her face in her hands as her shoulders heaved with the force of her muffled cries.

How in the blazes did one comfort a weeping woman? He felt beastly. He had broken the poor lady's heart. Here she was all alone in the world without a man to take care of her. How could he have been so insensitive?

What could he do to quell her hysteria? He was even more out of his field of expertise with sobbing females than he was at tracking stolen books.

Pitiably hunched over beside him, she seemed so tiny and helpless. Unaccountably, he found his arm extending across her back, his hand gently clasping her shoulder that was furthest from him.

His action resulted in her brushing against him and dropping her tear-streaked face against his chest as she proceeded to wail.

He sat there as helpless as a newborn foal for a considerable period of time, wishing like the devil he knew what to do. He patted her back and murmured in much the same way as he had murmured to the pups Her Whiteness had given birth to last month.

The wails eventually lessened to whimpers, but she still seemed decidedly forlorn. Which made him feel beastly. He would do anything to bring back her smile.

Then he thought of what he could do to make this crying of hers stop.

$\mathcal{C}$hapter 2

All her life, Catherine had been possessed of the unfortunate propensity to cry whenever she was gravely disappointed. The ripping of her dress hem could reduce her to tears as easily as the heart-wrenching view of a cripple limping toward Bath's healing waters. Her exasperated mother had spent years trying to coach her eldest daughter to control these outbursts. It was surely the only thing at which her dear mother had ever failed.

Catherine most definitely needed a handkerchief. What a difficult position she had put poor Mr. Steffington in. (Not to mention the state of his moist cravat. She must offer to have her abigail iron it for him.)

But first, she must figure out a way to gracefully extricate herself from this settee without him seeing her blotchy face. Distraught she might be, but not so distraught that she did not care what she looked like.

"I say, Mrs. Bexley, I did not mean to so offend you." The tone of his voice was so tender, it sounded almost as if he were speaking to a small child. "If I can be of assistance, I shall happily endeavor to be your servant."

What an exceedingly delightful man! She sniffed deeply, then mumbled, "You're too kind." If only her tears would dry of their own accord. She really could not allow the man to see her ravaged face. She had her pride—as shredded as it was at the moment. Sniff. Sniff. "Pray, Mr. Steffington, have you a ha-a-a-nd. . ." Sniff. ". . .kerchief?"

He cleared his throat, and she realized she needed to peel herself from his person in order for him to extricate the handkerchief. "I believe I do," he said.

Her face still buried in her hands, she returned to her former position—spine straight—on the settee.

"Here."

From the corner of her eye she saw the proffered linen, gratefully claimed it, and proceeded to dab at her face, eyes, and squirting nose. What a pitiable sight she must be! She continued to hold the handkerchief to her nose while she gathered her wits enough to speak to this kindly man. (It was bad enough he'd have to observe her watery eyes, but she was determined the handkerchief would hide her hideous nose from his perusal. Nothing could be uglier than a lady with a bright red nose.)

"I shall never forget your generosity of spirit," she finally told him.

"If I am to help you, I shall need to know everything you can tell me about the missing manuscript."

She stood, grateful to escape his pitying stare—at least for a few minutes. "I suggest you follow me to the library. I shall show you the exact spot where it used to be kept."

He followed her across the drawing room's Axminster carpet, back down the stairs he'd so recently climbed, along the Carerra marble corridor and through a paneled door into the library which not so very long ago had been her husband's domain.

It was an inviting room with its warm colors, dark woods and a fire glowing in its hearth. Unlike the brilliant, shimmering whites that dominated the wood moldings in the rest of the house, the wood in this library was a honeyed dark brown. Tall bookcases stuffed with finely bound leather volumes lined the walls at either end of the room. Though the books looked most handsome, Mr. Christie had informed her they would not fetch much at auction. Such a pity.

She strolled to the place of honor in the room. Many years ago Mr. Bexley's father had Sheraton construct a classical, gold-leaf table that resembled an altar, and its surface was domed with a clear glass box. The empty table looked as incomplete as a debutante in her chemise and curl papers. "Sadly, this is where the manuscript was displayed."

She noted that his gaze had swung around the entire chamber before settling on the gilt table. "It was stolen from here?"

"Yes."

"When did the theft occur?"

"About four months ago."

He winced. "The thief's sure to have found a buyer by now."

"I'm not as knowledgeable as you are about such things, but wouldn't a potential buyer who knew that there were less than five of these in existence also know who owned them?"

"While there's much merit in what you say, not all collectors are scrupulous."

"There is that."

He proceeded to walk around the table, then he

dropped to his knees and raised his head to look beneath the table. "You did not have a mechanism to lock the glass case?"

"I don't believe there was one. Very careless, I know. The manuscript was purchased by my late husband's father before he lost his sugar plantation in the West Indies. He's the one who commissioned the table as well as this house."

"Were you present when the book was stolen?"

She shrugged. "I don't precisely know when it was stolen."

He quirked a brow. She noticed his eyes were so dark a brown they looked black. Like his hair.

"When the maid noticed the manuscript gone, she thought I'd taken it away or sold it, so she did not mention it to me. And to be perfectly honest with you—and in the strictest confidence—I must tell you that just before it went missing, Mr. Christie had come from London to appraise it."

"I'll wager he thought it far more valuable than that Shakespeare folio sale he brokered four years ago."

She was so proud of this gentleman's knowledge, she forgot about covering her nose with his handkerchief. Turning to him, she smiled radiantly. "You would win the wager, my brilliant Mr. Steffington! I cannot tell you how exceedingly happy I am that I've found a man possessed of your knowledge to assist me."

He held up a hand in protest. "Oblige me by *not* referring to me as *brilliant*."

She pouted. "Very well, but you can't keep me from thinking of you as brilliant."

He cleared his throat, his brows squeezing together. "It is significant that the theft occurred after Mr. Christie came to Bath. It cannot be a coincidence."

"Surely you're not suggesting Mr. Christie is dishonorable?"

"No. The man's reputation is above reproach." His dark eyes regarded her with intensity. Even though the Steffington twins were identical, she thought this one more handsome. Perhaps it was his somber countenance. He was the antithesis of her late husband. Which was a very good thing. There was something utterly masculine about his near-black eyes and near-black hair that when combined with his tall frame and deep voice commanded her complete trust. This was a real man. He would serve her gallantly, whether it be finding the thief, or slaying dragons.

"I also know how slim is the probability of coincidence," he continued.

Mr. Steffington was not only exceptionally well read, he was also possessed of a mathematic bent. She recalled her Papa using the word *probability* with great regularity, and Papa was most decidedly possessed of a mathematical mind.

Perplexed, she peered up at him. He was a full head taller than her. "Then how can the two events – Mr. Christie coming here and the subsequent theft of the Chaucer manuscript – be connected?"

"That is what we must discover."

We? She thought she rather liked that he was going to allow her to participate in his queries. "Where do we begin?"

"First you must tell me in what ways you have attempted to locate it."

She felt most inhospitable standing there facing him in the cozy library. "Pray, Mr.

Steffington, please have a seat on the sofa." The damask sofa of asparagus green was the only thing in the library which she had chosen—and then only because the one it replaced had been threadbare.

Once he sat, she took a seat on the opposite end of the sofa. "The first thing I did—after nearly suffering apoplexy—was to question all the servants."

"And how many have you?"

"Not so many as when Mr. Bexley was alive. I've got my abigail, a Frenchwoman named Jeannine; my footman, who showed you in and whose name is Simpson; my cook, Williams; and a maid, Hathaway."

"No servants have left your employ since the time of Mr. Christie's visit?"

Oh, dear. "The housekeeper, who had been Mr. Bexley's housekeeper before we wed, took her pension and retired to her sister's in Cheddar, but I assure you she's incapable of dishonesty."

"It would be helpful if we could assure ourselves that she's not shown any evidence of coming into a large sum of money."

Catherine liked that his mind was so thoroughly latching onto her problem, but she did not like for him to think ill of Mrs. Higgins. "In order for my former housekeeper to have come into a fortune, the manuscript would have had to have come on the market, and I have not been able to learn that it has."

"I've not heard of that, either. Perhaps Mr. Christie has. Have you written him to apprise him of the theft?"

"Not actually."

His gaze narrowed. "Pray, madam, what did

you *actually* apprise him of?"

She stiffened. "I didn't apprise him of anything. I merely wrote to him to ask if he'd addressed any inquiries about our *Canterbury Tales.*"

"Why did you not tell the man it had been stolen? If anyone in the kingdom is in a position to find a buyer for it, Mr. Christie would be the man!" He sounded as if he thought her a complete idiot.

"I have not wished to advertise the fact that the Chaucer has been stolen."

She could tell by the intensity of his expression, he was carefully forming his response to her. Mr. Steffington struck her as a man who did everything carefully and methodically. "It would be to your advantage to let it be known throughout the three kingdoms that a nearly priceless manuscript has, indeed, been stolen from you."

So he did think her a moron. "You're right. I understand that, but I have my reasons for silence."

"Since I am already privy to so much private information, might I ask what reasons could possibly motivate you to do something so counterproductive?"

"The first reason is that my late husband's siblings were naturally disappointed that the manuscript was left to the eldest son. The five of them had hoped it would be sold when their father died, and the proceeds split six ways. I can't imagine how upset they must have been when the family's treasure came to me. And if they learned I'd lost it. . . "

She hesitated before continuing. Her solicitor, her sister Mary Alice, and Felicity were the only three persons who knew the truth about Mr. Bexley's fortune.

"And your other reasons?" he inquired.

She drew a breath. "I don't like others to know that my late husband was not as wealthy as he presented himself to be. In fact, he wasn't at all wealthy. This house is heavily mortgaged. On his deathbed, Mr. Bexley confessed he had nothing to leave me except the Chaucer manuscript. He made me promise I would sell it and live on the proceeds for the rest of my life."

She dare not allow herself to remember those final hours when Mr. Bexley tried to atone for his hedonistic ways, or she would erupt into a crying fit again.

Mr. Steffington's voice softened. "I will do everything in my power to restore the manuscript to you."

Drat! Tears once more seeped into her eyes.

"But not if you're going to continue being a water pot!"

There was a knock at the library door. "Madam?" the footman said, pushing open the door.

"Yes?"

"A Mr. Longford is at the door. Should you like me to show him to the drawing room? He says he's here to collect you for the park. He's arrived in as fine an equipage as I've ever seen."

She drew an exasperated sigh as her glance darted to the clock upon the chimneypiece. It was three o'clock. She had completely forgotten she had agreed to go to Sydney Gardens with him. "Please tell Mr. Longford I've had some business..." She stood, shaking her head. "No, I'll tell him myself." She turned back to Mr.

Steffington. "If you'll excuse me, I won't be a moment."

Upon her doorstep, Mr. Longford stood like a pup with its tail between its legs. "I'm terribly sorry, Mr. Longford," she greeted. "My footman should have shown you in."

As his foot crossed the threshold, she apologized. "Unfortunately, something of grave importance has come up which prevents me from joining you this afternoon."

His glance flicked to a tilbury tethered in front of Number 17.

"Please forgive me." She offered him a smile. "Tomorrow afternoon?"

He could not have looked any sadder had she announced the death of his favorite hound. "I thought after last night. . . after you responded so affirmatively to my . . . my declarations. . ."

Declarations? To what had she responded to so affirmatively? She cast her memory back to the previous night when this gentleman had proceeded to sit beside her and watch the dancers at the Upper Assembly Rooms. Unfortunately, she hadn't paid the slightest heed to what the poor man was babbling about. He was so outrageously boring. Always had been. Even when he had attempted to court her before she married Mr. Bexley.

She would never subject herself to his company if it weren't for the fact they were related. His mother, after being widowed, married Catherine's father's brother, who happened to be Catherine's favorite uncle.

It would serve her right if Mr. Longford had misunderstood her affirmative remark, whatever that affirmative remark was. How deplorable that she never listened to him, and it certainly put her in a quandary now. Should she own up to her lamentable shortcomings and confess that she had not been listening? Doing that, though, might offend the poor man. He already looked woefully sad.

Hopefully, when next she saw him, she would be able to use his contextual clues to know just what she had agreed to the previous night. But, of course, she would have to listen most politely. Which was beastly difficult for her to do when she was with Mr. Longford.

Postponing the trip to Sydney Gardens might allow her to dream up a plausible-yet-inoffensive excuse for not having paid attention to what the man was saying the previous night. She bestowed what she hoped was a sweet smile upon him. "My dear Mr. Longford, I shall greatly look forward to our meeting tomorrow. Now, with the greatest disappointment, I must return to my pressing business." The bit about her disappointment ought to appease him.

Melvin looked up when she re-entered the chamber. That halo thing around her dark golden locks had vanished, but she still exuded an elegant countenance. She was fair and slender and looked like she needed a man to take care of her. He was surprised that he'd had no difficulty whatsoever speaking with her, even if she was a female.

"Now, where were we?" she asked, returning to her seat on the sofa. She sat upon the cushions, tucking her feet beneath her skirts, then she faced him in the same relaxed way his 13-year-old sister did. But in no other way did she resemble

Lizzy. The expression on Mrs. Bexley's face convinced him that she found him interesting. No woman had ever before been interested in what he had to say.

But, then, most women didn't like discussing classics and rare manuscripts.

"Permit me to ask how you think a thief gained entrance to your house," he said.

"He must have come when no one was home."

"And when would such an occurrence be?"

"The only time all the servants are gone at the same time is on Sunday morning."

"When they go to church?"

"Yes."

"And what do you do on Sunday mornings?"

Her dimples creased. "Why, I go to church, too."

"That is the only time when your house is not inhabited?"

"Yes, though I suppose the thief could steal in during the night while we slept."

"But how would he get past your locked doors?"

"Actually, I'm not altogether certain the doors were kept locked—though they are now."

He would refrain from chiding her. The poor woman had obviously suffered a great deal because of that omission.

"I know what you're thinking," she said, glowering at him.

"You couldn't possibly."

"You believe I'm an imbecile."

"I do not!"

"Yet you're thinking that not seeing to the locking of my doors was the most stupid thing you've ever heard of."

"I'm sure I must have heard of something more stupid." His dark eyes flashed with mirth.

And she burst out laughing.

He, too, laughed, and when he was finished, he eyed her seriously. "You have shown me where the manuscript was kept. You gave me an approximate date of the theft. You told me what servants are here, and which one has left since it went missing." He met her intent gaze. Yes, her eyes were an aquamarine. Quite lovely eyes. If one were interested in such things. "And the only other fact I have learned from you—save for your lamentable negligence in not locking the doors—is that Mr. Christie came to appraise the manuscript not long before it went missing."

"And you don't believe in coincidences."

He nodded. "The question now is how would one go about trying to sell so valuable a manuscript?"

She hopped up and scurried across the chamber's Turkey carpet to the desk where she snatched a plume and a piece of velum. "I propose to make a list."

Unlike his twin, Melvin had never made a list in his life. He saw no reason to when it was ridiculously easy to remember anything that would be put on a list.

She came back to the sofa.

"Now," she said, "what shall we list?"

He would refrain from complaining about her unnecessary list. "Most importantly, you must query Mr. Christie. Nothing of value in England is brokered without the man's hand in the pie."

She wrote the numeral one and put *Christie* beside it.

"Next, I would proceed to search through every

Times that has been published in the last four months."

She had started to write number two, but paused. "I've already done that."

"Every single edition?"

Nodding, she added, "Every single paragraph, no matter how insignificant it looked."

"Of course the *Times* isn't the only newspaper."

"But it may be the one most appealing to a discriminating collector of great literary works."

She wasn't stupid as he'd first thought her. "True. We must now endeavor to go back over the other major newspapers published the last four months. Fortunately, our friend Appleton never throws anything away. I believe he subscribes to the *Morning Chronicle*."

"Capital!" She wrote the numeral two and next to it, *newspapers*.

"Now, about your former housekeeper. How can we learn if she's living beyond the means of a retired servant?"

"I can hardly ask her."

"I know that."

"Perhaps—if the perusal of the *Chronicles* isn't productive—I could dispatch you to the city where she lives."

He nodded. "I could make inquiries."

She nodded as she wrote number three and next to it, *Mrs. Higgins.* "And you're so intelligent, I know you'll think of the most clever way to do so. Though I assure you, the woman doesn't have a dishonest bone in her body."

"Hopefully our investigation won't progress to your former housekeeper in Cheddar."

"Do you have any other lines of inquiry?"

"If none of these actions yield a clue about the

manuscript's location, I shall have to seek permission to view some of the great private libraries in Britain. With Dr. Mather's help."

"I suppose he's one of the men of letters at Oxford?"

He nodded.

"You'll have him write letters of introduction for you?"

She really wasn't stupid. "Yes." He cleared his throat. He seemed to do that a lot when he was with this woman. "I should like to make a request."

Her brows lifted.

"I beg that you not speak of my. . . my purported intelligence or. . .forgive me if I sound conceited, my brilliance."

"Do you mean when we're visiting the private libraries—if it comes to that?"

He nodded. "Yes, of course, but I shouldn't like for you to say those things to me. Makes me deuced uncomfortable."

She sighed. "I shall endeavor to abide by your wishes—decidedly difficult as it will be." She took up her pen and proceeded to write number 4, *private libraries*. "I assume we can eliminate Lords Spencer's and Oxford's libraries because they already have Chaucer manuscripts?"

"Yes, I think it best to eliminate those."

"Lord Agar?"

"This will give me the opportunity to see his library."

"I must go with you."

His eyes widened. "That would be most improper."

A flash of anger singed her eyes. "I am not a maiden, Mr. Steffington. I can rent a carriage, and the two of us could travel. We might need to use false names."

"And when we reach the libraries? Am I not to extend my letters of introduction?"

That pouty look reappeared on her face. "Could we not say I was your wife?"

If the wealthy—and probably titled—owners of the libraries had ever gazed at Mrs. Bexley before, they would not be likely to forget her. (He realized other men were not as ambivalent as he to a pretty face.) "Is there not a chance that you might have met some of these gentlemen previously?"

She put hands to hips and stared at him. He was learning that she did this with great regularity. "I suggest we cross those bridges when we come to them."

Of course, she was right. He met her gaze and nodded almost imperceptibly.

"There is one more thing I must ask of you," she said.

He effected a mock bow. "I am your servant."

"I shan't want anyone to know what the nature of our relationship is. You cannot mention the Chaucer to anyone." She paused, her voice softening. "Not even to your brother, with whom I know you're exceedingly close."

He could understand how distressing it would be for her if Bexley's siblings learned of the theft. "My brother is not given to gossip."

"I am sure your brother is all that is gentlemanly, but I would rather he not know exactly what we are doing. He could inadvertently let something slip."

"I will not lie."

"I'm not asking you to."

He got to his feet and peered down at her. "Will

that be all for now, madam?"

"There is the matter of me weeping on your cravat. Won't you allow me to have my maid iron it for you?"

He raised a flat palm. "It's not necessary. My brother and I share a most capable valet."

She walked him to the front door. Unaccountably, he disliked leaving the library. He could never remember being in a cozier room.

$\mathcal{C}$hapter 3

When Melvin entered the library in their Green Park Road house, Elvin leapt to his feet and threw down the newspaper he'd been perusing (the reading of which was a most unusual occurrence for his brother, to be sure). "Well?"

"Your tilbury has been restored to you intact."

"That's not what I want to know," Elvin said with impatience.

Melvin looked askance at his twin. "Pray, what do wish to know?"

"What the bloody hell did Mrs. Bexley want with you?"

Owing to his promise to the widow, Melvin was not at liberty to tell his brother. Yet, in their seven and twenty years, he had never once lied to Elvin. And he could not do so now. Melvin did not like doing anything dishonorable, and lying to the person he was closest to would cut him to the quick.

He had neither anticipated that Elvin would be curious, nor had he thought of how he would explain the day's meeting at Number 17 Royal Crescent – or the subsequent investigations he would conduct on the widow's behalf.

"Mrs. Bexley is consulting me regarding some research into old documents. I daresay it would bore you to death if I told you anything more."

"Does this mean you'll stay in Bath?"

"For now."

"Then I shall be indebted to Mrs. Bexley."

The beastly thing about taking a position in a library would be the separation from his brother. Despite their vast differences, they were exceedingly close. He offered his twin a smile.

"She's paying you?"

"We haven't actually come to exact terms with that at present." Which wasn't a lie. Even if he was able to earn the fifteen percent fee, neither he nor Mrs. Bexley knew how much the rare manuscript would fetch.

Elvin cleared his throat. "So. . . did you find her attractive?"

Melvin shrugged. "I hadn't thought of it."

"How could you not? She's very pretty. Do you not remember the Season she came out that I was rather taken with her?"

"As good as my memory is, it is incapable of remembering all the females you've been *taken with* this past decade." If a lady was possessed of a single attractive feature, Elvin was certain to be attracted to her.

Just another way in which the brothers differed.

"I cannot believe you don't remember how unhappy I was when Harold Bexley and Maxwell Longford started dancing attendance upon her." Then he spoke as an aside. "That was when Papa was alive, and I had no money of my own with which to compete with those two gentlemen."

And apparently Harold Bexley's fortune was all a sham. Except for the Chaucer. "You believe she was a fortune hunter?" He was disappointed in that.

"What woman isn't?"

"She repelled you?"

"No. It's just that I didn't think I stood a chance of competing with them, and I dropped back and worshipped from afar."

"I daresay not for long. I can remember at least two dozen other ladies you worshipped—many of them definitely *not* from afar." He wondered if his brother was still interested in Mrs. Bexley. "Are you still seeing that actress?"

"Mrs. Harrigan?"

Melvin nodded.

"No. She had the opportunity to go to Drury Lane."

Which probably meant Elvin had been tiring of her.

"If you were interested in Mrs. Bexley—when she was Miss Hamilton, that is—you should not have stepped aside. You're a far better man than either Bexley or that bore Longford."

That face he knew so very well smiled upon him. "And you're the kindest and most brilliant of brothers."

"You know I don't like you to say I'm- - -"

"Brilliant."

Melvin's lids—and his voice—lowered. "She said it, too."

"Mrs. Bexley?"

Melvin nodded.

"I am told women are attracted to brilliant men."

"I assure you, my arrangement with Mrs. Bexley is purely business."

Elvin dropped onto the sofa and peered up at his twin, a cocky smile on his face and devilment in his eyes. "Did she call you Aristotle?"

Melvin glared. "I pray she never hears about

that."

"Then you must ensure she doesn't cross paths with any of our friends."

"Speaking of friends, is Appleton in Bath?"

"Yes, in fact we're going to a cock fight this afternoon. Care to join us?"

Melvin regarded his brother through narrowed eyes. "You know better than to ask."

"I know you haven't been in an age, but you did enjoy a good cock fight when we were at Eton."

"I was a lad of thirteen!"

"Why did you want to know if Appleton was in town?"

"I wish to consult his copies of the *Morning Chronicle*."

"I believe we've got the past three or four days here."

Melvin was surprised his brother had noticed. It was usually just Melvin who read the *Chronicle* cover to cover every day. As thorough as the *Times* was, it still appealed to Tory tastes. And Melvin was most decidedly a Whig—the party appeased by the *Morning Chronicle*. "I'm a bit more interested in the past three or four months, actually."

"Appleton's the man to see, then." Elvin shook his head morosely. "I pity his poor parlor maids. It's a nearly impossible task to tidy up after him."

"Without throwing out what looks to the rest of us like rubbish."

"Will you go to see him today?"

"Yes. In fact, I thought I'd go now."

"I'll just get Suskins to fetch my hat, and I'll join you."

* * *

Less than three hours after he had left Number 17 Royal Crescent, Melvin returned. By the time he climbed the staircase while carrying a box piled high with newspapers, he had quite lost his breath. Mrs. Bexley was writing at a little French desk when he entered the drawing room.

She looked at him, her brows lowered with concern. "My dear Mr. Steffington, you did not need to carry that heavy box up here!" She put down her pen and stood. "Come, let us go to the library. I perceive you've brought back copies of the- - -" She peeked into the box. "The *Morning Chronicle*."

"I've two more boxes."

"My footman will bring them. I wish to use your brain every available moment and allow Simpson to be the brawn." She looked from his chest to the tip of his head, which made him feel deuced uncomfortable. "Not that you're not possessed of both."

So she thought him brawny? How was he supposed to respond to a remark like that?

He chose to ignore it.

Within a few minutes, Melvin and Mrs. Bexley were seated at a large desk facing one another over a stack of yellowed newspapers. "We should be able to cut the work in half with both of us doing it," she said. "Do you have an efficient method you'd recommend? Surely someone who has the discipline to earn a Doctor of Letters knows much about the best way to manage one's time."

"I have stacked them by month. I thought perhaps we could each take two months. I'll start with July. You take August. When I finish July, I'll take September."

"As I move to October. It's good, I think, that we'll use chronological order."

He nodded. He handed her the stack of August editions. "Have a care. They're rather heavy."

She plopped her stack in front of her. "I do hope the thief is not a Whig."

Why was the exasperating woman babbling about Whigs when they were in search of a thief? Did her comment mean this lady was sympathetic to Whigs? Very surprising. Had her late husband not stood as a Tory in the House of Commons? "Pray, madam, why do you say that?"

She peered up from the August 1st edition she was now perusing. "It's just that in my mind, I had the thief pegged for a Tory because I find I don't like them as well as I like Whigs – though I could not own to such an opinion while my dear Mr. Bexley was alive."

Odd that she and her husband had been so diametrically opposed, but Melvin was happy she felt as she did since he, too, had a long-standing abhorrence of Tories.

Before she got too intent on the task at hand, he needed to broach an awkward subject. He cleared his throat. "I should like to bring up a rather personal question."

She stopped thumbing through the newspaper and regarded him with dancing eyes. "You don't strike me as the type of man who bombards one with personal questions."

"Oh," he said in an apologetic voice, "it's not a personal question that actually pertains to *you*."

"That's comforting."

"It's more about your . . . I suppose it's about your financial situation. I noticed that you have not replaced your housekeeper. Would it be impertinent of me to ask if you plan to?"

"No. My mother served as housekeeper of our large home most ably, and since Mrs. Higgins left, I have taken over her duties. Thanks to my hard-working staff, this has been a most agreeable arrangement."

She was obviously too proud to tell him she could no longer afford a housekeeper. He felt compelled to say something that would compensate for the brutally honest reply she'd given. "Then you have hidden talents. Your home appears to be run by a most efficient person."

She bestowed a wide, dimpled smile upon him, then returned to August 1st.

His attention was once more directed at the box in front of him as he ruffled through the pages to give her the other half of the August editions. "You said you read through every word in the *Times*, but I don't think that's necessary. I wouldn't expect, say, to see an advertisement for a Chaucer manuscript in the middle of an account from Parliament."

She started to giggle. At first he did not understand why, then he realized the humor in his own last comment. Melvin had no sense of humor. No one had ever accused him of being funny. But now, he realized that what he said could be considered humorous, and he, too, began to laugh.

"Are you always right, Mr. Steffington?"

He did not lie. Looking her squarely in the eye, he said, "Usually."

During the next twenty minutes as they went through the papers, the only sound punctuating the silence was the turning of the oversized pages.

"This is really too shabby!" She flung down the

paper she had been reading and met his gaze. "Can you credit it? His friends have launched a subscription to help poor, penniless Robert Sandworth!"

Did everyone in the kingdom know Sandworth had foolishly lost his fortune at the gaming tables? This woman obviously did. "It speaks well for a man when his friends think so highly of him."

She put down the paper. "Tell me, Mr. Steffington, do you enjoy play?"

"I play, but I fail to understand the appeal of high stakes gambling."

"How sensible you are!"

"It seems we've found still another thing upon which we are in perfect agreement."

She gave him a quizzing look. "Pray, what was the first thing upon which we so perfectly agreed?"

He cleared his throat. He wasn't used to declaring his opinions to others unless those opinions concerned Greeks who died 2,000 years previously. "Actually, I am not overly fond of Tories myself."

"How delightful." Her attention returned to the newspaper she'd been reading. "Forgive my outburst. I shall try in the future to behave myself."

She spoke of herself as if she were an errant child, and despite that she must be the same age as he, he had been struck that sometimes there was a childish aura about her. The pouting. The foot stomping. The tucking of her feet beneath her as they sat upon a sofa. Exceedingly immature behavior. The propensity to thrust out her elbows while planting hands at her hips and glaring at him. All of these habits were something Lizzy might do.

Yet in spite of all the lady's semi-transgressions, he found Mrs. Bexley enjoyable to be around. Was that because it was the first time in his seven and twenty years he'd been able to speak coherently to a female? Perhaps it was her child-like qualities that made him feel so at ease with her.

Of course, he didn't have an inkling how he was supposed to act around a lady of quality. He supposed he was going to have to seek advice from Elvin. His twin never had any humiliating lapses when talking with women. In fact, Elvin was popular with the ladies. Very popular.

Then again, Melvin might not need assistance from Elvin or anyone. As long as their conversations dealt with the missing manuscript, he was comfortable conversing with this woman.

During the next hour, the sun slowly left the chamber. Each of them was so intent on searching their respective newspapers they hadn't realized there was only barely enough light to read.

Before the library was in complete darkness, Simpson came and lighted the various candles throughout the chamber.

"Forgive me," she said to Melvin, "for having you sit in a dark room. I tend to get entirely too caught up in what I'm reading."

"It's the same with me."

"That makes three things!"

Had the woman gone mad? Then he knew very well the three things she referred to were their three mutual commonalities. He offered a false laugh. "Right-o."

She sighed, put down her newspaper, and eyed him. "What date are you on?"

"Just the seventh."

"Me too. It's slower going than I'd expected."

"At least it's not tedious, like studying Latin verbs or something dull like that."

She turned up her nose. "That does sound dull." She yawned, covered her mouth, then stretched. "I daresay we need a break. You must dine with me. I shall be ever so happy of the company."

He hated to think of her eating all alone. And, besides, the smells from the kitchen had made him quite hungry. "That sounds very good. I just realized I've not eaten a bite since breakfast."

She stood and stretched some more. "I shall probably continue this work after dinner, but you mustn't feel pressured to do so. I truly don't mean to monopolize all your time."

He straightened. A break was most welcome.

Catherine Bexley made a discovery at the dinner table that night. Brilliant he might be, but Mr. Steffington was particularly clueless at the art of conversation, especially polite conversation with a person of the opposite sex. When she broached the weather, his responses were of a single syllable. When she asked if he enjoyed shooting, his response consisted of but one syllable. When she asked if he were enjoying residing in Bath, he answered her in a single syllable.

The subjects at which she thought he might speak with proficiency, unfortunately were ones at which she was likely to be inept. But she decided to take a stab. "Pray, Mr. Steffington, you must tell me who your favorite authors are."

He glanced up from slicing his mutton. "Contemporary or classical?"

She had stuck a vein! A Y-shaped vein, at that. "You must tell me both." When he did not respond, she prompted him. "Start with contemporary books."

"I don't like poetry or works of fiction. I like to read about what men think. Philosophy."

Now she hesitated. She wasn't knowledgeable about philosophy. As in Aristotle. But he was discussing contemporary thinkers. Would political theory fall under philosophy? "Do you mean authors like Paine?"

His dark eyes flashed. "I find much to admire in Paine."

"I do as well. Pray, who else do you find who's of a similar mind?"

"Burke is a most logical thinker who also expresses himself most eloquently."

"And what about Voltaire?"

He shrugged. "He and Rousseau led the Enlightenment movement, so their influence has been monumental."

She wrinkled her nose. "But I daresay you don't read their poetry."

He chuckled. "No, I don't. There is one more type of contemporary work I greatly enjoy."

"What is that?"

"England has some demmed fine historians." His hand flew to his mouth. "Forgive my vulgar language. I'm. . . not used to speaking to women."

She peered at him over the rim of her wine glass. "I have heard that particular adjective used with such frequency by my late husband that I had quite forgotten it was not acceptable to be used in mixed company." She set down her glass. "Which historian do you admire most?"

"Gibbon."

"Oh, but Mr. Gibbon writes about the ancients!"

"But he is a contemporary."

"There is that."

"Have you read him?"

How humiliating for her to admit she had never read *The Decline and Fall of the Roman Empire*. "I was just about to begin." She sighed. "I would think that's the kind of work a man like you would like to have written."

"Indeed."

For the rest of the meal they were able to converse in a most amiable fashion. After the sweetmeats were laid, she smiled upon him. "Do you know, Mr. Steffington, I marveled that anyone could tell identical twins apart, and now that I've been talking so much with you I believe I can easily differentiate between you and your brother simply by hearing you talk. There's a vast difference in the way you speak."

"The most difficult thing about being a twin is that everyone assumes you are identical in every way."

"I wonder if that explains why you embarked upon scholarly pursuits? Perhaps that was your way to become your own person."

He shrugged. "I suppose it could have been an unconscious decision to blaze my own path, so to speak, but my interest in the classics was inherent."

"And I take it your brother does not share your interest?"

"We have few interests which are the same. As

lads, though, we did everything together."

"I'm sure you must be very close to him."

He nodded. "He is not only my brother. He's also my best friend."

She helped herself to sugared fruit.

"Another way to tell us apart is that I am an inch taller."

"That hardly helps one to know which of you is which when you're not standing next to one another."

"A brilliant observation, to be sure."

She began to giggle, and once he realized she found his comment humorous, he smiled too.

When the sweetmeats were gone, he met her gaze, a solemn expression on his face. "What will you do if we can't reclaim the Chaucer?"

"I shall be forced to be dependant once more. This time upon my dear brother—who already has twelve mouths to feed."

"Your brother has twelve children?"

She shook her head. "He has eight children, a sweet wife, my mother, and my youngest sister. I had hoped to bring my sister to Bath, where I could present her." She shrugged.

"So, you're like me. You want your independence."

She never wanted to be dependent upon a man ever again. "Indeed I do." How did Mr. Steffington do this? In their few hours of acquaintance, he had come to understood her better than anyone ever had. She was coming to believe that overhearing Felicity's conversation the previous night was going to be one of the most fortuitous events in her life.

$\mathcal{C}$hapter 4

As Mr. Longford handed Catherine into his open barouche, she cautioned herself to be attuned to what the man was saying—which was always an arduous task but much more so now that Mr. Steffington so fully engrossed her thoughts.

She felt incredibly guilty that she would be off riding through the lovely gardens on this uncharacteristically sunny November day while poor Mr. Steffington continued toiling over old copies of the *Morning Chronicle* in her library.

It was bad enough that he had stayed in her library until past midnight the previous night. His every waking moment was now taken over with her problem. What if they could not locate the manuscript? She had no other way to compensate him for all his trouble. The poor man's significant efforts would be for nothing.

"'Twas so fine a day, I had at first planned to come to the Royal Crescent in my phaeton, but I decided upon my barouche. That way, my coachman can concentrate upon the driving, which will enable me to give you my full attention."

Another thing she disliked about Mr. Longford (besides his unceasing flow of boring words) was that he was given to boasting about his wealth. She was quite convinced the preceding comment was made so that she would know he possessed a variety of conveyances.

Before she had the opportunity to respond to his comment, he launched into another topic— which was his custom. "Pray, is that not the same tilbury which was at your house yesterday?"

As they drove off, she glimpsed at the tethered vehicle, which looked exceedingly modest next to Mr. Longford's fancy barouche. "I take no notice of such things."

"I trust the business which prevented us from going to Sydney Gardens yesterday has been satisfactorily completed?"

"Not actually."

Unbelievably, he remained silent for a moment. Which was a feat as rare as the multiplication of loaves. A full minute passed before he continued. "Might I inquire if yesterday's caller at Number 17 is still there today?"

She glared at him. "I hope you don't believe I would have a man spending the night!"

"Oh, no, I assure you, I know you're a very fine lady. I would never consider you would do anything that could tarnish your good name. If I thought such a thing, I would not be honoring you by allowing everyone in Bath to see you sitting by my side."

"What makes you think my visitor is a man?"

"I know of no women who are given to driving throughout Bath in a tilbury."

"If you must know, a man is assisting me with that personal business I had to deal with yesterday and which has not been satisfactorily completed as of yet."

"If there's any way I can be of assistance, pray, you have only to ask. Since you have no man to take care of you, I feel obliged to."

"I shouldn't like you or anyone to think I'm a helpless woman."

He drew her hand into his. "My dear Mrs. Bexley, one has only to set eyes upon you to realize how delicate you are."

Before she could protest, he continued on. "In fact, I would be most agreeable to sending over my secretary to assist you. Somerfield is a most capable man. Why, there's no end to the things the man is able to accomplish."

She shook her head. "I am quite pleased with the person who's currently assisting me." Indeed, she had hardly been able to sleep the previous night for thinking of her good fortune in finding Mr. Steffington.

Mr. Longford cleared his throat. "Would that gentleman be someone I know? A resident of Bath perhaps?"

Were Mr. Longford a woman, Catherine would have thought him the greatest busybody in all of Bath, but one did not usually think of a man as a busybody. (Though Mr. Longford was certainly a very great busybody.) It was difficult for her to conceal her impatience with this man.

She glared at him. For some peculiar reason, she didn't like to admit her connection to Mr. Steffington. At present, their relationship was something that only the two of them knew about. She could not remember ever sharing a mutual goal with anyone else before in her entire seven and twenty years, and she did not want anyone or anything to intrude upon them. The introduction of another person into their private sphere could be toxic.

Nevertheless, it was only a matter of time

before Mr. Longford learned who the man assisting her was. "You know Melvin Steffington?"

His brows lowered. "That's the smart twin, is it not?"

Funny, that's exactly how she would describe him—though Mr. Melvin Steffington would not like her to call him smart. She nodded.

"Then I daresay he must be assisting you with the late Mr. Bexley's library. I heard he was seeking a post."

It was easier to allow him to think what he wanted to think. "Indeed." That was as much as she was going to say on the topic.

"If you're thinking about selling the late Mr. Bexley's books, I might wish to have them for my property in Coventry."

And she'd vow he would probably pay a hefty price for them because he liked to flaunt his wealth. "I shall remember that when I'm ready to sell."

"Then I suppose it was his brother I saw at the cock fights yesterday, since Melvin Steffington was engaged with you."

Picturing the bookish Melvin Steffington at a cockfight was as incongruous as picturing their seventy-year-old queen dancing upon the stage at Drury Lane. "I daresay you're right."

"Even if I do say so meself, I am uncommonly good at picking the victors. Won eighty quid yesterday just because I happen to be as intuitively knowledgeable about cocks as I am about horseflesh. Take the matched bays you see before you. Turned down Lord Townson when he offered me five hundred quid for the pair."

Her thoughts drifted away as she planned what she could do were she to get her hands on five hundred pounds. Even the eighty guineas he won yesterday could have been put to good use by her.

And as the carriage wound its way along the streets of Bath, she thought about her dire need for funds and about the bankers clamoring for her to pay on the mortgage and about the tradesmen whose bills she owed.

Unfortunately, in spite of her best intensions, she was not listening to her companion. But, really, the man was droning on and on about roosters fighting! Could anything be less interesting?

After they crossed Pulteney Bridge and neared Sydney Gardens, they began to nod greetings to a number of acquaintances. Some of them were walking along, the women tucking their hands into furry muffs, and many other couples were riding in phaetons. Some single men sauntered along on horseback.

Even as he nodded to acquaintances, Mr. Longford's tongue never slowed. "Take Mr. Horton's nag. Why would a man allow himself to be seen with so common a horse?"

"What does it matter, if it gets him where he needs to go?"

"My dear woman, it matters a great deal. How can a man be thought to have good taste and breeding if he is not discerning about horses?"

For the next ten minutes, while inclining his head from time to time at passersby, he continued on about his impeccable taste in horseflesh, frequently mentioning the various members of the aristocracy who had tried to buy his horses.

Catherine deemed horses as interesting as roosters and wished herself back at Number 17 with the competent Mr. Steffington, who never bored her.

When she eventually returned there, Mr. Longford once again claimed her hand. "Pray, may I call upon you again tomorrow?"

"Tomorrow I shall be extremely busy." She still hadn't dispatched that letter to Mr. Christie. Mr. Steffington wasn't going to be happy when he learned of her omission. Not paying attention to Mr. Longford's rambling, she started drafting the letter in her head while smiling vacantly at Mr. Long*mouth*—er, Mr. Longford. Felicity had told her that her brother and his friend referred to Mr. Longford as Long*mouth*. But not in front of him, of course.

"Will you be at the assembly tomorrow night?"

Unconsciously, she wondered if Mr. Steffington danced. She knew his brother did. When she realized Mr. Longford was awaiting a response, she said, "I beg your pardon. What was that you asked?"

"I asked if you would be at tomorrow night's assembly." He did not look happy.

She had told Felicity she would meet her there. "Yes, I believe so."

There was a distressed look on Mrs. Bexley's face when she swished into the library, apologizing. "You must forgive me for leaving you here to do all the work whilst I was traipsing across Bath."

He would hardly call suffering Longford's company traipsing happily around the city. The poor woman earned his respect for putting up with the walking soliloquy. Then he thought of what Elvin had said about her that Season she came out. *Was she a fortune hunter?* That would explain why she bestowed her attentions on Longford. The man was obscenely rich.

He stiffened as he looked up to address her. "There's nothing to forgive. What you do with your time is nothing to me."

She stood statue still, a pout on her face. "There's more to confess. I forgot to dispatch that letter to Mr. Christie."

He didn't like to stare at her, but it was really quite remarkable that her frock was that same blue/green as her eyes. Remarkable eyes. Snapping out of his momentary stupor, he said, "I hope you don't believe I would try to tell you what to do. It's just that it would be helpful to learn if anyone has approached Christie."

"Of course, you're right. After all, it was number two on our list."

Our list? He did not like being associated with anything so frivolous as a woman's list, but he would not protest. He shrugged. "It looks as if number one is much more time consuming than at first thought."

She came to sit across from him at the big desk. "That's because you are likely doing what you told me not to do."

He chuckled. "I confess, I have veered off course when something interesting catches my eye."

"It's only natural to do so." She lifted up October 1st. "You'll be happy to know I would not allow myself to go to bed last night until I finished August."

"I am *not* happy to learn neither of us has found anything to bring us a single step closer to the culprit."

"There is that." She read on for a moment, then addressed him. "Do you dance, Mr. Steffington?"

What in heaven's name had brought up that subject? He regarded her from beneath lowered brows. "Do I dance?"

"Yes, that's what I asked."

He shrugged. "I suppose I do. I'm a bit rusty."

She thought perhaps if Mr. Steffington were to ask her to dance, she might cast off the last of her mourning. "Why do you not come to the assemblies anymore?"

He did not answer for a moment. "If you must know, I'm not very good at dancing."

"Oh, I see. You don't like to do anything if you can't be the best at what you're doing!"

How could she possibly know that about him? They'd only been in each other's company the last four and twenty hours. "I wouldn't say that." *Even if it was the truth.* He was not going to act like an arrogant ass, like Longford.

"You shouldn't let it bother you if you're not a great dancer. With your height, it shouldn't matter to any woman. Has it escaped your notice that ladies adore having tall men for dancing partners?"

"But ladies do not adore having their feet trampled."

She giggled.

He was growing to like the tinkling sound of her frequent laughter. "Pray, madam, what is so funny now?"

"I was picturing you stomping on a lady's feet." She shook her head. "I know it's not funny, but I seem to have a perverse sense of humor."

That very perverse sense of humor suddenly struck his funny bone, and he began to laugh.

She clapped a hand to her mouth.

"What's wrong?"

"I keep going back to number one because. . . as you said, it's much more interesting than reading a list of Latin verbs. However, I need to put the interesting work aside for a few minutes in order to compose a letter to Mr. Christie." Then she opened a drawer, took out pen and paper, and began to draft the letter.

He was struck by the excellence of her memory. She had remembered him referring to Latin verbs the previous day. He knew few people who remembered things as well as she. This young woman whom he at first thought to be empty headed wasn't nearly so vacuous as she presented herself.

As he continued reading into September, she scratched out a letter. When she was finished, she held it up from the desk. "How does this sound?" And she began to read:

Dear Mr. Christie,

It grieves me to inform you that the lovely edition of Canterbury Tales that you so kindly came to Bath to appraise was stolen not very long after your visit. I am writing because of all those in the kingdom, you are the one person who's in the position to know if it has come on the market.

I don't need to tell you that the lawyer I consulted told me even if it is sold to another party, it is legally my possession.

Has anyone approached you in these past months about its sale?

I depend upon your discretion that news of its theft not be revealed to anyone else.

Yours ever most sincerely,

Catherine Bexley

"Very good," he said.

"Can you think of anything I've forgotten?"

He shook his head.

Simpson knocked at the library door. "I've brought you the post, madam."

"If you'll wait just a moment for me to address this, I'll have you post it."

When she finished, she and her footman exchanged letters, and he went off to post his mistress's letter.

Not wishing to appear nosy, Melvin refrained from watching her as she read the single post.

But he could not block out the sound of her distress. Her breath hitched, then he once again heard her whimpering noises, which caused him to spin around and face her.

He couldn't bear to see a woman cry, but he could hardly ignore her. "Pray, madam, what is the matter?"

"N-n-nothing." She turned her face away from his scrutiny as if she were embarrassed for him to see her cry. "May I trouble you for a hand. . ." Sniff, sniff. ". . .kerchief?"

He extracted one from his pocket and handed it to her.

Not normally one to pry, he now felt it his responsibility to try to alleviate the poor lady's suffering. What gentleman wouldn't? "Now see here, Mrs. Bexley, you are *not* fine! You must tell me what's wrong."

His comment had the effect of making her cry even harder. Her sobs reverberated throughout the chamber, her shoulders quivering with each new wave of cries. Good lord, had his comment sent her off into a fresh torrent of tears?

Obviously, his commanding tone had not achieved the desired result. He sat there for a considerable period of time, all the while trying to decide what he should do next. Did one put his arms around a sobbing woman? Did one murmur sweetly? He was so destitute of experience in this arena that it put him in quite a quandary.

Yet two times in as many days he had found himself in the awkward position of trying to comfort the same weeping woman.

He exercised his new-found habit of clearing his throat, then gentled his voice in much the same way as he did with Her Whiteness's new pups. "Forgive me if I've made things worse."

Her face still buried in her hands, she shook her head vigorously. "No-o-o-o-o."

So she wouldn't forgive him?

Then she continued. "You did not. . ." Big sniff. ". . .make things worse. In fact. . ." She paused to blow her nose. "You have been my sole bright spot."

He felt as if he'd grown a foot taller. "I do so want to help you."

"No one can help me. Read this." She handed him the letter.

$\mathcal{C}$hapter 5

The letter was indeed bleak. It was written in the neat script of a professional clerk, this one in the employ of the Coutts Bank in the Capital. Though it was couched in legal terminology, two things were very clear: the date, November 22—which was less than two weeks away; and the fact that if Mrs. Bexley had not paid the overdue amounts owed on the mortgage of Number 17 Royal Crescent by that date, she would be forcibly evicted from that location.

What was the poor woman to do? Melvin—possibly better than anyone—understood her need to stand on her own. She loathed the notion of being a burden to her brother—another trait she and Melvin shared.

Though she fiercely wished to take care of herself, there was some inherent quality in her fair femininity that elicited in him a need to help take care of her. Not like a husband, of course. More like he felt about Lizzy.

But entirely different. Very perplexing.

Perhaps because she had only recently left Longford, Melvin's first thought of extricating her from this dire circumstance would be for her to wed the man. But he quickly dismissed that line of thinking. He liked Mrs. Bexley far too well to wish her united to such an oaf.

He turned to her and spoke with a conviction

he was far from feeling. "I will do everything in my power to locate your manuscript before that date."

She peered up at him, her moist eyes red, her voice quivering. "But there is no way we could have a buyer for it that soon—even if we should find it."

"I assure you, Mr. Christie would be more than happy to advance you a portion of the money anticipated from the sale—if you have obtained possession of the Chaucer."

She blew her nose once again (in a most dainty fashion), wiped at her eyes, and attempted to gather her composure as she met his gaze. "You truly are the brightest star in my galaxy, Mr. Steffington."

Now he felt as if his chest had expanded by six inches. "I may not prove worthy of your trust, but it will not be from lack of effort." His attention returned to the stack of newspapers in front of him on the big desk. "Now, back to the task at hand."

He scanned every page with one very specific goal. He was determined not to divert his attention by reading the articles. His thoughts *were* diverted by the heavy burden he'd put on his own unworthy shoulders. What did he know about locating stolen manuscripts? What if he let her down? What if she lost her home because she'd erroneously placed her faith in the wrong person?

Why had he made her such a promise? Next, he'd be telling her he could walk on water. The *probabilities* of him doing either were nearly the same.

As the footed wooden clock on the chimneypiece ticked away, the afternoon passed, page by yellowed page. His hopes extinguished. Neither of them had found anything promising. Light slanting into the library from the tall, velvet-draped casement grew dimmer. Just like their prospects.

He cleared his throat. "I regret to say that I'm finished with my two months of *Morning Chronicles*, and I have found nothing. How go you?"

She frowned. "I'm on October 29th, and I've not found anything either."

His lips folded into a grim line. "Then I go to Cheddar tomorrow."

A pair of incredibly solemn blue/green eyes met his, and she spoke morosely. "Number three on our list."

He'd never felt so impotent. "Here, I'll take the 30th." He reached across the desk and took the final edition.

As he'd come to expect, they found nothing in the last three newspapers. "I'm sorry number one proved so fruitless."

She shrugged as she lighted the oil lamp which sat upon the desk. To his surprise, she began to speak like a young girl during her first Season instead of a woman on the verge of being thrown out in the streets. "Please say you'll come to the Upper Assembly Rooms tonight."

The only thing he disliked more than assemblies was dancing at assemblies. Why in the bloody hell did he have such a difficult time turning down this woman? He met her hopeful gaze. "Will I have to dance?"

"I have not danced since before I lost Mr. Bexley, but I find I should like to stand up with you."

"Then it will be my honor to stand up with you, madam."

While Catherine watched the beautiful Felicity dancing with her husband, Thomas Moreland, she nodded most agreeably to Mr. Longford, who sat beside her, continuing to ramble on. She had tried to listen attentively to him, but, really, the topics on which he spoke were vastly uninteresting. Granted, the weather was a universal conversational gambit, but after lamenting that that day's fine blue skies had turned to gray rain clouds, how much more could one say?

Not to be deterred from his linguistic dominance, Mr. Longford transitioned from weather in Bath to the disastrous effect such rains would have on his massive farming interests. "You may be surprised to learn," he said, "that I am the largest non-aristocratic landowner in England."

Before she could inquire about those vast farming interests, he proceeded to tell her he was now in possession of nearly 900,000 acres. "Since my father died, I've added two nice parcels, one sixty thousand acres, and the other 100,000 acres."

No doubt Mr. Longford would think her late father's 30,000 acre farm as insignificant as a cricket field. "Then I pray the rain doesn't endanger your harvest." She spoke without removing her gaze from Felicity and her handsome husband.

They were the loveliest couple on the dance floor—and certainly the most in love.

Theirs had been a true love match. Felicity had

saved a young, dying Thomas when he'd been left for dead one night on the London Road. He had gone on to India and made his fortune but always remembered Felicity with singular affection. After he returned to England, he rescued her family's ancestral lands and captured her heart in the process.

Every time Mr. Moreland's eyes rested upon his wife's blonde beauty, it was impossible to conceal his adoration of her.

Perhaps the Morelands were the reason why Catherine had vowed never to marry again. Her marriage to Mr. Bexley had, unfortunately, not been a great love match. She often wondered why he had married her when he obviously preferred spending his time with other bloods. Or doxies. She supposed she was merely a pretty object he wished to possess, much like the richly illustrated *Canterbury Tales*.

Since a love like the Morelands' was a rare occurrence, Catherine knew the probability of embarking on a loving relationship was so low as to be out of consideration. *Probability.* Mr. Steffington's use of that mathematic term reminded her so much of her dear Papa. Papa, too, loved books, but he especially loved mathematics, and frequently discussed *probability.*

At the end of the dance, Thomas Moreland escorted his wife back to the settee where she'd been sitting beside Catherine, then he excused himself to return to the card room.

Why did Mr. Longford not choose to go to the card room? The man was most provoking! "Do you not agree that the Morelands are the loveliest couple to grace these Assembly Rooms?"

Catherine asked him.

He leaned forward to flash a smile at Felicity. "Indeed. A most handsome couple."

Felicity bestowed a smile upon the gentleman who sat on the other side of Catherine. "Thank you, Mr. Longford." Returning her attention to Catherine, she said, "Have I told you my sister is increasing?"

"You hadn't told me, but from something you said earlier, I surmised that she was. I've been hoping this time it will be a son. There are only so many mirthful names to bestow up on little girls."

Felicity tossed her head back and laughed heartily. "Yes, I suppose our family has overdone it a bit with Felicity, Glee, and Glee's little Joy." She sighed. "I do hope Blanks gets a son. Thomas so adores our boys."

There was a tap upon Catherine's shoulder. At first she thought it must be Mr. Longford, but then she noticed Felicity's gaze lifting, and Catherine turned around, tilting her head to peer up at Mr. Steffington.

Actually, there were two Mr. Steffingtons, and owing to the fact one was bent toward her, she couldn't tell who was who because she quite obviously couldn't see which was the taller—the surest way to differentiate the identical twins. Her brows raised.

Still bent toward her, he spoke into her ear to ensure he would be heard over the hum of voices and trills of laughter that surrounded them. "May I have the honor of standing up with you the next set?" Both twins were eying her. Which twin was this? Because she had turned down Sir Elvin Steffington at the previous assembly, she felt this one must be *her* Mr. Steffington. Melvin

Steffington.

"It will be my pleasure, Mr. Steffington." She placed her hand into his and tried to avoid Mr. Longford's open-mouthed gawk. *Oh dear.* How would she apologize to the poor man? Why was she always having to worry about hurting Mr. Longford's feelings? Would that she didn't have to put up with the man at all. Every minute in his presence was tormentingly tedious.

It was quite the opposite with the man who was leading her onto the dance floor. He never bored her, even though he spoke little. She always felt so comfortable with him.

How handsome Mr. Steffington looked dressed in impeccably tailored black coat, snowy white cravat, and subtle gray pantaloons. She supposed his brother had a say in how his twin dressed for these assemblies for Sir Elvin dressed in perfect taste; his brother's daytime attire had indicated a careless disregard for dress.

The other women must have found his appearance agreeable because nearly every lady in the ballroom was watching him.

Once they took up their position on the dance floor, most of the dancers lifted their gazes to the gallery above as the musicians took up their instruments and began to play. Catherine was particularly happy the dance was to be a waltz. That would enable them to converse, and she knew if she could just be engaged in conversation with Mr. Steffington, she would immediately know without any doubt which twin she was dancing with.

He clumsily drew her into his arms, murmuring. "I pray I don't trample your feet."

There was something utterly masculine in his

exotic sandalwood scent. She was almost certain this twin was Melvin. *Her twin.* "If you should step upon my feet, any pain would be offset by my pleasure at dancing with you."

He peered down at her, his brows squeezing together. He was a great deal taller than she was. The tip of her head barely came up to his shoulders. "Do you know which twin I am?" A devilish glint sparkled in those black eyes of his.

"Of course I do. You're Melvin Steffington."

"You must have seen us standing next to one another."

"I did not!"

"You told me you would be able to tell us apart by our speech, but I don't think *May I have this dance?* qualifies."

She started giggling.

"May I ask what it is you find so amusing?"

"You, my brilliant Mr. Steffington, gave yourself away."

He laughed too. "So I did." Then lifting a brow, he asked, "Did I not also tell you I disliked you referring to me as *brilliant*?"

"Even when the *brilliant* is in jest?"

"So madam enjoys poking fun at a humble scholar?"

"Madam finds it difficult to believe there's anything humble in a confident scholar such as you."

"There are many areas in which my confidence escapes me—dancing being the first to come to mind."

She would not confirm his statement, even though he was not a natural dancer. While he knew all the steps, he was perhaps the most awkward dancer with whom she had ever stood up. Not at all like Mr. Bexley.

Thank goodness.

Mr. Bexley had danced with the same elegance at which he interacted in society. Those types of pursuits were vastly important to him, especially the nocturnal pursuits, though Mr. Bexley did not confine those bedchamber activities strictly to nighttime.

He had been known to not-so-discreetly keep his carriage outside Mrs. Baddele's House of Cyprians in the morning as well as afternoons. Though he most certainly visited that establishment at night, he preferred giving up his nights to his other mistress, Faro.

Despite that they lived in the same house, she rarely came face to face with her husband.

Try as she might, Catherine could not imagine Mr. Melvin Steffington crossing the threshold at Mrs. Baddele's, nor could she see him wagering large amounts of money at the Faro tables.

There was something ever so solid about him. Not at all like Mr. Bexley.

"But, Mr. Steffington, of all the men in this chamber at present, I would rather be dancing with you."

"I assure you, my brother is a much better dancer."

His brother did remind her a great deal of Mr. Bexley. Not physically, but in their personalities. Sir Elvin was comfortable and confident in the presence of women, and he gave every indication that his other interests mirrored those of her late husband. "Your brother possesses many of the same qualities my dear Mr. Bexley possessed." It was a conscious effort on her part to always speak favorably of poor Mr. Bexley in some lame way of compensating for the inferno which he must be inhabiting at present.

"I didn't know him well."

"Mr. Bexley was fifteen years older than me, and I suspect that's one of the reasons you didn't know him well. You must be near my own age." She would not bring up the other reason the two men were not familiar to each other—that the men had no shared interests.

"I'm seven and twenty."

"As am I."

Neither of them spoke for a few moments, then he cleared his throat and said, "Thank you for what you said."

She found herself squeezing his hand. "About preferring you to all the others?" *What have I just said?* The meaning was vastly different than preferring to dance with him more than all the others. Oh, dear. Mr. Steffington was sure to think her flirting with him when that was not her intent at all.

He peered down at her, his black eyes smoldering with emotions she knew he could never express in words. And he nodded.

After that dance, she owed an explanation to the patient Mr. Longford. "Forgive me, Mr. Longford. I should have favored you with my first post-mourning dance. It was only today I decided to put the last vestiges of mourning behind me, and I lamentably forgot to tell you." She was mildly ashamed of herself for saying something she didn't mean, but her mother had always told her white lies were acceptable when used to spare someone's hurt feelings.

For once, someone else beat Longford's response. "I am most happy to hear that," Sir

Elvin said. "Pray, Mrs. Bexley, I beg that you do me the honor of standing up with me."

What could a lady do? She placed her hand into Sir Elvin's as he led her onto the dance floor for a country set. Before they took their places, he said, "I was happy that your commission will keep Aristotle in Bath."

"Aristotle?" As soon as she repeated the name, she realized just who was referred to by the Greek scholar's name. Immediately, she thought she could latch onto it. It suited Mr. Steffington far better than Melvin. Of course, she would continue to call him Mr. Steffington.

"My brother."

The orchestra stuck up the tune, and there was no more opportunity for them to talk. Aristotle was right about his brother. Sir Elvin danced most elegantly. Because they were not conversing, she gazed upon him, realizing he looked exactly the same as his twin. She had come to appreciate their appearance. Of course, she was not in any way interested in men in a romantic way.

Just as Sir Elvin was handing her off in exchange with another partner, her gaze connected with Aristotle's as he stood at the far end of the chamber, broodingly handsome as he solemnly watched her dance with his brother.

Her breath hitched.

Chapter 6

Though he'd been a twin for seven and twenty years, Melvin had never before considered Elvin identical, but as he watched his brother dancing with Mrs. Bexley, the queer feeling that he was watching himself rushed over him. That she peered up at his twin with laughing eyes felt oddly disconcerting.

He was struck by how well the two of them went together. Mrs. Bexley and the elegant dancer. Mrs. Bexley and the personable brother. Elvin was just the sort to win her heart. Even she had remarked on how similar Sir Elvin was to her *dear Mr. Bexley.*

Melvin swallowed hard as he watched them. He suddenly became cognizant of his brother's many references to the widow over the past two days. Could it be Elvin was especially taken with her?

Though he was exceedingly fond of his brother, Melvin did not like to think of his brother courting Mrs. Bexley. He shouldn't at all like to see Mrs. Bexley hurt. She was so delicate. His twin was notoriously fickle with women: both ladies and demireps. He discarded women as some discarded old invitations, their usefulness spent.

A raging heat pored over him as he stood stone still behind the obnoxious Long*mouth*—a name the twins' friends had used for years to describe Longford. Not to his face, of course. The heat in the chamber was insufferable. There must be a thousand people or more crammed into this ballroom.

Why in the blazes had he come to this place he loathed so? His hands fisted. *Because of her.* He rued the day he had met Mrs. Bexley. He disliked what he had become since the morning he first knocked upon the door to Number 17 Royal Crescent.

She had the most mortifying effect upon him. He could refuse her nothing. Thank God she was respectable for if the lady requested that he strip naked and dash through the streets of Bath, he was apt to peel off every stitch of clothing and begin to sprint.

No sooner had Elvin restored her to the seat beside Long*mouth* than that tiresome man claimed the poor woman for the next set. Why could he not have given her a chance to cool off? Could The Nuisance not see how vigorously the unfortunate lady was fanning herself?

Even in school, Long*mouth's* perceptions had been as flawed as a blind man's paintings. Melvin glared at the couple. The sparkle he'd earlier detected in her remarkable eyes had vanished, and no smile lifted her face now.

She not only gave the appearance of being tired, she looked disinterested. Who could blame her? While Melvin was contemplating her change in demeanor, it occurred to him that her sweet smiles had only been meant for Elvin.

His hands fisted with resentment. How could she appear so happy with Elvin when just moments before she had told Melvin she would choose him over any man in the chamber?

His brother came to stand beside him. "She's

lovely, is she not?"

Melvin ever so slowly met his brother's gaze with steely eyes. "To whom do you refer?"

"Mrs. Bexley!"

"You know I take no notice of such things."

"How fortunate you are to be able to spend so much time in her company."

"Were you in my shoes, I daresay you'd tire of her in a matter of days."

Elvin folded his arms across his chest and was incapable of removing his gaze from the widow. "Care to make a wager?"

Did this mean Elvin was falling victim to the lady's rather sweet ways—and not unpleasant appearance? "You know I dislike wagering."

His brother was far more quiet than was his nature. He seemed mesmerized by the vision of Mrs. Bexley gracefully gliding across the dance floor. Her shimmering silver dress stood out in the sea of black jackets and pastel gowns. "I believe my brother needs assistance in his current endeavors with the pretty widow."

Melvin disliked turning down his brother. When Elvin hurt, Melvin hurt. It had always been thus. As children, when Elvin cried because he wished to ride the pony Melvin sat upon, Melvin would relinquish the beast in order to bring a smile to his twin's face. When the lads were at Eton and Elvin was ravaged by fever, Melvin had to leave their chamber so his brother would not see him cry. Under normal circumstances, Melvin would always defer to his brother's wishes. But Mrs. Bexley had specifically asked that he not tell his twin about the stolen manuscript.

Melvin had given his word. "You would perish from boredom."

"I think not."

Once more, Melvin slowly and icily met his brother's gaze. "You're willing to rise before three in the afternoon?"

The baronet twin shrugged. "I am certain I could manage to be out of bed by noon. If I had such an incentive." He could not remove his eyes from Mrs. Bexley.

Melvin gave a bitter laugh. "Do you realize I rise at eight each morning and arrive at Mrs. Bexley's at nine?"

"Dear lord!" Elvin's face screwed up. "A baronet's son does not rise with the chickens."

"Tomorrow I rise at five in order to perform a particular commission for the lady." If he meant to travel to and from Cheddar in the same day, he could leave no later than half past five.

Elvin's eyes widened, his mouth gaped open. "Then I daresay I don't wish to see Mrs. Bexley that badly."

This time when the lady returned, she dropped onto the settee next to Felicity, exhausted. It was at this time Melvin did something he had never before done. He moved to her and offered to procure for her refreshment.

She gazed up at him, her eyes once again smiling. "That would be ever so kind of you, Mr. Steffington."

She had not called him Sir Elvin, which he had half expected. How in the blazes was this woman able to distinguish between him and his twin?

Feeling as if he were charged with a commission of great importance, he went to the stifling tearoom and waited patiently in line to avail himself of two cups of tea. When he returned, Felicity had moved to the dance floor, and Elvin had confiscated her seat on the other side of Mrs. Bexley.

That lady was at present favoring his twin with the exact same smile she had so recently bestowed upon him. Melvin moved to her and cleared his throat loudly, not really expecting that he could be heard over the throngs.

He was mildly surprised that she looked up at him. "How very kind of you, Mr. Steffington," she said, taking the cup. "My throat is ever so parched."

"It is exceedingly hot in here," Elvin said.

"And the lady has not been allowed to rest." Longford glared at the twins.

She quickly drank the liquid. "I shall, indeed, be allowed to rest for I plan to take myself home at present."

"The poor woman is not accustomed to such strenuous activity." Longford narrowed his gaze at the two men he perceived as his rivals. "I shall be happy to send round for my carriage to convey you back to the Royal Crescent."

Longford was one of a handful of men in Bath who was rich enough to have his own chaise and four—and the man never missed an opportunity to make sure everyone knew it.

The lady sighed. "I would be most grateful. I declare, I do not think I have the strength to walk home."

At half past five the following morning, Melvin donned his oilskins and beneath still-dark skies went to the livery stable to hire a horse for the long ride to Cheddar. He dared not risk one of his family's beasts for so grueling a mission. As it was, he would have to change horses two or three times.

He had asked that his servant deliver a note to Mrs. Bexley after nine o'clock. The note merely reminded her that he was headed to Cheddar to investigate Mrs. Higgins. *I will apprise you of what I learn at the earliest opportunity*, he had concluded, before signing himself *Yours ever truly, M. Steffington*. She had provided him with Mrs. Higgins' address at Pleasant View Cottage.

It was a pity they had to race against the clock—and Coutts Bank—because Melvin would have liked the luxury of waiting until the rainy skies cleared. Instead, he mounted the gray filly and began to charge into the southeasterly winds and the steady drizzle, hoping like the devil the storm would not gather any more strength.

The first half hour was the hardest. The piercing winds cut through him like frozen steel. His face stung from the harsh, cold wind, and his ears became numb. His fine leather gloves did little to protect his chilled fingers, and even his ribcage—like his teeth—quivered from the brutal cold. He could not remember the last time he had been this miserable.

As the murky light of dawn stole over the distant horizon, the cold was less palpable. The second hour of the journey he grew accustomed to the misery. Accustomed, but not accepting. He kept asking himself why he was doing this, why he had encouraged the widow to put her trust in him.

He was so out of his expertise, he wished to God he'd never responded to her initial note. Just a few days earlier, his life had been far less complicated. Far less exasperating.

It was difficult to believe that just a few days

previously they had been favored by blue skies and mild temperatures. Which reminded him that Mrs. Bexley had gone with Long*mouth* to Sydney Gardens that day while he stayed in her library searching yellowing newspapers for something that wasn't to be found.

A gnawing feeling that they would never find the Chaucer manuscript kept eating away at him like hungry maggots. *But I've given her my word.*

By the time his mount made its way through the mire to Radstock, it became abundantly clear that traveling to Cheddar and back on the same day would be difficult under ideal weather conditions. Under these conditions, it could take three or four days.

Three or four days they didn't have, especially this time of the year when the days were already so short.

While he was waiting to change horses in Radstock, he consulted the folded map in his pocket. He suddenly realized why there were so few towns between Bath and Cheddar, and his stomach somersaulted. As the crow flies, the distance between the two cities was not great.

But he had failed to notice on his map the vertical script that identified the Mendip Hills. He had never before felt more like a moron. He should have known better than go off half cocked to where he'd never tread before.

He pitied the poor horse which would have to climb the muddy hills.

But more than anything, he pitied himself.

He had let down Mrs. Bexley. She would lose her home.

When Sir Elvin called upon Catherine that

afternoon, she almost thought it was his brother who came strolling into her drawing room, even though Simpson had just announced the baronet. He was the image of Mr. Steffington.

As she looked closer, the differences between the two became more apparent. Her Mr. Steffington was not nearly so careful in his dress. He had come to her in Hessians that were not freshly polished, and his cravat had not been precisely tied. He had been comfortable in brown woolens.

His brother, on the other hand, looked as if he'd spent two or three hours of preparation with a gifted valet. From his charcoal pantaloons, to his claret silk waistcoat, to his rich velvet jacket, he presented a courtly appearance. How had he managed on so rainy a day? He must have been protected in a carriage or hackney.

"Won't you sit across from me?" she said.

He took a seat upon a damask settee that matched the one she sat upon. His gaze circled the chamber. "My brother is not here today?"

So Mr. Steffington had complied with her request not to mention the Chaucer manuscript to anyone. Had he not told his brother anything about what he was doing today? She feared that her version of his activities might conflict with Mr. Melvin Steffington's; therefore, she said as little as possible. "No, not today."

"I say, my brother's been rather quiet about the nature of the research he's helping you with."

She had known since that first day she could put her trust in Melvin Steffington – Aristotle. He had not betrayed that trust by confiding in his twin brother. She cocked her head and regarded him with dancing eyes. "I would be very surprised to learn that your scholarly brother was ever terribly communicative."

He chuckled. "Right-o. He has always been more given to reading than to talking."

His speech was really nothing like Aristotle's. The timbre of their voices was the same, but Sir Elvin's speech exuded the same confidence peculiar to those firstborn. Like Mr. Bexley. Melvin. Steffington, on the other hand, chose his words carefully and sparingly.

She was convinced she would never mistake Sir Elvin for his more sober twin, though as she peered at this one, she was astonished at how much the two looked alike. Astonishing, too, was her disappointment that he wasn't Aristotle. This was the first day she hadn't seen Mr. Steffington since their association had begun.

"What about you, Sir Elvin? Do you enjoy reading?" She wished to steer the conversation away from Melvin Steffington for fear her information might conflict with what he had told his brother.

He shook his head. "I've always preferred being out of doors. I'd rather shoot than anything – another difference between me and my twin brother."

"Yet you two are close?"

"Very. I cannot bear to think of him taking a post and moving away from me. The very thought is almost as painful as a death in the family."

She could not imagine Melvin Steffington ever confiding something so personal. Yet, because Sir Elvin had spoken of something so deeply emotional, she liked him far better than she had expected she would. He was not shallow like Mr. Bexley had been.

Oddly, she understood how Melvin's absence could disturb. For she greatly missed seeing him today. In a very short time she had become accustomed to and comfortable in his presence. "I understand."

"Forgive me, madam, for speaking of death so soon after your mourning has ended."

He displayed wonderful manners—as did most accomplished dancers. A pity he wasn't his brother.

There was a knock upon the door, and Simpson announced Mr. Longford. A moment later, that gentleman entered the chamber, his shiny boots still wet from the day's rain but the rest of him remarkably dry. She supposed his oilskins puddled on her marble entry hall.

Ever gracious, Sir Elvin replaced a cringe (displayed briefly after hearing Longford's name spoken) with a friendly greeting.

Mr. Longford wasn't nearly so gracious. He was unable to conceal his disappointment that Sir Elvin was calling upon the widow he so favored. After stiffly shaking the baronet's hand, he turned to Mrs. Bexley, bowing as he offered her a nosegay. "Allow me to offer these roses that match the bloom in your lovely cheeks."

"How thoughtful of you," she said.

The gentleman could not have looked more pleased with himself had he just placed a crown upon the queen's head. "That is the very same floral arrangement my brother procured for his betrothed, Miss Turner-Fortenbury—cousin to Lord Finchton, you know." He came to sit beside Sir Elvin.

Just to facetiously please Mr. Longford, she turned to Sir Elvin. "That would be Viscount

Finchton, a sixth cousin, twice removed of Miss Turner-Fortenbury." Returning her gaze to Mr. Longford, she asked, "Pray, when is you brother to marry Miss Turner-Fortenbury?"

"Next month." Mr. Longford then faced his rival. "I daresay I know not which twin you are."

"Forgive me," she said. "It didn't occur to me to introduce you two."

Mr. Longford glared at the man beside him. "We need no introduction. We were at Eton together."

She smiled at them. "Then you're friends?"

Sir Elvin shrugged. "I wouldn't actually say we're friends."

Mr. Longford shook his head. "No, not friends."

"Though I daresay we have no ill feelings toward one another. None whatsoever."

Her hand flew to her mouth. "Oh, dear, I still haven't disclosed the identity of the twin beside you, Mr. Longford. Which of the brothers do you think it is?"

"It must be Melvin because I understand he's been assisting you in some way only a scholar like he could."

"Actually, I am Sir Elvin."

Mr. Longford's countenance underwent a metamorphosis, and a smile lifted the corners of his mouth. (Even a man with the lowly rank of baronet merited Mr. Longford's admiration.) "It's a pleasure, Sir Elvin."

A short silence followed.

"Nasty day, is it not?" Sir Elvin's gaze swung from Catherine to Mr. Longford.

Mr. Longford nodded solemnly. "I had hoped to ride in Sydney Gardens today."

"I can't help but to worry about my brother. I'm

not precisely sure what he's doing today, but since he rose at five this morning, I had a feeling he was going on a journey." He eyed Catherine. "It's a frightful day to be on the road on a lone horse."

"He'll be fine," Mr. Longford said.

Sir Elvin frowned. "We lost one of our younger sisters to lung fever after she got soaked in a rainstorm."

Catherine's pulse soared. Was Aristotle all right?

Long after her callers had gone and long after night fell many hours later, she kept hoping to hear from Mr. Steffington. Hadn't he said he would apprise her of his findings at the first opportunity?

She had difficulty sleeping. Hour after hour she lay in her bed gathering her blankets around her, the wind howling and rain beating against her window. Her thoughts kept coming back to the fact the Steffingtons' young sister had taken lung fever and died after being in the cold rain.

When she did finally go to sleep, she awakened frightfully, every part of her trembling. She could not dispel the horrifying vision of Aristotle's body beneath sodden skies in a muddy ditch. It had taken her a minute to realize where she was, to realize it was just a nightmare.

Nevertheless, she could not go back to sleep.

Rain continued all of the following day. She never left Number 17 Royal Crescent—not only because of the foul weather but mostly because she did not want to miss Mr. Steffington when he called upon her.

When he did not come that day, then that

night, she grew alarmed. *Something has happened to him. And it's all my fault.*

$\mathcal{C}$hapter 7

After changing horses and eating cold meat and a bumper of ale at the coaching inn in Radstock, Melvin left that establishment's warmth behind and braved the steadily increasing rain and chilling winds. The road which slithered through the Mendip Hills was nothing more than a muddy quagmire, and progress was incredibly slow. Already it was two in the afternoon, and he'd not covered half the distance between Bath and Cheddar. What a fool he'd been to think he could have made the trip there and back in a single day. No matter how early he had risen that morning.

When planning the journey, he'd no way of knowing he would be inundated with unrelenting rain. Had he to do it all over again, would he have waited? Probably not. Time was more precious than gold. They had but eleven days in which to locate the Chaucer manuscript, and not a single clue had yet been uncovered.

With the rain and mist, his visibility was impaired. But he did not need to clearly observe the miles and miles of verdant hills around him to know how alone he was. That he'd not seen a single traveler since he left the inn three hours earlier could be attributed to the wretched weather. The weather could not be blamed, though, for the absence of houses along the way.

By four o'clock, night was already beginning to fall. How could he expect his weary mount to continue on when they would not be able to see their way? *I can't give up.*

With the departure of the murky daylight, the temperatures began to drop. It could freeze. He could freeze. To death. He thought of Charlotte, his favorite sister who caught lung fever and died after making her way home from the village in freezing rain. It had been years since he'd allowed himself to recall that painful loss.

I must keep on.

Whenever he thought of trying to take shelter, he would picture Mrs. Bexley lying on a wet street, rain pounding down on her, after she'd been forced from her home. In one of those odd transpositions the mind often plays, Mrs. Bexley's face was interchangeable with Charlotte's.

Because of that vision, he continued on throughout the night.

Ladies did not call upon unmarried gentlemen, but Catherine was far too worried about Melvin Steffington to have the slightest care for her reputation. So there she stood upon the step to the Steffingtons' house on Green Park Road, her cloak completely saturated. Hopefully, it had protected the gown beneath.

The gray-haired servant who opened the door looked askance at her. No doubt he thought her a doxy. "I am Mrs. Bexley, and I must speak to Sir Elvin." Her voice was uncharacteristically strident.

The man's eyes widened. "Won't you step in out of the rain?"

He left her removing her hood and shaking off

her cloak in the entry hall while he began to mount the wooden stairs.

A moment later, Sir Elvin raced down that same stairway, his eyes never leaving hers. From the stricken expression on his face, she realized he knew no more about his twin's location than she. "Have you news of my brother?"

A morose shake of her head was her only response. She felt like collapsing into a crying heap.

He recovered enough to assist her with the sodden cloak, which he handed off to the male servant. "Please, won't you come into the library where it's warm? You must be frightfully cold." She was cold, but she had a warm house to go into. What of poor Mr. Steffington? She kept thinking of his sister who had perished from the cold.

During her sleepless night, she had come to the decision that she must share with the baronet the details of her relationship to his brother.

He indicated a silk brocade sofa which was closest to the fire. "Please, won't you sit here."

"I feel so guilty sitting here when your brother is being exposed to all the worst elements. Because of me."

"Do you know where my brother has gone?"

I must not cry. She gave a solemn nod. But as she began to speak, she was incapable of keeping her voice from cracking with emotion. "He's gone to Cheddar."

"But that's across the Mendip Hills! In this weather?"

"He left early in the morning the day before yesterday."

His eyes, so much like Melvin's in every other

way, were as cold as anthracite. "Yes, I know when he left. What the devil was he doing going there?" His heated expression softened. "Forgive my language. I'm not myself. Deuced worried about Melvin."

"As am I." She drew a deep breath to keep from bursting into tears. It seemed to work. "Your brother is the most noble man I've ever known."

"You don't have to tell me that."

Of course his twin would know every nuance of Mr. Steffington's most agreeable personality. "I believe he's exposing himself to untold danger in order to keep a roof over my head." A sob broke free.

He quickly moved to the sofa, sat beside her, and placed a gentle hand upon hers. "Pray, you must tell me everything."

She told him about the stolen Chaucer, about the nature of the work Mr. Steffington was doing for her, and ended by telling him that when his twin learned of the letter from Coutts Bank, he promised to do everything in his power to find the manuscript.

"I take it a manuscript like that is worth a great deal of money?"

"There is no book in the English language that is more valuable. Selling it would take care of all my needs for the rest of my life. Even the fifteen percent your brother would get could be a great deal of money." Her lids lowered as she said a silent prayer for his safe return. She hadn't the heart to voice her fears to Sir Elvin for he was clearly as worried about his brother as she was.

It was best to change the topic of conversation. "I must beg that you not tell anyone about the stolen manuscript. Your brother gave me his word he wouldn't,"

"My brother's word is as good as money in the bank. And, of course, if you don't want to speak of it, I won't tell a soul."

He looked distracted, then suddenly stood. "I beg your pardon, but I must send for my coach and try to find Melvin."

"I have to come with you."

He paused, giving her a queer look. "That would hardly be proper, madam."

"I wouldn't be standing here if I were concerned about what was proper."

Their gazes locked and held, and in those few seconds when she peered into his dark eyes, she knew their shared concern for Melvin united them. "I am hardly a maiden, my dear sir, nor am I a girl. I am as old as you. Do you think that young?"

"Of course not."

"As distressing as it is to bring this up . . . what if your brother has fallen ill? I have some skill caring for the infirm. I want to be there in case your brother needs me."

Their eyes locked. It was a moment before he responded. "Very well."

After traveling all night, Melvin arrived at the posting inn in Cheddar, exhausted, cold, and thoroughly wet. The innkeeper had been most accommodating in leading him straight away to a warm room and sending up a hot meal. By the time Melvin had taken a long nap, his clothes— hung by the fire—had dried.

He dressed and went down to the tavern to initiate a conversation with the innkeeper. Melvin had already planned how he would approach the subject of Mrs. Higgins. "I say, I've a friend whose former servant has taken up lodgings at Pleasant View Cottage. Do you know them?"

The older man wiped away a dribble of ale from the counter. "That would be old Mr. Higgins' place. Poor fellow had seven daughters."

"How many sons had he?" Melvin asked.

"Not a single one. To make matters even worse, five of his daughters never married. They weren't a pretty lot, if you know what I mean?"

Melvin nodded.

"Poor man," the innkeeper continued. "Two or three of them went into service, and one of them—can't remember which—is back now, living with the oldest, who never left home and who is getting way up in years. Mr. Higgins confided in me that in his old age he grew thankful he had no sons."

"I daresay all parents end up being pleased with the gender of their offspring."

"It was more than that, actually. He said if he'd had a son he would have had to leave his small farm to the eldest, and there would be no place for his girls to live once they were pensioned off."

"So now the old maids have a home." Melvin needed to introduce his topic. "I suppose they live in the lap of luxury, what with one having been in service to the gentry." He needed to know if Mrs. Higgins had been spending wildly.

The innkeeper shook his head. "I don't think that's the case. The one what was in service—the healthiest, she is—has recently begun coming into town to sell eggs. If you ask me, she's desperate for money. Old Mr. Higgins had nothing to leave them. In his later years he weren't able to farm."

"Did he lease his land?"

The man nodded. "It's still being leased, but since it wasn't very large, it can't bring in much income."

Mrs. Bexley would be relieved to know her former housekeeper was innocent of the theft. No elderly woman would be making a long trek into town to sell a few paltry eggs if she hadn't great need of money.

On the other hand, Mrs. Bexley would be sad to know that her Mrs. Higgins was not comfortable in retirement.

If only they could get their hands on the stolen manuscript. Mrs. Bexley would be in a position to help her old servant.

Before he left Cheddar, there were two things he needed to do. First, he would post a letter to Dr. Mather. Those interested in expanding their libraries often consulted Melvin's old mentor. It was looking as if he—and possibly Mr. Christie—were their last hope of tracing the elusive thief.

With that letter dispatched, Melvin went to Pleasant View Cottage to give Mrs. Bexley's regards to her old employee—and to see for himself if she was living in reduced financial circumstances.

She thought she would go mad throughout the journey in Sir Elvin's coach. Relentless rain, graphite skies, and a sullen travelling companion were distressing enough, but her added worry over Melvin Steffington made her lower than an adder's belly. When the rain ceased midway through the afternoon, the sun stayed hidden behind heavy, dark clouds. Under these conditions, it would be days before the muddy roads would dry enough for travelers to speed along.

All of her life, Catherine had been terrified of riding in a coach at night. Even the insensitive Mr. Bexley would always have his coachman find an inn as soon as night fell in order to keep from subjecting Catherine to the dark roads where highwaymen lurked. Strangely, on this night, she ignored her own fears—except those fears for Mr. Steffington's well-being.

After ten hours they finally approached the Mendip Hills. Their inquiries at the coaching inn in Radstock had netted them the information that a man fitting Melvin's description had indeed changed horses there two days earlier. They remembered him well because no other lone travelers had braved such treacherous weather that day.

Which made her feel wretched. It was all her fault poor, noble Mr. Steffington was putting his person in jeopardy. She did not want to think about the misfortune that had fallen upon his poor sister many years ago.

Skies darkened after they left the inn. "Are you sure you want to continue on?" Sir Elvin asked. "You understand if our carriage should become stuck in the mud it could be many, many hours before another traveler happens along our road."

Worse than being stranded was the fear of the cold in the wee hours of the morning. But that same cold is exactly what pushed her into an affirmative answer. She couldn't bear to think of Aristotle alone and cold. Because of his perceived responsibility to her. "I'm sure."

Throughout the journey, the normally congenial Sir Elvin was much too disturbed to make pretty conversation with her. She knew, too, he resented her for endangering the person he was closest to on earth.

What a transformation had come over him. Two nights earlier he had been unable to remove his gaze from Catherine, hovering around her the duration of her time at the Upper Assembly Rooms. Then the following day, he'd rushed to call on her home.

She was relieved that she wasn't going to have to repel the baronet's advances. She had not the least desire to spend the rest of her life subservient to any man. Especially a man who shared many traits with the late Mr. Bexley.

Now Sir Elvin acted as if she were invisible. Was his silence because he hated her? She wouldn't blame him if he did.

The interior of their coach was in nearly total darkness when she finally lifted the velvet curtain. Under the faint moonlight she could see ahead about twenty feet. Thank God the rain had stopped.

Sir Elvin had insisted the driver stay off the rutted roads where they were certain to get stuck. Instead, he asked that the coachman drive on turf. He had more than once expressed his hopes that they were on the same path taken by Mr. Steffington.

By peering from the window she hoped she might be able to see if Mr. Steffington was . . . coming home or if he was in need of assistance. She prayed it wasn't the latter, though she kept finding her gaze fanning along the hillside, dreading to see a lifeless figure.

"I suppose you and I are both being very foolish in our worry over Melvin," he said.

Her brows lifted.

"If we look at it rationally," Sir Elvin said, "Considering the wretched weather, we should not have expected Melvin to be home so soon. Under such conditions, he would be lucky to make it from Bath to Cheddar in two days, certainly not to go to and from Cheddar in a single day. I cannot believe my brother so foolish as to think it a single-day trip."

"There is the fact that he'd never before been to Cheddar."

"I daresay he forgot about the Mendip Hills."

"Your brilliant brother?"

"Don't call him that to his face. He hates it."

"I know."

"He's not always brilliant. Just most of the time."

"I know." Her gaze continued to scan the landscape, searching for the missing twin.

"I truly hope he's not fool enough to ride over these hills on a cold night like this."

She gave a false laugh. "Is that not what we're doing?" As she spoke, she saw something dark moving toward their coach. Her heartbeat accelerated. The dark outline which she couldn't make out came closer. She had no idea what color of horse Melvin Steffington would be on or what he would be wearing, but as the dark silhouette of man on horse against the horizon drew nearer, she nearly lost her breath in anticipation. "I see something! Please, have the coachman stop!"

Sir Elvin drove his walking stick into the roof of the coach. "Stop!"

Even before the carriage came to a complete stop, she swung open her door. "Mr. Steffington!"

* * *

When he first heard the voice calling out in the night, he feared he'd gone delusional. It sounded like Mrs. Bexley. Had he been thinking of her? Is that why he thought he'd heard her voice? God knows he'd been through enough physical discomfort these past few days—and still was bloody, bloody cold. Such misery could drive a sane man mad.

Surely, though, his eyes weren't playing tricks on him, too. He was certain a pair of horses were leading a coach in his direction. Why would anyone be trying to cross these hills at night when the dirt roads that had been there were now rivers of mud?

He drew up his mount in order to listen more attentively. He heard his name again.

And this time he was sure it was Mrs. Bexley's sweet voice. What the devil?

The coach came a bit closer, then halted, and a door swung open. "Is that you, Mr. Steffington?"

Those were the sweetest words he'd ever heard. "Yes! Is that you, Mrs. Bexley?"

A second door flew open, and a man leaped from the coach. "Thank God, Melvin!"

It took Melvin a few seconds to piece together what was going on. From the tone of his twin's voice, he could tell he was upset. Which meant these two were out on this frightful night looking for him.

Elvin was prone to worry, and he had obviously worried about him. Melvin suddenly felt remorseful he'd left town without telling his brother where he was going. "Forgive me for not telling you about my journey," he said to Elvin.

By then Elvin had rushed up to him. "How are you? I was beastly worried about you."

Melvin was so happy to see his brother—and to hear Mrs. Bexley's voice—he forgot all about being cold. A warmth burned deep inside him. "I've had a pretty wretched couple of days, but I am fine now. The inside of your coach is most alluring. Where'd you get it?"

"I hired it."

Mrs. Bexley approached the brothers. "I have been worried to death about you—so much so I went to your brother and told him everything."

"Everything?"

"Yes. Even about that horrid letter from Coutts."

Elvin slung his arm around his brother, and they moved toward the coach. "Three heads are better than two. I will help you and Mrs. Bexley. Pray, what did you learn in Cheddar?"

He hated to own up to his futility, to slam another door on their search. "Mrs. Higgins is not the one."

"I am happy to have that confirmed," Mrs. Bexley said. "Though it is so very discouraging that we can't see any opening in this dark tunnel."

The coachman took Melvin's mount and tethered it behind the coach before the three of them piled inside. His brother sat next to Mrs. Bexley, who handed off the rug to Melvin. "Here, Mr. Steffington, you take this. You must be chilled to the very bone."

He was too blasted cold to deny what she offered. "I feel as if I shall never thaw."

"I should never have let you go off like that. I knew Mrs. Higgins was incapable of dishonesty."

"By the way, she sends you her regards." He proceeded to tell them what he had learned about the former housekeeper's dire financial situation. "I daresay when we do find the Chaucer manuscript, you'll have to increase the poor lady's pension."

"That's a very good suggestion."

Though he could not see them well, Melvin was swamped with the feeling that his brother and Mrs. Bexley had grown very close during their journey.

It should come as no surprise to him. She had been struck by the similarities between his brother and her *dear Mr. Bexley*.

They rode on in silence. Melvin was with the two people whose companionship he enjoyed the most. Then why was he growing melancholy? Just a few minutes previously, he'd bubbled with a deep sense of well-being.

For some odd reason, seeing his brother and Mrs. Bexley so comfortable together saddened him. He did not like to think of Elvin tiring of Mrs. Bexley as he always tired of his ladybirds. She was too fine a woman to be taken lightly.

There was also a little niggling disappointment strumming through him. She *had* told him he was her most favored man. Now it seemed she obviously preferred his brother.

$\mathcal{C}$hapter 8

The last person she wished to see upon returning to Bath was Mr. Longford, but there he sat in his fancy coach just as the Steffingtons' rented chaise was bringing her home. As quickly as she scurried from the chaise, he was faster, reaching the top step just before her.

Owing to his lack of height, she stopped on the step just below him so as not to call attention to his short stature.

She could feel his gaze raking over her. Being the fashion conscious person he was, he would be sure to realize from her heavily wrinkled dress that she'd worn it for the past two days. He was also bound to wonder why she needed the heavy, hooded cloak on a sunny day like this one had become. She felt ever so dowdy standing beside the impeccably dressed man of small stature.

"Good day to you, Mrs. Bexley." His eye flicked to the rented coach. Any hopes he'd had of discovering who she'd been with were dashed when the driver flicked the ribbons and sped off.

She knew just what to do to avoid his prying questions. She spun around to stare at his coach and four. The coach itself was shiny black with gilt paint edging the doors and rich claret velvet curtains. The four black horses looked identical. And they were beauties. Why in the world one would need four matched beauties like those to take him the distance of half a mile within the city of Bath? "I declare, Mr. Longford, I have not seen your magnificent conveyance in daylight before. I already thought your barouche the most elegant ride possible, but this is just too magnificent!"

The man positively glowed. "I commissioned it from the carriage maker to the Duke of Clarence."

She attempted to effect a look of appreciative amazement. "How fortunate I am to have ridden in it. I declare, I shall feel connected to the Royal Family."

"It was my intention to take you for a ride in it this very day."

"You are frightfully kind, but alas, I cannot today. I have a great many business matters to attend to."

His smiling face fell. "I have been attempting to see you these past three days."

"My affairs are in a state of flux at present, and they demand my immediate attention." She whirled toward the door. "I'm sorry I won't be able to visit with you today."

"Have you been with Melvin Steffington?" He nearly sneered the words.

She slowly turned back and gave him a cold stare. "Actually, I have been with both of the twins, but I fail to understand why that should concern you." She rushed into the house.

In the entry corridor, Simpson met her. "Welcome home, madam. Should you wish to see the post?"

"Indeed I would." She prayed that Mr. Christie had responded to her letter. She picked up a short stack of letters from the sideboard and quickly examined them. Her heartbeat drummed when she saw Mr. Christie's distinctive handwriting. She rushed to the library, which was quite dark, and drew open the celadon-colored damask draperies. Now the light was good enough to read. She sat down at the desk that had belonged to Mr. Bexley. Really, she must start thinking of these things as *her* possessions.

She carefully unfolded Mr. Christie's letter and began to read.

My Dear Mrs. Bexley

It is with unimaginable disappointment that I read your letter informing me of the grievous loss of your nearly priceless manuscript of Chaucer's major work. It would have been the greatest acquisition I'd ever presided over.

Equally as shocking to me is that I never heard of it coming on the market. It is a rare occurrence when something of that import is not presented to me.

I feel it my duty to point you toward two of the newest, most enthusiastic book collectors in the kingdom in the hopes that one of them can assist you where I have failed. (These would be in addition to Lords Oxford and Spencer, both of them known far and wide for their extensive collections of books.) One of the new collectors is Thomas Whitebread, and the other is Lord Seacrest. I pray this information is of assistance to you.

It grieves me that the theft occurred shortly after my visit. Such an occurrence has the ramification to impugn my character. I have tried to remember to whom I may have spoken of your treasure, but my memory is not so sharp after the passage of four months. If my recall should improve, I vow to contact you at once. Allow me once again to say how very sorry I am over your loss.

Yours ever truly,
J. Christie

By the time she had bathed and changed into fresh clothing, Simpson announced another caller: Mr. Steffington. This caller was far more welcome than Mr. Longford had been.

She understood why he would have been the top pupil in his class. He was possessed of a slavish determination to complete his tasks successfully. Not for the first time, she congratulated herself for having chosen him.

Though she normally saw callers in the drawing room, she felt most comfortable with Mr. Steffington in the library. They had spent so many comforting hours there with each other. "Please show Mr. Steffington to the library."

When she entered that chamber a few moments later, he stood. Her gaze swept from the top of his dark head, along his clean-shaven face, to his freshly starched but inexpertly tied cravat, and his chocolate-colored frockcoat, buff breeches that molded to his long, muscled legs and terminated in a pair of soft cowhide boots that were in need of shine. No doubt, his brother would cringe over his careless appearance.

"Mr. Steffington! I did not expect to see you today. Did I not tell you to climb into bed and catch up on the sleep you have missed?" *Because of his loyalty to me.*

"We've only ten days."

She was so touched that he shared her heavy burden.

Her face brightened. "I have a lead!" She went to the desk, got Mr. Christie's letter, and offered it to him.

He scanned it, then looked up at her. "Do you know either of these men?"

She shook her head.

He went to the desk. "I shall write to each of them, apprising them of my scholarly pursuits and inviting myself to see their collections. I had originally hoped to have Dr. Mather open the doors for me, but we haven't time now."

She went to the shelf for her *Debrett's* and looked up Lord Seacrest's seat. "Lord Seacrest's home is Granfield Manor in Warwickshire." But how was she to discover the direction of Mr. Whitebread?

"I go there today." His square jaw set firmly, and she thought he looked more masculine than any man of her acquaintance.

"*We* go there," she said in her most authoritarian voice.

His head cocked as he regarded her from beneath lowered brows. "A lady does not ride on horseback for more than a hundred miles."

"We are not riding on horseback, nor are we taking a post chaise. I shall hire a coach. I'll send Simpson over to the livery at once."

His hand seized her arm. "You are certain you wish to come with me? It will be a long and grueling journey – not to mention the impropriety of it."

"I should die of curiosity were I to stay here." She started for the library door. "I do hope your brother can come with us." Traveling with two men was far more respectable than just the two of them. "Where is he? I thought he had taken an interest in assisting us."

"My brother collapsed on his bed. He has always needed sleep more than me."

She knew the strict discipline which guided Mr. Steffington's life deprived him of anything he considered frivolous – even sleep. "Do you think we can persuade him to journey with us?"

He shook his head. "As it happens, he has promised to preside over our sister Annie's debut tomorrow night. It's the sort of thing that falls into the realm of duties of the firstborn."

"I do believe you're happy not be the firstborn."

"You know me too well, madam."

"There is one thing I must request that you do on our journey."

His brows elevated.

"You are not to go without sleep. We will stop at coaching inns along the way. You've already forsaken too much sleep on my behalf."

"If you insist upon sleep, then I dictate the hours of rising."

"Fair enough."

"First, I know just the man who can tell me where Mr. Whitebread lives. I will dispatch both letters today on the overnight post. Then after I pack a few things I shall return here. Early afternoon."

Curiously, Long*mouth's* expensive coach and four was in front of his house on Green Park Road when Melvin returned. Why in the blazes was he there? Elvin would never willingly suffer the man's company.

As Melvin went to enter his home, Longford was leaving. The two men nearly collided. Longford gazed up at him, his eyes narrow. Melvin had never realized how short the man truly was. His nose was directed at the center of Melvin's chest.

"Ah, you're just the man I wished to see," Longford said. His booming voice exuded the manliness his body lacked.

Now it was Melvin's turn to narrow his gaze. "Pray, why would you need to see me?"

"Because you have been spending a considerable amount of time with the woman to whom I am betrothed."

"I don't know what you're referring to. The only woman who's been in my company is Mrs. Bexley."

Longford's green eyes chilled. "Precisely."

Melvin could not have been more stunned had the man declared he was a triplet to Melvin and Elvin. A shorter, more verbose triplet. His thoughts flashed to the last time he had seen Mrs. Bexley with Longford when they had danced. She had been so disinterested in what her partner was saying that she did not even try to maintain eye contact with him. Melvin thought listening to Lizzy discourse on her new bonnet might be more interesting than Long*mouth*. Er, Longford.

It suddenly occurred to him the reason Mrs. Bexley was keen to recover the Chaucer was so she would not be forced to unite herself with Longmouth.

He couldn't blame her.

Yet he blamed her for agreeing to marry a man she could never love. All for money. Melvin's good opinion of her lowered.

Melvin's hostile gaze locked with the other man's. "What is the purpose of this visit?"

"I, ah, I just wanted you to know the lady is promised."

"You think I want her for myself?"

"I daresay she would hardly give you the time

of day. After all, you are merely a younger son."

"But you're wrong Longford. She's given me more than the time of day." With that, Melvin entered the house and slammed the door on the other man.

Perhaps she should have stayed back in Bath. What good could she possibly be to this expedition? It was obvious Mr. Steffington had no use for her. He didn't even want to engage her in conversation. They had been traveling for four hours, and he had said fewer than a dozen words during that time.

She wondered if his silence was because he so exceedingly enjoyed the book he was reading or if it was because he found her as boring as she found Mr. Longford. A pity his brother hadn't come. At least he displayed all the courtly traits his twin lacked. He was just as smooth as Mr. Bexley—which might explain why she had heretofore preferred the quiet brother.

"Your book must be very good," she finally said. "Might I inquire what it is?"

He closed the book, keeping his index finger there to mark the page and glared at her. "Euripides."

Her nose scrunched. "No doubt it's about some kind of ancient war. Is it Greek or Roman? I never can remember all those foreign-sounding names."

"Euripides was Greek, madam." He re-opened his book.

"You are very fortunate that your stomach does not prevent you from reading in a moving carriage."

He gave her an impatient look. "Enlighten me, please, as to the relationship between your stomach and reading."

She began to giggle. She laughed so hard, tears began to stream along her face.

"Pray, what is so funny?"

It was a while before she could compose herself enough to answer, and when she did, her sentence came out in pieces. "I was picturing. . ." She broke into laugher again. ". . .a stomach with eyes."

He gazed at her as if she were mad. Then the expression on his face softened, and he, too, began to laugh. A moment later, he confessed. "I visualize a statue of Buddha with eyes protruding from his belly."

"And an opened book facing that huge belly!" She laughed anew.

When the pair of them eventually recovered, he asked, "Why do you link reading and stomachs? This is a new amalgam to me."

"Have you never heard of reading while in motion causing an upset stomach?"

"Never." He studied her. "You are cursed with this malady?"

She nodded ruefully.

"That is a most severe deprivation on a long journey like this." A moment later, he asked, "What do you do for amusement while traveling?"

He had to ask? "When I am not alone. . ."

He removed his finger from the book and firmly closed it. "Forgive me. I have been a most rude traveling companion. To quote Lord Chesterfield, I lack *the Graces*."

"At last, Mr. Steffington, we have both read the same book."

"Tell me, did you laugh when you read *Lord Chesterfield's Letters to His Son*?"

She started giggling again. He must think her the silliest woman there could be. But, really, she had laughed aloud when she'd read Lord Chesterfield's admonition to his son regarding the . . . picking of noses, which of course, was not a topic she could discuss with the man sharing her carriage.

"*Under no circumstances are you to look at the finger. . .*" Mr. Steffington stopped himself from completing his lordship's words to his son. "Forgive me, 'tis a most indelicate topic to bring up with a lady."

She started laughing again. "It *was* awfully funny."

He tried to look serious, but he too began laughing. "My brother and I passed the book around Eton."

She nodded. "It is just the sort of thing lads of that age would especially love."

"I know the man was heavily criticized—posthumously—but never was a parent more obsessed that his offspring should achieve perfection."

"It is touching. Sad, but touching."

"The letters do have the benefit of improving lads who read them at Eton."

The carriage went quiet again.

"I am sure there must be other books we both have read," he finally said.

"But you don't like poetry, and you don't read novels."

"Certainly not novels such as those written by Walpole or Monk Lewis, but I do like Mr. Scott's historical novels."

She was smiling so frequently now, it was difficult to believe she had been melancholy just minutes before. "As do I, ever so much. I love to read about knights of yore."

"'Tis the same with me."

"See, we do have shared interests."

"What of Longford? Do you share many interests with him?"

She had the distinct feeling Mr. Steffington was glaring at her. What could she have said or done to cause his manner to change so abruptly? "I don't know Mr. Longford all that well. Have you forgotten I only recently came out of mourning?"

"I may be ignorant of *the Graces*, but is it not customary for one just coming out of mourning to wait for some time before embarking upon another marriage?"

"I believe that is customary—and certainly the proper way for a widow to conduct herself."

She was now certain of it. He was glaring at her. It was the kind of glare that might greet an *I'm-frightfully-sorry-I've-accidentally-shot-your-dog* statement. Oh, dear. What had she done to anger him?

Well, two could play that game. Her gaze flicked to his book and she spoke icily. "Pray, don't let me keep you from reading about ancient Greek carnage." With that remark, she lifted away the curtain with a trembling hand and began to peer at the countryside under twilight's dim glow.

What had he done to raise her hackles? It was he who should have his hackles raised. After all, the woman had gone and gotten herself engaged to a man she could not pretend to be in love with. And this, after she had told Melvin he was the brightest star in her galaxy.

He hadn't thought her the sort of woman to

idly ingratiate herself with every man who came into her sphere. He had actually liked her. In much the same way as he liked Annie and Lizzy.

But altogether different.

He supposed she was one of those practiced flirts who made each fellow she was with feel as if he were *the brightest star in her galaxy*. His brows lowered, and he stiffened as he moved away from her and practically ripped open his book. Though he made out as if he were reading, he wasn't even on the same page he'd been reading when she interrupted, nor could he have concentrated on it had he been.

This journey was nothing like their last had been. She and his brother had chatted like magpies. She was bound to be decidedly disappointed that Elvin hadn't come with them. Unlike himself, Elvin was possessed of *the Graces*.

He found himself wondering if Elvin fancied the lady. They had certainly gotten on well yesterday and earlier today. More than once she had commented on how very much Elvin reminded her of *dear Mr. Bexley*. He sighed. Yes indeed, the woman made a habit of praising men. Anyone who imparted praise and flattery so easily certainly could not be sincere.

Even though she had been the one to get snippy with him, he felt wretchedly rude. As a gentleman, he should be gallant to his companion, no matter how irritating she was.

Or how often she doled out false flattery.

They rode on in silence beneath skies merging from daylight to night. With nightfall, the interior of the carriage became uncomfortably cold. He noted that she stuffed her hands into a huge fur muff. Ermine, was it not? Elvin would know.

His guilt over his rudeness gnawed at him until their coach was in complete darkness, and he closed his book. "How do you feel now? The motion is not making you sick?"

"Not as long as I'm facing forward."

"You mean if you were seated where I am, you would get ill?"

"Just thinking of it makes me queasy. Oh, Mr. Steffington, I don't know what I was thinking when I inflicted myself upon you. I am the worst sort of traveling companion there could be."

"Now, now don't say that. You're perfectly. . . acceptable."

"I haven't told you another reason I wish to stop for the night."

"Go on."

"I'm frightfully afraid of travelling the main posting roads after dark."

"Why?"

"I'm terrified of highwaymen. My aunt and uncle were murdered by highwaymen when they didn't readily hand over their jewels."

He winced. "Does that mean you wish to stop at the next village that has an inn? It is not even five o'clock yet."

"Yes." Her voice sounded even younger than Lizzy's. The poor lady. She must be petrified.

At once he got the coachman's attention and told him to be in search of a coaching inn as soon as possible. Then he faced her. "You realize we will be wasting valuable hours?"

"I know." A moment later, her voice sounding incredibly frail and youthful, she added, "There's more."

"Pray, madam, are you afraid of dragons?"

She started to giggle again.

What was there about her giggle that whenever he heard it, he was powerless not to laugh with her? In fact, he had laughed more the past week than he had in the past two months. "What do you find so amusing?" he asked.

"The notion of dragons. A learned man such as yourself knows there's no such thing as dragons."

"While they might be as mythical as a minotaur, they are readily referenced in English literature." His voice sombered. "Forgive my levity, Mrs. Bexley. What else is there that frightens you?"

She hesitated a moment before answering. "I am terrified of sleeping alone at a posting inn."

"Now see here, madam, I cannot share your bed!"

She started giggling again. "I didn't mean for you to share my bed. Surely you know I'm not that sort of woman. But can you please demand to have the chamber next to mine? Then I wouldn't be so afraid."

"Certainly." He had already planned to do that. He did not like the notion of a defenseless woman being alone in a strange inn.

"And I thought perhaps you and I could sit before the fire in the private parlor and chat until one of us gets sleepy."

His presence would keep her from being frightened. "As you wish. I think to protect your good name- - -"

"We should use false names."

"Exactly."

Chapter 9

He had thought this night would bring him nothing but remorse over the precious hours lost, but nothing could have been farther from the truth. He could not remember when he had more enjoyed an evening. He and Mrs. Bexley—who were at present answering to the name Mr. and Miss Smith—were ensconced in the cozy parlor adjacent to her bedchamber, a good wood fire burning at the stone hearth. While sooty coal fires always brought to mind the teeming Capital, the smell of wood burning always brought to mind fresh country skies.

Because the night had become inky black with an icy sting in the air, and angry winds howled beyond these windows, the warm little chamber cocooned them most happily.

He and Mrs. Bexley had long discussions over Mr. Scott's historical novels and Mr. Burke's political—and atheist—beliefs while leisurely eating an excellent country dinner of roasted pork and potatoes. The innkeeper even procured for them a bottle of claret.

After dinner, they carried their wine goblets to the little chintz sofa near the fire and continued their discussion. Since the sofa was really more the size of a settee, they were very close. Physically. Her upper arm kept brushing up against his. It only then occurred to him how improper this was. Mrs. Bexley's good name would be ruined if anyone ever learned that they had traveled together with not even a lady's maid to lend propriety. And if it were ever learned they had actually slept at an inn under false names, she would never again be welcome in the homes of respectable people.

No one must ever know. He would protect her reputation in the same way he served as her protector in other respects. The poor lady had no man to take care of her.

"Really, Airy," she said, "could you not have come up with a more convincing name than Smith?"

"Did you just call me Airy?"

She gazed at him with laughing eyes, her cheeks dimpling—and making her look incredibly young. She fluttered her lashes as she nodded.

"A derivative of Aristotle! Who told you?"

"Do not all of your friends refer to you by that name?"

That was true. "I dislike being called Aristotle."

"It suits you far better than Melvin." She scrunched up her nose. "Not just because you're veddy, veddy smart."

Good lord! The lady was foxed!

She set down her goblet and eyed him. "But I prefer Airy."

"That is without a doubt the silliest name I've ever heard."

Placing her hands on her hips, she glared at him. "You dare to say my father's name is silly? My father was the most intelligent man I've ever known. Until I met you."

"Your father's name was Aristotle?" He found that incredible.

"No, you silly man. My father's name was Harold."

"I thought you said—no, implied—that his name was Airy."

"It was. Almost. Everyone called him Harry. Do you not think that a remarkably masculine name?"

"Yes, it is."

She stared at him, her lips pursed. "Melvin just doesn't suit you."

He actually found himself agreeing with her. He hated their twinly names. But he wasn't about to call himself Aristotle. How arrogant would that be? Besides, this was Georgian England, not ancient Greece. "Since only my siblings ever refer to me by my Christian name, it's hardly worth worrying your pretty head over."

He had called her pretty. Melvin had never in his seven and twenty years told a female who was not his sister that she was pretty. He hoped she hadn't noticed, or she was apt to think he was trying to seduce her.

"Oh, Airy, do you really find me pretty?"

He found himself staring at her. The flames sparkled in her golden hair, and the heat tinged her cheeks pink. He had always been acutely aware of the unusual color of those magnificent eyes, but he had not noticed how long her lashes were. But then, he'd never been so close to her. Her faint lavender scent had become as much a part of her as her trilling laughter.

This was entirely too intimate. "Of course you're pretty," he snapped. "But really, you shouldn't address me by my first name."

"Silly, I'm not. I refuse to call you Melvin."

What a sad situation he was in when an

inebriated woman made more sense than him. "For the sake of making my point, madam, let's say my first name was Harry. You are not to address me as such without drawing censure. Why, you don't even refer to your late husband by his Christian name!"

"It didn't suit him. Only Mr. Bexley would do."

"May I suggest you only call me Mr. Steffington?"

She lowered her voice in an effort to mimic him. "You may suggest anything you like, but on this journey I shall only refer to you as Airy. Are we not pretending to be brother and sister?"

"Well, yes. . ."

"Then I shall call you Airy for the duration of this journey." She yawned and folded her head against his shoulder. "Have you heard anything about Lord Seacrest's library?"

Should he ignore that her head was quite intimately resting upon his shoulder? If he said something, she might remove it. He wouldn't like that. Even though he knew it was wrong, he felt as comfortable as when he was as a lad in his Grandmama's big, curtained four-poster. "Actually, after I thought about it, I realized he must have been the earl Dr. Mather had visited in Warwickshire. That peer was keenly interested in Shakespeare's folios and was determined to use his fortune to acquire one for each play."

"So he's very wealthy?"

He nodded. "In addition to owning a huge piece of Warwickshire, he also owns coal mines in Wales and a sugar plantation in the West Indies."

She held up her hand. "Say no more! One who owns coal mines controls the world."

"I learned one more interesting thing about

him."

"What?"

"He is a recluse."

"Then there will be no possibility he will recognize me!"

She was quick witted. She neither read Latin nor Greek nor had an interest in those two ancient civilizations that thrilled him, but she was possessed of uncommon good sense, and she displayed good understanding of the books she had read.

Altogether, he thought her intelligence superior to that of his sisters, but that was no great compliment, owing to the fact his sisters were far more interested in reading Ackermann's than the *Edinburgh Review.* Still, it was enlightening to him that women were not as dull as he'd once thought them.

All of a sudden he realized this woman whose head had softly rested upon his chest was affianced to another. He stiffened, took two firm hands and removed her from his person, then angrily rose.

All the nice feelings he'd had for her vanished with the realization this woman was nothing more than a flirt and even worse—a fortune hunter. Both were abhorrent to him. "You are tired, and we must rise early. I bid you goodnight, madam." With that, he grabbed what was left of the wine bottle and stormed from the chamber. He had a very good mind to get thoroughly foxed himself!

"Night, night, Airy. Sleep tight, and don't let the bedbugs bite."

A steady tapping upon her chamber door awakened her the following morning. It took her a moment to remember where she was. There was no sign of the green silk bed curtains she was accustomed to seeing the first thing each morning. She rose on her elbows and gazed around the austere cream-colored chamber with its huge wooden ceiling beams. Her fire had died out, but the room still held its warmth.

"Who is it?"

"Melvin Steffington. I've brought you breakfast."

As soon as she heard his name, a flood of memories from the previous night embarrassed her. She had insulted him by saying she disliked his name. Worse yet, she had called him Airy! She had a lamentable habit of saying the most stupid things when she consumed wine. What must he think of her?

It was bad enough that he would think her ill-mannered, but now he was apt to also think her a lush. She was sure, though, that there was wine left when Mr. Steffington left the chamber, and since he too was drinking, she could not have drunk more than two glasses—which was one more than what was customary for Catherine.

When she went to move from the warm bed, pain surged to her temple. Another casualty of the wine. She stepped cautiously toward the door. Each step vibrated to her throbbing head. "That is very kind of you," she said to the door that separated them. "Please go ahead and eat. Perhaps by the time I'm dressed, I will feel more like eating than I do just now."

He cleared his throat. "If there's a need, I've brought tisane."

"There is need," she groaned. *A very great need.*

"If you'll just open the door a bit, I'll hand you

the glass. It's our valet's own special decoction which my brother swears by to banish the bad head after. . ."

She was utterly mortified. "After one has imbibed too much?"

"I wouldn't necessarily say that." His voice was ever so polite. "You scarcely had two glasses."

"You are too kind, Mr. Steffington." She inched the door open and stuck out her hand for the elixir.

It tasted nasty, but if it would rid her of the wretched headache, it would be well worth it.

Because she was unaccustomed to dressing herself, it took her longer than normal, and still her hair was a disaster. Fortunately, Mr. Steffington wasn't the sort of man who would notice. As she peered at herself in the looking glass, she unaccountably wondered which of her features he would take notice of. If he were apt to take notice of any.

This was not her best day. Her eyes were dull, and she looked pallid. And she prayed he would not notice that no matter how hard she had tried to arrange her hair, it still looked as if she had just climbed from her bed.

When she finally made her way to the adjoining parlor, her head still throbbed.

He stood as she came through the doorway, and she inclined her head ever so slowly so as not to jar it and send her into agonies of pain. Her glance flicked to the plate in front of him. He had eaten every bite.

The very sight of her own plate with toast and hog's pudding sent her stomach reeling. She could not even sit in front of it. Instead she remained standing, even though he indicated for her to sit in front of untouched plate full of food.

When she didn't move, a sly smile lifted one corner of his very agreeable mouth. "Allow me to guess. Could Mrs. Bexley be feeling poorly today?"

"Your amusement does not amuse me, Mr. Steffington, for it comes at my cost."

"Forgive me, but you were so. . .so delightful last night."

Her eyes narrowed. "In what way?"

"Have no fear that you've done anything less than expected of a lady."

That was a relief. "So, in what way was I delightful?" Uh, oh. She vaguely recalled placing her head against his chest. Oh, dear. Crimson hiked into her cheeks.

He shrugged. "Allow me to say that you behaved as if we were very old friends."

She certainly hoped he meant *friend* and not *doxy*. "I feel as if we are old friends." Truly, he'd been more loyal to her than any man she'd ever known. Even Mr. Bexley.

She frowned. Especially Mr. Bexley.

"If you're not going to eat, we need to carry on."

Because the sun had not risen high in the sky when they first started their journey, it was cool enough to have Catherine stuffing her gloved hands within her muff—after throwing a rug across her lap. As skies brightened, she was able to throw off the rug.

A pity she couldn't get rid of her headache that easily. "I thought you said your valet's elixir of tisane always brought relief to your brother."

His brows lowered. "It's not helping you?"

"Oh, it's helped lessen the intensity of the pain."

"I'm terribly sorry. It's my fault for continuing to fill your glass."

"You didn't pour it down my throat. I really should have known better. It's just that I have not had a single drop of wine in these past fourteen months. It didn't seem right while I was in mourning."

"That would explain why after so small amount, you . . . experienced the effects of the spirits."

"I know you're trying to be the perfect gentlemen by reassuring me, but I would prefer to speak of my embarrassment no more."

"As you wish. What would you like to speak of?"

"Our quest. When shall we arrive at Lord Seacrest's?"

"I hope to be there by three this afternoon."

"If you read the map correctly." She flashed a smile. "You did account for hills, dales, and mountains this time?"

He tried to look angry, but he was unable to suppress his smile. "Allow me to make a proposal. I won't speak any more about your . . . wine binge if you won't speak about my mapping mishaps."

"Wine binge?" she shrieked.

He started laughing, and she was powerless not to join him. She loved to laugh. Always had. It had been a great disappointment that Mr. Bexley had neither a sense of humor nor was he clever enough to know when she was teasing.

In spite of her dull headache, she was nearly swamped with a feeling of well-being. Mr. Steffington was so very good for her. Perhaps, though, her happiness was connected to the emerging sun. Sunshine always had that effect upon her.

What a pretty site all those red and gold autumn leaves made as they scattered beneath the blue skies. Even the stark branches of the beech and oak were lovely to behold on this cheerful day.

If only the motion of the carriage did not disturb the contents of her stomach. If only her head did not throb.

"I think when we arrive at Granfield Manor, you ought to stay in the coach. That is," he said, eying her muff. "If the weather doesn't turn too cool. We are going north."

"So it is expected to be cooler."

He shrugged.

"I don't wish to stay in the carriage." She folded her arms across her chest.

"Then what is it you would like, madam?"

"I want to be your wife."

$\mathcal{C}$hapter 10

What the devil! *She wants to marry me?* Their gazes locked and held. For that one moment, he fancied that she really did wish to marry him. But as quickly as she had uttered the words, he realized she didn't want to be his wife but wanted to be his fake wife for an afternoon.

For some odd reason, the truth deflated him. Not, of course, that he wished to be married. He had no desire to be shackled for life to some empty-headed female. It was just that. . . well, the notion of a lovely thing like Mrs. Bexley being attracted to him couldn't help but please any man.

Good lord, that was the sort of reasoning that ruled his twin—not the serious, pragmatic brother. He had best push away such destructive thoughts.

He met her gaze squarely and shook his head. "No, no, that won't do."

She gave him that pout she had so successfully employed in the past to get exactly what she wanted from him. "Give me one good reason why it won't."

"Your good name. There's one good reason."

"Lord Seacrest need never find out my true identity."

"You couldn't possibly know such a thing."

She eyed him with a smug look that

accentuated the dimple in her cheek. "But there is the *probability* that he will never learn who I am. Are you not a believer in mathematical probabilities, Mr. Steffington? Are you not given to looking at life in terms of mathematics?"

He was, so much so that he had once seriously considered being a mathematician. Before he realized he loved books more. How was it this woman knew him so well? It was deuced awkward having a woman getting so close. He cleared his throat. "You know I am."

"Then there you have it!"

"No, I don't. Why can't you just stay in the coach and let me do what you came to me to do in the first place?"

"I have a very good reason for not wanting to stay in the carriage. Unless Lord Seacrest has the Chaucer on display under glass as did my late husband and his father before him, determining if Lord Seacrest has the Chaucer might take a concentrated bit of deduction. It could be hours. It's not like you can just waltz in there and demand to see the Chaucer. You must go about searching for it in a polite manner. Have him think you're looking for something else."

"I had hoped to play to his vanity and make it appear I have come to see one of the finest libraries in the kingdom."

"Oh yes, I am certain he'd like that. Man doesn't collect not to share."

"Dr. Mather said the very same thing." And Mather was one of the most intelligent men he'd ever known. He cleared his throat. What was there about this woman that had him prefacing so many remarks with a rumpled cough? "And what if we discover the Chaucer in his possession? Then will you reveal your true identity?"

She puckered her lips in thought. "That's a very good question." She sighed. "I shall have to cross that bridge when I come to it, but if I must claim it, then I'm ever so happy to have a strapping man like you with me."

Strapping man? No one had ever referred to him in that way before. Elvin had likely been referred to in such a manner. And he supposed they did look exactly the same to most people. He *was* even the tallest twin by an inch.

Suddenly, he grew suspicious of her comment regarding his size. Why should his size matter? Did the lady want him to seize the book and fight off the peer's servants as he and Mrs. Bexley made a getaway? He could see he was going to have discuss this further with the woman.

But first, he needed to address what she'd said just prior to the *strapping* praise part. "Now see here, you can't just say *I'll cross that bridge when I come to it*. The key to any successful mission is a well-thought-out plan." Now he folded his arms across his chest. "I refuse to step one foot inside of Granfield Manor without a plan."

"There are some things in life for which one cannot plan."

One minute ago he was a strapping man whose company she desired, and now she spoke icily as if she must wish him to Coventry.

"I always have a plan."

She glared. "It's impossible to be prepared for every contingency. I like to get the lay of the land before I decide upon a course of action."

"Then it is very good thing you are not leading men into battle because you could lead your troops to slaughter."

Her eyes narrowed. "You are accusing me of gross incompetence."

"Do you know how ridiculous you sound? You're not a general, Mrs. Bexley."

She started to giggle. Her laughing increased. She laughed so hard, rivulets streamed from her lovely eyes.

Once again, her laughter was contagious. Why was it she made him laugh so easily? No one had ever had such an effect upon him.

After a considerable period of time, she wiped away the last of her tears and faced him. "It really is too funny imagining me as a general! You do say the silliest things." She drew a breath. "But to return to our discussion, can we not reach some sort of compromise? Partial plan, partial improvisation?"

"Would you care to elaborate?"

"All right. Let's say that as soon as you enter his library, you see the Chaucer prominently displayed. Let's form a plan on how we would handle it. On, the other hand, if it's not readily discernible at first, we form a plan on how to discover it."

He nodded. "Exactly what I'd like to do."

"Good. So plan away, Mr. Telford."

Very good. How many women would know the name of England's greatest engineer? "First," he said with a nod, "what should we do if the manuscript is on display? Will you wish to immediately reveal your identity and claim it? I did some investigation of my own which substantiates what you had learned about the rightful ownership of stolen goods."

"Legally, it is mine, is it not?"

"It is."

"Then I think I would—under those circumstances—reveal my identity and claim it."

"If that's what you wish, I will back you up."

"But—owing to the fact you want to plan for every contingency—what should you wish to do if he summons big, burly footmen to take it away from you after you've taken it away from him?"

"I would bloody well get out of there."Oh oh. He wasn't supposed to say bloody in front of a lady. His mother was forever chastising the twins for using such language in front of their sisters. "I beg your pardon for my choice of words."

"I assure you, my husband often said much worse, and he never asked for forgiveness."

What a beast the fellow must have been. Why would she continue to refer to such a man as *my dear Mr. Bexley*?

"Since you wish to make a thorough plan," she continued, "how many burly footman would it take to have you racing from the house? Two? Three? Five?"

"I should have to see them."

"Ah ha! See, some things just cannot be calculated ahead of time."

Now it was his turn to glare. "You have made your point, madam."

She held her head high, a smug smile crossing her face. "Now, let us discuss how we react if the Chaucer is not readily visible."

"I thought I would say that it is my desire to see the rare editions that are in his possession and for which he is so noted."

"Playing to his great vanity, again," she said with a nod. "Very good."

"Surely if he had the Chaucer, he would reveal

it at that time. As you said, one does not collect who does not wish to display."

"And so, if he then reveals it, we go back to the initial plan, declare ownership, claim it, and leave—unless you find the size of the footmen giving chase too terrifying." She gave a little giggle.

"Now see here! I never said I would be terrified." He sat rather straighter and expanded his chest in an attempt to appear as manly as possible. "In fact, I daresay if I ever thought you in peril, I could defend you most adequately."

"Would you really, Airy?" Her voice had gone all youthful again.

"You must guard your good name, Mrs. Bexley. It is improper for you to address me by my first name."

"Oh, but I didn't really address you by your first name. 'Tis just a little name I choose to call you when it is just the two of us."

"You will give me your word not to use it in the presence of others?"

She nodded sheepishly.

At that point he realized he had actually consented to allow the woman to address him by that ridiculous name. A name he disliked. A derivative of Aristotle. He was mad at himself for not holding his ground better with her.

He pulled open the carriage curtains at peered at the hilly Warwickshire countryside. Already the sun was waning. Their timing could certainly have been better. If they tarried for long at Granfield Manor, it would be dark when they left. Having their coachman traveling strange roads at dark could be problematic. And what if there were no posting inns? This was a most aggravating situation. He certainly had not planned very well.

"As much as we are racing against the clock—and Coutts Bank," he said, "perhaps we should find a posting inn for the night and show up fresh in the morning at Granfield Manor."

She gave him a somber look. "I understand your concerns, but I think we won't be long at Granfield. Shouldn't we be there shortly?"

"According to my calculations, we should be there in the next half hour."

"Pray, Mr. Steffington, don't worry about getting stranded at night. If anyone should worry, it should be me—the world's biggest coward—and I know we'll be safe tonight."

"How, madam, can you possibly know such?"

"Women' intuition," she said without a second's hesitation.

He frowned. "That's just like something a woman would say. There is no logical foundation whatsoever for what you've just said."

"Are you saying that women are stupid?"

He thought what she said was very stupid, but only a fool would tell her that. "Of course not. You know who Thomas Telford is. You are not stupid, madam."

"But I'm illogical?"

"Well, actually, yes!"

She turned to peer from her window, presenting him the back of her head. For the first time he noticed that her hair did not look quite the thing. In fact, it rather looked as if she hadn't brushed it this morning.

"I refuse to speak to you, Mr. Steffington, until I must when we reach Granfield Manor."

"As you like it, madam."

* * *

By the time their coach reached the gatehouse to Granfield Manor, the sun was slipping behind the distant hills, casting a deep shadow over the wheat-colored parkland that spread out before the Elizabethan structure that had to be Granfield.

While not as large or as magnificent as Burleigh House, Granfield was a grand old house anchored on either side with stately ogee-topped towers. As they drew closer, she realized it was built in the old courtyard style of architecture.

Their coachman pulled into the courtyard and drove to the large, timbered front door. A footman came and opened their door.

Melvin cleared his throat, then spoke in a most strident voice. "Dr. and Mrs. Melvin Steffington to see Lord Seacrest's library."

"He is expecting ye, sir?"

Melvin shrugged. "I'm not sure. A letter was dispatched to him earlier in the week."

"If you will just come into the morning room, Dr. Steffington," the footman said, "I shall tell 'is lordship ye are here."

In the morning room they each sat in one of the two large velvet-covered chairs that faced the fire. The chairs' wooden arms gave a bit of a throne effect. Despite the fire, the room was bloody cold with its icy stone floors and a cool draft whistling around the closed, Gothic looking windows.

Melvin noted that Mrs. Bexley's hands were trembling. Perhaps she should not have left off her muff. Even though it was not yet four o'clock, night was falling fast. The farther north they went, the earlier night came this time of the year.

Presently, a man he assumed was Lord Seacrest emerged from a doorway at the opposite end of the long corridor, a smile on his face. Though Melvin had expected the peer to be a stooping white-haired man, he was anything but. He was only slightly older than Melvin and was in possession of a thick head of light brown hair. He dressed well. Melvin was sure Elvin would approve of his wardrobe choices.

Melvin and Mrs. Bexley stood as he approached.

"Dr. Steffington! Allow me to introduce myself. I am Lord Seacrest. I received your most welcome letter just this morning. I must say, I hadn't expected you so soon."

His attention then turned to Mrs. Bexley.

Melvin cleared his throat. "Allow me to introduce my, er, wife to you, my lord."

Lord Seacrest effected a bow. "Very good to meet you, madam. Won't you both come to my library?"

"It will be our pleasure," she said, slipping her arm through the crook in Melvin's arm.

Seacrest's gaze swung from her to Melvin. "Do you know, Dr. Steffington, I had already heard of you?"

"Is that so?" Melvin was shocked.

"Yes, when Dr. Mather was here during the summer, he said if I ever lost the services of my man of letters, he would highly recommend you."

"He actually named me?"

"He did, indeed." Lord Seacrest opened the door to the library. "This is, as you surely know, my obsession."

"Ah, we speak the same language," Melvin said as he moved into the chamber and stopped, his gaze slowly taking in as much as he could of the room. Nothing about it looked Elizabethan. Vastly different from other libraries Melvin had toured, it was a huge, square room. Scarlet draperies had been pushed away from the three casements which provided a view of Seacrest's park. It would have been even more stunning at mid-day when the sun sparkled over what Melvin suspected was River Avon.

All four walls of the library were lined with beautifully bound leather books. Thousands of them. At the far end of the chamber, a fire blazed in the huge marble chimneypiece, where a half a dozen throne-like chairs formed a cozy semi-circle facing it. Some half a dozen other intimate seating areas scattered across the chamber's huge red Turkey rug.

Melvin moved to the nearest section of the library and began to read titles, some of which he unconsciously translated from the Latin or Greek to English: Homer, Aristotle, Euripides, Plutarch, and many other ancients.

So mesmerized was he examining the library, so happy was he to be viewing this wondrous collection, he almost forgot his reason for coming. He abruptly quit looking at titles and ran his eye around the chamber once more, this time seeking a prominent display worthy of something as significant as the Chaucer.

On the wall to his left, he spied a glass enclosed bookcase and began to stroll toward it. As he came closer, he noticed it was locked. Very good. Whatever was in there was indeed valuable.

"What have you here, my lord?"

Lord Seacrest shadowed him. "That, Dr. Steffington, features the choicest *jewels* of my collection." He extracted a key from a small pocket in his yellow silken waistcoat and inserted it into the lock of the glass-doored case.

At closer inspection, Melvin realized this was no common glass but appeared to be extraordinarily thick.

"Your Shakespeare folios?" Melvin asked, disappointed as he came closer and saw the quarto books with which he was so familiar. There was nothing else there, save more than a dozen of these exceedingly valuable two-hundred-year-old books.

"Indeed." It was impossible for Lord Seacrest to tamp down his surging pride in his voice.

"Why, you must have the most extensive collection of these in the entire kingdom," Mrs. Bexley exclaimed.

Oh, she was good at playing to men's vanity.

Melvin should know. As did Elvin. And Long*mouth.*

Seacrest shrugged. "That is my goal, Mrs. Steffington, but alas, Lord Spencer's collection is far better than my own."

"Lord Spencer is much older than you," she said, smiling up at the earl. "It's taken him decades to achieve what he's got. And look at how young you are! To think you've done all of this in so short a time."

Oh, she was good! Melvin glared at the flirt in action.

The earl was doing anything but glaring. Were he bird, he would be a peacock at this moment, preening under her praise as he cast admiring glances at her.

The peer spent the next half hour gloating over his folios, insisting that his visitors don gloves and examine them, and talked to them rather as if they were uneducated baboons. Melvin decided he did not like Lord Seacrest. Especially since the man addressed nine comments out of ten to Mrs. Bexley and swept his approving gaze from her face then slowly down the length of her torso, pausing appreciatively at her breasts.

Melvin decided that her dress was much too low cut in front. It was a wonder he hadn't noticed it that day as they rode together in the carriage all those hours. Why did she not pull together her cape about her throat? She was apt to take lung fever from being so inadequately dressed.

It was difficult for Melvin to get excited over these Shakespeare folios, given that he was well acquainted with others like them. They were not all that rare. Nothing like an illustrated Chaucer manuscript. Getting his hands on that—even if he'd never met and agreed to help its female owner—would send Melvin's pulses surging with excitement.

Once the last folio was restored to its special place on the glass shelf, Melvin said, "I assume these are your most rare books?"

"I believe so." Lord Seacrest turned to Melvin (finally realizing her husband had accompanied the lovely lady with whom he was so enchanted). "Though I am in possession of a Bible, the origin of which your Dr. Mather was unable to assist me in establishing. Pray, come here and let me show it to you. Perhaps you shall be better able to date it for me."

Melvin followed the home's owner, his gaze flicking to the tall windows. Uh, oh. It was already pitch dark outside with nary a moon to offer brightness.

Lord Seacrest unlocked a small, built-in

cabinet made of walnut and withdrew a fat Bible, then placed it in Melvin's still-gloved hands. "Feel free to flip through it and tell me what you think."

The worn leather binding gave no clue as to its age because often books falling into disrepair were rebound in such a manner. Not having original binding, of course, decreased the value of items like this.

His eyes narrowed as he carefully opened the book and started to read at around the thirty percent mark. It took no more than a page for him to pinpoint the date. He looked up at Lord Seacrest. "I'm surprised Dr. Mather was unable to date this."

"He said that books covered in this manner weren't very old."

"He must not have gotten much farther than the cover, and I will own that having a contemporary-style cover does devalue the book, but one has only to read a few pages of the old English to date it." He handed it back to Lord Seacrest. "Congratulations. Your Bible predates your Shakespeare."

A smile flashed across their host's face. "Then I am very happy you have paid me a visit today. Now I wish to repay you with dinner. I know I may sound boastful, but my chef is one of the finest in England. He's French and was formerly chef to the Prince Regent in Brighton." No doubt, Seacrest was accustomed to getting whatever he wanted. His pockets were undoubtedly deep enough.

"We really can't," Melvin said.

At the same time, Mrs. Bexley said, "We should love to!"

Melvin bowed to her. "A wise husband defers to

his wife." He was grateful for the opportunity to remind Seacrest that Mrs. Bexley was married to him. Sort of.

Over the three-hour dinner, Melvin kept looking at his pocket watch. Another day was almost gone, and they hadn't gotten any closer to finding the Chaucer than they were on the first day.

He was concerned, too, about traveling these strange roads so late at night, particularly because of his wife's fear of highwaymen. Well, not exactly his wife, but the earl needn't know that.

To his consternation, he learned there was no posting inn near Granfield Manor. "You'll have to travel all the way to Redditch to find one," their host said.

"And how far is Redditch?" Melvin asked.

"Twenty-five miles."

They were no longer on flat land. Those twenty-five miles could take many hours to traverse.

"Do not worry, Dr. Steffington. I've had a room freshened for you and Mrs. Steffington to stay the night."

$\mathcal{C}$hapter 11

Mr. Steffington closed the bedchamber door behind him. "Now see what you've gotten us into? We should have left when he invited us to dinner. Why did you accept?'

"Because I was starving! Recall that I hadn't eaten all day." She had been ever so unwell that morning that even the sight of food was enough to have her casting up her accounts.

He frowned. "And now we're stuck in this room together. Why could you not have been my sister as we were at the Duke's Arms last night?"

"But you are mistaken, Airy. I wasn't actually your sister at Duke's Arms."

"You know what I mean." Her gave her an I'd-like-to-gag-your-mouth-with-a-used-handkerchief look.

She attempted to out stare him.

Mumbling something incoherent beneath his breath, he looked away, his gaze fanning over the unexpectedly plush room. Broadloom carpet in pale gold covered the floor. A fire blazed in the Carerra marble fireplace over which a gilt mirror hung. The chamber's two tall windows were draped with gold silk. Her gaze then followed his to the bed, where more silken draperies hung from the big four-poster.

Oh, dear.

"Of course, I shall sleep on the floor," he said.

"Of course." She shrugged. "It does look softer than most floors. And I shall insist you take the counterpane to fold into a little mattress."

"Will you be warm enough without it?"

"Oh, yes. I shall have the bed curtains closed to hold in the warmth."

"I suppose they shall also give you privacy."

"True. I shouldn't like you to see me sleeping. I mean, what if my mouth gapes open like a moron—meaning no disparagement to those poor afflicted souls."

"I cannot imagine you ever looking anything but ladylike."

"Oh, Airy, that is so kind of you." That he was incapable of staying angry with her, endeared him to her. The girl who would one day capture his heart would be very fortunate. Very fortunate, indeed.

As she directed a smile at him, his lashes lowered. She was certain his compliment now embarrassed him. He was not the smooth-talking, bed hopper she'd wager his twin brother was. She rather pitied the girl who married *that* twin. Reflecting over her own smooth-talking, bed-hopping late husband, she was now happy that he'd been possessed of those traits. Otherwise, his demise would have been too, too painful.

She sighed. Yes, the girl who married Mr. Steffington would be most fortunate.

"You must allow me to make your bed," she said. "I am ever so experienced. Whenever my little nephews visit me in Bath, I make them a pallet on the floor of my bedchamber." She set about to remove the quilt from the bed, fold it lengthwise, and place it on the floor beside her own bed, just as she had done with her nephews.

Then her gaze traveled over him from head to toe. "I fear you may be too tall."

"My feet won't mind hanging off."

She started to giggle.

He cracked a smile. "Allow me to guess. You are now imagining my feet talking."

Still giggling, she nodded.

"You are possessed of the silliest sense of humor." He eyed the pallet. "Perhaps you shouldn't put it so close to your bed. What if I snore?"

"I am accustomed to men snoring." Her hand clapped around her mouth. "I didn't mean to imply I've slept with multiple men. Only one, actually."

His dark eyes flashed with mirth.

And they both laughed.

He went to the pallet and moved it from its position parallel to her bed and placed it in front of the fire, parallel to the footboard of her bed.

"I'm not a bit sleepy." She eyed the room's little floral loveseat. "Should you like to talk for a bit? I promise I'm not inebriated tonight." She moved to the love seat, sat on it, and patted the cushion beside hers. "Please, sit beside me."

"I never said you were inebriated."

"Because you're too nice."

After he sat, she said, "Are you satisfied that the Chaucer is not in Lord Seacrest's possession?"

"I am. A man as proud of his library as he would not hide its crowning jewel."

"I suppose you are right, but did you not have the urge to look behind the library's various doors to see what was concealed?"

"I always wish to look behind the doors to see

what treasures are to be found in libraries, but something as magnificent as a one-of-a-kind, illustrated *Canterbury Tales* would be proudly and prominently displayed."

"But what if Lord Seacrest knows it was stolen? He may even be the one who stole it. Or had someone steal it for him."

"While I did not exactly warm to the man, I don't think he would be capable of criminal theft."

"Why did you not warm to him? I thought he was charming."

Mr. Steffington frowned. "You would. He shamelessly flirted with a married woman!"

"Well. . .I'm not actually a married woman."

"He doesn't know that!"

Mr. Steffington's deep sense of morality touched her. She gave him a puzzled look. "I hadn't noticed Lord Seacrest flirting. He was merely being friendly."

"Only to you. He was jealous of me."

"Why would he be jealous of you?"

"Because I had the good fortune to marry you." He shrugged. "At least, that's what the man thinks."

"Oh, Airy, that is so sweet that you think being married to me is a good thing."

"I didn't say that."

"Oh."

He stiffened and slid in the opposite direction from her. It was obvious he did not want any part of their bodies touching. He was such a proper gentleman.

"Allow me to change the subject," she said. "What did you think of his library?"

"I thought it an ostentatious display of wealth."

"But was it a good library?"

"It was a good library."

"But?"

"But I thought he was more concerned about the bindings on the *outside* of the books than the contents *inside*."

"You must own, it was a very attractive library."

"I prefer ones with upper galleries."

"Now see, you too are concerned with aesthetics."

"I'm not *concerned* with aesthetics, but since you asked my opinion, I voiced it."

"What criteria do you use to judge if a library is good or not?"

"I look at the collections, and I must say Seacrest's collections are good, and they cross all the important time periods in philosophical thought."

"You will lose me if you go into philosophical thought. I did note that there was a section in the library dedicated to poetry—which I adore."

"Yes, he even had good translations of Virgil—including one of mine, though he didn't remember my name in that context. I get the feeling his librarian handles his acquisitions."

She was astonished. "I did not know you translated Virgil! I must have a copy."

"It will be my pleasure to present you with one. The ones I own are not bound in fine leather like Seacrest's."

"I don't care. I shall treasure it. I am so honored. I have never before shared a room with one who wrote books, and now I'm actually sharing a bedchamber with one! This is so exciting."

"Pray, Mrs. Bexley, don't tell anyone you and I

have shared a bedchamber."

She nodded. He was so noble to be so concerned over her good name. "But you told me you didn't like poetry when you obviously like Virgil's."

"I do read poetry, but then I read everything. Except Byron. I never had any interest in reading about so hedonistic a central character."

"I do believe you're a prude. You judge Lord Byron's poetry by the man's low moral principles."

"I am not a prude." He glared.

She thought of the company he and his brothers kept in Bath and decided perhaps he was not a prude. Felicity's brother, Lord Sedgewick—before becoming a family man—had been quite the rake. In fact, the whole lot of them had led the life of privileged bloods. They gambled, went to race meetings, and frequented Mrs. Baddele's House with great regularity. Everybody knew.

Her entire demeanor brightened. "I have an idea."

"When you get that look in your eye it disturbs me."

He was getting to know her entirely too well. "What look?"

"The look that says I'm not going to like your idea."

He was likely right. "After the house quiets and everyone is asleep, we can stealthily make our way downstairs and look behind all those locked doors in Lord Seacrest's library."

"That is a ridiculous idea."

"Why?"

"Because it's a good way to get shot."

"Why would Lord Seacrest shoot us? You said

yourself he fancied me."

"Then he'd have a good reason for killing me!"

Her brows lowered. "I shouldn't like that."

"I appreciate that." He looked at her with skepticism. "You realize, don't you, that a man who invests so heavily in his library is not likely to leave it unguarded?"

"Perhaps not. Remember, I had the most valuable book in all of England, and I did not have it guarded. I'm not even sure if our doors were ever properly locked."

He inclined his head. "I rest my case."

"So you think it's my fault the Chaucer was stolen?"

"Actually, I do. If it had been in my possession, the library would have been locked at all times, and the house would never be left unguarded."

Of course he was right, but she didn't like him acting like a scolding father. Her gaze narrowed, then swung away from him as she glared angrily at the flickering fire. "I happen to be a trusting person. I like to think the best of my fellow man. It never occurred to me that someone would steal the Chaucer from my home."

"I would be shocked if Seacrest were a trusting person. I noted the special locks he'd had installed on the windows."

"So you're saying you're not interested in a late-night excursion to the Seacrest library?"

"Under no circumstances would I do something so unethical. It's bad enough that I've already lied about my relationship with you."

Very well. She would wait until all of them—including Airy—went to sleep, then she would go herself.

She feigned a yawn. "I suppose I am rather

tired."

His glance flicked to her valise, then to his beside it. He cleared his throat. She was coming to learn that he cleared his throat every time he was about to say something that he thought might be construed as too intimate. "Would you like me to leave the room whilst you dress for bed?" He was unable to meet her gaze.

"You don't have to leave the room."

His gaze absently lowered to her bodice, then whipped away. "Then I vow to turn my back and close and my eyes whilst you . . . ah, remove your. . . well, you know."

"You don't have to close your eyes."

Those dark eyes of his rounded. "Oh, but I must. You're a lady, and I'm a gentleman."

She stood. "That won't be necessary. I'll pull the curtains around my bed and then disrobe."

"Capital idea!" He looked exceedingly relieved.

She went to her valise, removed her night shift, then crossed the room and climbed on top the big bed.

"Here," he said. "I'll close the bed curtains for you."

It was much easier for him because of his height. He closed the ones to the right, then the ones at the foot of the bed, then when he closed the ones on the left she was in total darkness.

She sat on that left side of the bed and listened to his footsteps move away. "Thank you, Airy. Good night, sleep tight- - -"

"And don't let the bedbugs bite," he finished.

"I doubt Lord Seacrest has to worry about bedbugs."

"You're likely right."

While she was removing her clothing, she

unintentionally pictured Airy standing in front of the fire removing his shirt, the firelight glistening along the length of his bare torso. Her mouth went suddenly dry, and she fought the urge to peek through the curtain at him.

What a magnificent sight he must be. She found herself wondering if he slept nude but realized even if that were his custom, he would never do so in the same room with a lady of good birth. He was more noble of character than any man she had ever known. Except her father.

Once she had changed into her night shift and got beneath the covers she called out to him. "I'm decent now, but I find I don't like the dark. If you weren't in the chamber with me, I would be terrified."

"Should you like for me to crack open your bed curtains?"

"Please."

"I, ah, shall need to restore my shirt first."

How she would love to see him without his shirt. "Don't bother. I'll close my eyes."

"Are you sure?"

He needn't know if she peeked. After all, it was quite dark within the cubicle of her bed. "Certainly!"

"Forgive me. I didn't mean to imply. . ."

"Of course you wouldn't."

He quietly moved across the carpet. "Where should you like the sliver of light?"

"The foot of the bed will do nicely, thank you." And would afford a glimpse of him.

Seconds later, a buttery vertical light striped the foot of her bed, and she stealthily watched as he moved back to his pallet with the powerful majesty of a panther. Firelight glanced from the tawny length of his long, lean—and wonderfully bare—torso.

Yes, she thought to herself, her breath a bit ragged, the girl who snared dear Mr. Steffington would indeed be fortunate.

One side of her face smashed against the pillow, she listened for the change of breathing that would tell her he'd gone to sleep.

He must have been very tired for less than five minutes after he laid on the pallet, he started softly snoring. How long should she wait to assure herself Lord Seacrest and his servants were soundly asleep?

She remembered Mama's lamentations that women's cares settled on them in bed each night, but that men fell asleep as soon as their heads hit the pillow. That had certainly been the case with the late Mr. Bexley.

She forced herself to wait a considerable period of time before she crept from her bed, took an unlighted candle from the side of her bed, and tiptoed to the door where she unlatched the lock and quietly opened the door. It squeaked; she stiffened and turned toward Airy's pallet. He still slept soundly.

Easing the door closed behind her, she stood still in the darkened second-story corridor and listened. The house was eerily quiet. Her heartbeat accelerated. Her fingers coiled around the wax candle as if it were her lifeline. After a few moments, she stole to the stairway and stood statue still for several minutes, listening for any noise.

There was none.

Her pulses pounded as she began to descend the stairs, her bare feet as quiet as a cat's soft paws. By the time she reached the ground floor, she was relatively confident she was home free. Still, she moved slowly and with quiet movements.

Before the library's closed door, she paused and—remembering the late nights when Mr. Bexley had stayed in his library—listened. She heard nothing. But what kind of sounds could she expect to hear if a lone man were reading there? The very thought of strolling into his lordship's library in her night shift caused her no end of mortification.

Several minutes passed before she took a deep breath and opened the door. When she saw that no one was there, she let out a huge sigh and strolled into the chamber. To her relief, the fire had not gone out and still faintly illuminated the room. She went to the fire and stuck her unlighted candle into the flame until it lit.

Then she set about opening every closed cupboard or door within Lord Seacrest's prized library. The first cabinet was much deeper than she'd expected and contained tall stacks of various newspapers but mostly copies of the *Edinburgh Review*.

She moved on, opening each door along the west side of the chamber, then moved to the right and started examining each of the closed cupboards there.

The library door swung open so violently, it slammed against a wall.

Her gaze arrowed to the doorway. There stood Lord Seacrest. Even from the distance of twenty-five feet, she could see the anger singe his face. "May I help you, Mrs. Steffington? Or is that your real name?"

$\mathcal{C}$hapter 12

Elvin had told him he had a propensity to fall asleep within fifteen seconds of closing his eyes. This night it had taken longer. Without his intentions of doing so, once he closed the curtains around Mrs. Bexley's bed he was nearly overcome with images of her removing her clothing.

He was unaccustomed to such unwelcome thoughts foisting themselves upon him, but the more he thought of her smooth, fair body glistening in the firelight, the more welcome the images became. If that weren't bad enough, the notion of seeing the lovely woman disrobed did the most unwelcome things to his body.

What the devil had gotten into him? He hoped to God the lady never learned the he had such dishonorable thoughts.

He punched his pillow, rolled over, and willed himself to replace those images with architectural renderings of the Parthenon and Andrea Palladio's Italian masterpieces.

Then he fell asleep.

But the muffled sound of a door closing roused him. He leapt up, ready to defend Mrs. Bexley. "Who goes there?" he inquired.

When there was no response, he crossed the chamber, stood before the slit in her curtains, and addressed her. "Terribly sorry to disturb you, but are you all right?"

There was still no response.

He decided to take the liberty of lifting away her curtain. "I say, Mrs. Bexley- - -" What the devil? Her bed was empty!

In that instant, he recalled her insane desire to further search Lord Seacrest's library, and he knew where the stupid woman had gone.

The sound that had awakened him must have been their door closing. He had best hurry if he hoped to prevent her from jeopardizing their mission. Without taking time to put on his shirt, he sped from their bedchamber and as silently as he possibly could, he began to descend the darkened staircase.

He was not alone. Some distance in front of him, there was another footfall. It was much too dark for him to see who it was, but the footsteps were much too heavy to be hers. His heartbeat roared within the walls of his chest.

Melvin was her only hope. His step accelerated.

He came to the foot of the stairs, rounded the next corner and raced to the library, his pulse recklessly fast. A wedge of light spilled from the library's open door into the corridor. Lord Seacrest, with candle in hand, filled the doorway and was speaking in a most irreverent manner to Mrs. Bexley, er, Mrs. Steffington.

Melvin knew he must think quickly. He sped up to stand beside their host. "Please," he said, his voice low, "Allow me to handle this. Mrs. Steffington is possessed of the most lamentable habit of walking in her sleep. She manages to light candles and embark on the most nonsensical chores. She once put hot coals into the ice house and had no recollection of it the following day."

With that truly lame explanation, he crossed the chamber and scooped the lady into his arms. "It's all right, my darling, I'm taking you back to our bed."

Dr. Melvin Steffington had never in his seven and twenty years referred to a woman as *my darling*. And he'd said *our bed*, both of which were uncharacteristically brazen for a serious-minded bachelor like Melvin,

Surprisingly, his extemporaneous explanation seemed to appease their host. How could a man who so appreciated man's written word believe such nonsense?

"Terribly sorry to have disturbed your lordship," Melvin mumbled as he swept past the man, who was dressed in a long nightshirt.

Melvin's faux wife feigned faux sleep as he mounted the stairs. Though she was not very large, by the time he reached the top step he had some difficulty catching his breath. He would not recommend climbing stairs with a woman in one's arms.

He also had the devil of time trying not to think of her naked feet and not to think about her undergarments having been removed. Then there was his own state of nakedness. Both of their names would be ruined if anyone ever learned of tonight's transgressions. It would be difficult, too, to face her in the light of day tomorrow. Or was it already tomorrow? He couldn't wait until dawn— the earliest they could flee from Granfield. Melvin couldn't leave Granfield Manor soon enough.

If she were a child, he would spank her for her disobedience.

In their bedchamber (which seemed incredible that he was sharing a bedchamber with a woman to whom he was not married), he dropped her onto the carpet, then shut the door as forcefully as he could without slamming it.

"What the devil did you think you were doing?" He didn't care that he'd cursed in front of her. She deserved worse than *devil*. He didn't care that his voice was raised in anger. She deserved that too.

Her gaze traveled from his face down the length of him. He felt deuced awkward. "You were magnificent!"

He forgot that he was standing there half naked. His chest seemed to expand. "I was rather proud at how quickly I reacted, though I'm shocked that Seacrest seemed to believe me."

"Just because one's rich enough to buy the most expensive books in the kingdom doesn't mean one's smart enough to understand all those books."

Exactly what Melvin had been thinking about Seacrest. His eyes narrow, he glared at her. "You're mistaken if you think I can be duped as easily as Seacrest. My temper won't be assuaged by your flattery."

"I wasn't trying to flatter," she said softly, her gaze sweeping over his upper torso. "I was exercising my unfortunate habit of speaking my mind."

It was still flattery, unintentional as it may have been, and he wasn't about to fall for it. "It appears you also exercise your unfortunate habit of rash and illogical reasoning."

Now she returned his glare with vehemence. "And I thought you a gentleman! I'll have you know a gentleman would never say such horrible, insulting things to a lady." Her voice was cracking as it did when she was on the brink of tears—an action he'd observed too many times and would prefer not to see again.

A gentleman would apologize right now, but Melvin could not. If she hoped to continue their quest, he had to know she wasn't going to do other things as stupid as what she had just done. He refused to enter into an association with someone whose thoughtless actions could seriously jeopardize them.

He felt beastly if his harsh words made her cry, but they had to be said. "I will not be manipulated by your tears this time. You were wrong on so many levels I don't know where to begin. It should have been obvious to an imbecile that Seacrest does not possess the manuscript. None of those cupboards was either deep enough or secure enough to hold a prized manuscript like the Chaucer.

"If we're to be in this together, one of us does not stalk off independently. If it's your desire to investigate this by yourself with no help from me, just say the word, and I'll be happy to bow out."

Her eyes brimming with tears she somehow managed not to spill, she peered at him. "Just because I'm a female, you think me stupid."

"Your gender has nothing to do with your stupidity."

She started to wail. "You did-did-didn't have to say I was stupid."

"I didn't mean you *were* stupid. I've never thought you stupid, but your actions tonight indicated a complete disregard for sanity!"

"Make up your mind! Do you find me stupid— or just crazy?"

"Neither, madam. I think you're an impetuous

female who needs the guidance of a man."

She spun away from him as if she'd been burned, but a second later whirled back around, hurling a chair cushion at his head.

He ducked, deflecting the blow from hitting his face. "Why did you do that?"

"I wanted to demonstrate the actions of an impetuous, helpless female!"

He effected an exaggerated bow. "I rest my case, madam."

Anger apparently trumped tears. Her tears vanished. "*I rest my case*," she mimicked to herself as she presented her back to him and marched across the bedchamber, continuing to mimic him with each step. She climbed onto her bed and snapped closed the slender sliver where her bed curtains had parted.

"Good night, Dr. Steffington."

She had never before addressed him by his academic title. With it, she was erecting an iron barrier between them.

"If you don't object," he addressed her bed, "I wish to put Granfield behind us at the first light of dawn. I'll leave Seacrest a letter professing our profound gratitude for showing us his fine library, what an honor it was, etcetera, and of course, I shall apologize for my wife's intrusion upon his sleep."

She was still too angry with him to respond.

She was still trembling as she sat squarely upon the bed in total darkness. She had never in her life been so terrified as she was when Lord Seacrest threw open that library door and called her out. She'd stood frozen, incapable of speech but knowing he thought her a thief in the night.

When her then-shining star came to her rescue she could have planted a big, wet kiss upon his mouth. How clever he had been to extricate her from the mischief she'd gotten herself into.

Then he had to go and spoil everything. The memory of the manner in which her Airy had spoken to her upon returning to their bedchamber quite broke her heart. She had thought he was her ally. She had thought perhaps he did not think her an empty-headed female. She had even thought he was so kindly a gentleman (as he always had been previously) that he would never chastise her.

She had not expected the passive Mr. Steffington to so exert his opinions or to so thoroughly belittle her.

Another source of her mortification was her unguarded reaction to seeing the towering Mr. Steffington's bare torso. It had nearly robbed her of breath as she gawked at him standing just behind Lord Seacrest. Her lashes lowered, a huge lump lodged in her throat, and her gaze lazily swept from his subtly muscled shoulders down the long, lean curve of his manly chest, trailing to his narrow waist where a thin trickle of dark hair plunged beneath his breeches and had her heartbeat galloping even more than it already was.

Then back in their bedchamber, her impetuous tongue betrayed her thoughts when she blurted out that she thought he was magnificent.

How could she have done such a brainless thing? She did not even like men. She had no desire to ever remarry. She had no desire to take a lover. Then why in the whole wide world had she been so mesmerized over his body?

Even as she sat there in the inky black dark, her pulse quickened when she pictured him. She could not help but be aware of his close proximity, be aware of their intimate setting. Could this setting have unconsciously preyed on her traitorous emotions?

So Mr. Steffington would not only think her colossally stupid, he was also apt to think her a harlot!

How could she have gotten herself into this predicament? She had only wanted to recover what was rightfully hers. She'd been just female enough to think Mr. Steffington was her own gallant knight who would do anything to rescue the maiden—or in her case, matron.

Until tonight, she had been able to coax him into any action with the trickle of tears, but tonight he had totally exercised his manliness. He was no longer hers to command. Like other men, *he* wanted to command.

He'd even told her he would not continue their quest unless it was on his terms. Why did he have to act so beastly manly? Why did he have to *look* so magnificently manly?

Even as those thoughts penetrated, she was aware of a soft snore coming from his pallet. How could he just lie down and fall asleep after the angry words that had passed between them? She must have been sadly mistaken when she had thought him sensitive. She should have known a man who was not enamored of poetry could not be sensitive.

Her *Dr.* Steffington was just like other men (except for the part about not wanting to seduce her). She fought the *impetuous* urge to hurl a bed pillow at him.

She could weep at the fruitlessness of their entire investigation. Even a brilliant man like Mr. Steffington was ineffective in helping her reclaim the Chaucer. She was going to have to start resigning herself to the fact she was going to lose everything: the house she adored in the city she liked best; her independence; and even pocket money.

She would have nothing and be forced to live in her brother's overcrowded house in the wilds of gray Yorkshire where there would be no society other than her brother's gaggle of boisterous children. Eight of them. Six of them boys. She did adore them, but boys' interests were about as fascinating as a conversation with Mr. Longford.

At the age of seven and twenty, she felt as if her life was over. A wretched hopelessness stole over her as she lay back into the bed and covered herself. Her trembling had finally stopped, but her thoughts raced so quickly she knew sleep was as out of her reach as that fat volume of *Canterbury Tales*.

After an hour or two had passed, she decided she would watch for the dawn. Leaving Granfield at dawn's first light was one thing she and Mr. Steffington still perfectly agreed upon. She tugged open the upper right corner of her bed curtains. To her surprise, the darkest of the night had lost its intensity as dawn approached. She sat up and began to assemble the clothing she'd thrown off many hours earlier and started to dress.

By the time she had finished, it was time to awaken Mr. Steffington. She hopped off the bed just as he rose from the pallet.

She wasn't about to gush about how magnificent he looked sans shirt, but she could not help but to freeze to the spot and stare at the majesty of him.

"You're already dressed," he said.

"Yes, I wanted to comply with your wishes. Even though our relationship has come to an end."

His eyes rounded. "Then you no longer desire my assistance?"

"That's correct."

$\mathcal{C}$hapter 13

Because they'd gotten so early a start, they covered much more distance on the return journey than they had coming to Warwickshire, but they would still be required to spend the night at a posting inn. Judging from the view of the waning sun from her coach window, that would not be far off.

At first, she'd wondered if he would even remember her aversion to traveling at night on the posting roads, but she was confident with his exceptional memory, he would. Would he be willing to stop the journey so the woman who was no long his ally could assuage her silly fears?

How different this night would be than the night at the Duke's Arms. Then she and Mr. Steffington had enjoyed an easy camaraderie. They had even acted as if they were exceedingly fond of each other.

Now they acted like complete strangers.

All the gallantry she had once attributed to him had been in error. Obviously a man who could read his bloody Euripides for ten straight hours and say nary a word to his traveling companion was an insensitive lout. Like the rest of his gender.

Then, conceive that this . . . this lout rudely reads his Euripides knowing full well the woman with whom he's traveling is not possessed of the ability to read in a moving carriage. A gentleman would have put aside his own selfish pursuits in order to make himself agreeable to the lady with the unfortunate affliction.

But not Mr. Steffington.

Never mind that Catherine herself had precipitated this estrangement by severing their relationship in her momentary rage.

When dawn had arrived, her anger had abated, but she was too proud to apologize, and he had communicated to her only a few words and only when they related to their journey from Granfield Manor. His chilly demeanor precipitated their estrangement. He was likely thrilled now to be relieved of the onerous task he'd never wanted to undertake in the first place.

It saddened her to remember how intent he'd been when he was her greatest champion. He had seemed more worried about the Coutts deadline than she.

She thought too about the severe hardships he'd put upon himself when he traveled to Cheddar on her behalf. And she could not forget how worried she had been about him. When she'd thought him gallant.

The pity of it was she *had* come to rely upon him. She would miss that. But it was only right that a woman who planned to live on her own henceforth should not depend upon a man.

Except for her dear departed Papa, she'd never known a man upon whom one could rely. She *had* thought Mr. Steffington was one of that rare breed. Before he revealed his superiority. Just because he was so blasted smart did not mean everyone around him was stupid.

She kept watching as the sun sank further

behind the distant hills, waiting for him to suggest they stop for the night. He must be the one to show his concern for her wishes; she would not impose them on an unwilling man. She was through with manipulating males. Or trying to manipulate males.

When it was obviously too dark to continue reading, he finally closed the book and eyed her. It wasn't so dark that she only barely saw his impatient demeanor when he faced her. "I suppose you'll be wanting to stop for the night." Those were the first words he'd said since early that morning. *Odious man*!

"I would."

"I conveyed those wishes to the driver this morning. I said as soon as it became dark he was to begin looking for posting inns."

"Oh." Mr. Steffington at least could have told her. But, then, he could have at least been civil to her. Severing their relationship *had* been his idea initially. *Odious man.* "Do you have any idea if we're near one?" she asked.

"I've been trying to remember each of the towns in reverse order from our outward journey, and if memory serves me correctly, we should be coming to Chipping Campden."

If she were a wagering person, she'd wager his memory was correct. "When?"

He shrugged. "Within the next half hour." With that comment, he turned his attention to peering from his window as if there were something to see as darkness set on the rolling countryside.

He had no intentions of speaking to her. *Odious man.*

It was all for the best. Truly. She could bloody

well get that damned fiancé of hers to help find
the *Canterbury Tales*. The bloody bore was rich
enough to buy it for her.

Which begged the question: why had she even
cared about the manuscript if she were going to
marry one of the richest men in the kingdom?
Melvin had always assumed she was desperate to
find the Chaucer so she wouldn't *have* to marry
Maxwell Longford, the most insufferable man in
all of Bath. If not in all of England.

Every time Melvin thought of her consenting to
wed Long*mouth*, it lessened his opinion of her. Of
course, women entered into loveless alliances all
the time. The richer the man, the more attractive
his matrimonial prospects became.

But why did the threat from Coutts hurt her so
deeply if she were on the brink of marrying that
intolerable braggart? The only explanation was
that she did not want to marry Longford. Just like
Melvin, she must want to be independent. Relying
on others was abhorrent.

Soon the rolling hills of the Cotswold
countryside yielded to a village where buttery
squares of light glowed in the windows of the
cream-colored cottages they passed. Their
carriage slowed just as Melvin observed a hanging
sign for the Black Lion Inn. The coach turned and
passed beneath an old brick arch into an inn yard
which was surrounded by two-story buildings on
all sides. A lantern illuminated a second sign for
the Black Lion. One arrow pointed to a door
where humans could take respite; the other
pointed to the stable block.

When their coach came to a complete stop, he
turned to Mrs. Bexley. "You might wish to stay in
the carriage whilst I go make arrangements for

our chambers."

A fleeting look of some kind of emotion—was it fright?—reminded him of the woman's other request from two nights previously. He cleared his throat. "Does madam once more wish to ensure that I procure the room adjacent to you?"

"I would." Her scratchy voice sounded like that of a young girl.

He didn't wait for the coachman but opened the coach door and went into the inn. Because night had just fallen, there were no other patrons yet in the cozy, fire-lit chamber. Melvin easily procured adjacent rooms from a gray-haired proprietor who stood behind the tavern's bar. Melvin also requested dinner before returning to the carriage.

"There was no problem in securing adjacent chambers for Mr. Smith and his sister."

She faintly smiled at him as he assisted her from the coach. When they entered the tavern entrance, he was pleased to see the innkeeper had now lighted the wall sconce at the bottom of the narrow, dark stairs that would carry them to their rooms. "We have Rooms 1 and 2," he told her.

"You requested food?"

"I did. I assumed you'd be hungry." He certainly was.

"I'm feel as if I'm starving."

When they reached the relatively spacious Room 1, a youthful chambermaid was just finishing lighting the fire. "I'll carry on to Room 2 and see that it gets nice and warm too," she said as she left.

After a quick, unconscious glance at the curtained bed, Melvin turned toward the corridor just as the man from whom he'd requested their bed and bread came to the top of the stairs, lugging their valises. Though he was winded, the man managed to get the bags in the corresponding chambers and announce that his wife would be delivering the dinner in half an hour.

She had barely changed to her evening dress when there was a knock upon her door. She took a quick glance into the looking glass to make sure she looked presentable before opening the door to a plump matron who was balancing a tray crowded with their dinner offerings.

Mr. Steffington was behind the woman, offering to help her set up their food. He moved a refectory-style table from beside the window and placed it in front of the fire. The kidney pie, steaming turnips, cold mutton, bread and butter, and plum pudding were all placed on the small wooden table. "I'll be back with yer ale and 'ot tea in a moment," she said.

Mr. Steffington tucked two chairs under the table, then pulled out Catherine's without saying a word. Without saying a word, she took her seat. He sat across from her and started spooning food onto his plate, then silently passed the serving dishes to her.

"I will just allow myself a little bit of plum pudding first," she said. She couldn't help but to remember that her old nurse wouldn't allow them to have the plum pudding until they had eaten their other foods. Just another reason why she was happy to be grown and not have to answer to anyone. Especially to a man.

They continued on in silence even after their drinks were delivered. Quite naturally, her thoughts turned to that other night when they had taken dinner at the Duke's Arms and how different things were between them then, how easily they conversed. And laughed.

And now they acted as if they were at a wake for a much-loved family member.

In a way, she felt as if there had been a death. A death of what had been a comfortable friendship.

When they *had* been friends, she'd thought Mr. Steffington had only her best interest in mind. It had really been too selfish of her to expect him to put aside his own manly need to dominate in order to appease her.

How could she have believed any man could be so accommodating? Now she would lump Mr. Steffington in the same distasteful category with his rakish brother and the annoying Mr. Longford. He was, after all, a man.

And all men were louts.

Midway through their meal, Mr. Steffington's spine straightened, and he cleared his throat. He was the only man she'd ever known who prefaced his conversations with a short, masculine throat clearing. She gazed up at him, her brows raised in query.

"I say, Mrs. Bexley, just because we're not going to be working toward a mutual goal any longer doesn't mean we can't be civil to one another."

She glared. "Now you say that! Did you have a single thought for me while you read your blasted Euripides? You knew full well my. . . my affliction prevented me from reading, and if you were a proper gentleman you should have known I had to be exceedingly bored."

His dark lashes lowered and he spoke with remorse. "Forgive me. I thought that if you wanted me to talk with you, you might have initiated a conversation."

"You gave the impression Euripides was the most fascinating book ever printed. Far be it from me to disturb a scholar at work."

"I wasn't working. I was merely trying to keep from annoying you."

She didn't believe him for a moment. Had he any gentlemanly instincts he would have known how pitiable it was for her to travel upward of a dozen hours without a single word extended to her.

"I wish I could have read one of my own books, but sadly, that is not a luxury I am able to enjoy while traveling." She effected a martyred look. "I'm completely dependent upon the generosity of my traveling companions to lift my gloom through lively conversation."

Instead of the remorseful look she'd expected from him, he started to laugh.

"Are you laughing at me?" she asked angrily.

Still laughing, he nodded.

"Pray, Mr. Steffington, you must tell me what you find so funny."

"You, madam."

She stiffened. "Why?"

"I'm merely attempting to *lift your gloom.*"

He was mimicking her! As much as she wanted to throw another cushion at him, her rigidness bent, and she found herself laughing with him.

Why was it he so easily made her laugh? And vice versa?

After their laughing ceased, she eyed him. "I really was gloomy. Do you know how utterly and completely boring it is to have no person or book to enliven one's existence?"

"If you'd only initiated a conversation, I would have happily closed my book."

She put hands to hips. "But you're the gentleman—though you didn't act like one. You should have exercised your gallantry."

"And you're just a shy woman awaiting someone to amuse you?" He started to laugh again.

She was not amused.

"Forgive me," he said, "but you have never struck me as being a shy female. I believe, Mrs. Bexley, you're far too accustomed to having things your own way. That's really why you're angry at me. You wanted a man who would dance to your tune, no questions asked."

"That's not true!"

He studied her seriously from beneath lowered brows. "I think it is."

He was right, but she would never admit it.

"I've already lied because of you," he said, "and that was something I said I'd never do."

To Lord Seacrest. "I'm very appreciative that you did so, but I think you and I would both be in prison now if you hadn't."

He cracked a smile. "You're likely right."

She went all stiff again and directed a haughty look at him. "Well, you have no fear of ever again being required to do anything that's so distasteful to you." With that, she lifted the bumper of ale and drank half of its contents down at once.

She had no desire to continue their conversation.

There was no way they could ever rekindle that which they'd found two nights previously at the

Duke's Arms.

Once they settled in their carriage for the last day of their journey, she spoke first. "Pray, Mr. Steffington, would you care to estimate how long it will take before we reach Bath?"

He was rather relieved that she was speaking to him this morning. He would never understand women. First, she'd been angry that he hadn't spoken to her yesterday, then she purposely refused to speak to him as they neared the completion of their dinner. "If the weather stays fair, I believe we'll be in Bath before the sun sets," he answered.

She nodded, then began to peer from her window.

"You must note that I've not brought my Euripides this morning."

Even though she already thought him ungentlemanly, Melvin could not consciously be rude to a woman by reading his Euripides. Now that he knew it was not gentlemanly. He felt beastly that she'd thought him an ill-mannered bore the previous day. His knowledge of women was sadly lacking. He'd foolishly thought if she wished to talk with him she would have done so.

Her gaze shifted to him, and a smile lifted the corners of her very agreeable mouth. "I appreciate the sacrifice you're making in order to appease..."

"A poor, afflicted woman," he continued.

She started to laugh. "Really, Mr. Steffington, you're making it ever so difficult for me to stay angry with you."

"I'm still not exactly clear on what it was I did at dinner to alienate you." Would he ever understand women?

"You wouldn't," she said, frowning.

What the devil? Was she going to get all bristly with him again for reasons he would never comprehend? "Can we not behave as friends?"

Her incredible eyes misted, and her face turned away from him. "We were friends, were we not?"

"I shouldn't like to use the past tense." Wasn't that a gentlemanly thing to say?

"Then I appreciate that. It's a pity so much water has now passed under our bridge."

Why could women not speak plainly? Were they even capable of saying what they meant? He hadn't the foggiest notion that they *had* a bridge. "If you're referring to the termination of our partnership, may I remind you that was *your* idea."

Her eyes narrowed. "It was not!"

Perhaps she was right. "I merely said that if we were going to be working together, we must act like partners. Do you have any idea how dangerous your stealthy trip to Lord Seacrest's library could have been? You could have been shot."

She pouted very much the same as Lizzy.

"Madam, you are acting exactly like my youngest sister. She is thirteen."

"You've changed. You didn't used to chastise me."

"You didn't used to act as if you were thirteen." *Uh, oh.* That was not a gentlemanly thing to say. It was such a pity Melvin was not possessed of the Graces.

Without saying another word, she spun back to her window and ignored him for the next two hours. He wished to God he had brought his bloody Euripides.

At one o'clock she turned her attention to the basket of food they'd had the innkeeper's wife pack for them, and Mrs. Bexley solicitously began asking him what he desired and doled it to him in a most gracious manner. There were apples and big chunks of bread and country cheese and cold mutton.

When they were finished eating, she acted as if she'd never cut him several hours previously. If she'd suffered a blow to the head he would have attributed her sudden change of mood to amnesia, but the woman had been sitting right in front of him all morning.

"We must discover more books we have both enjoyed, Mr. Steffington. That is a topic which is most successful at stimulating conversation."

Now she wished to talk! He suppressed a retort. He was determined to conduct himself in a gentlemanly manner. "There's always Shakespeare."

Her eyes danced. "Do we agree that he's brilliant?"

"It is safe to say we must be in perfect agreement on that, madam."

"Let me guess. You like his histories best."

He nodded. "How well you've come to know me."

She screwed her mouth in thought. "Allow me to guess which you like best."

"Go on."

She thought for a moment before responding. "*Julius Caesar.*"

His eyes widened. "How could you know that?"

"It's your love of classics that gives you away."

"Now it's my turn to guess your favorite." He stared at her. "Romeo and Juliet."

She shook her head emphatically.

"I thought all women adored that romance."

"Why would I like a story with such an unimaginably horrid ending? Do you think I could take pleasure in death?"

"Sorry."

"Care to guess again?"

"So I take it you don't like the tragedies."

"That is correct."

"Then since you like Sir Walter Scott's historical novels, you must, like me, prefer the histories."

"It's not that I don't like the histories, it's just that I prefer the comedies."

He was at a loss to guess which of the comedies would appeal most to a woman. To him, they were all perfectly forgettable. Even if the writing was brilliant. After a significant silence, he shrugged.

She started to laugh. "You don't like the comedies, do you?"

"It's not that I don't like them. It's more that they're not so memorable."

"*As You Like It.*"

At first, he thought she was commenting on his opinion. "Oh, yes, it's a clever little play."

"If we're going to talk Shakespeare, I must tell you I never ever tire of his sonnets."

"I'm sure I must have read them at some point..."

She laughed. "And obviously, you did not find them memorable. After all, they weren't Virgil."

He found himself wondering if she still wanted him to sign a copy of his Virgil translation for her. Then he realized once they returned to Bath he wasn't likely to find himself in her sphere any more. He did not hang about the Assembly Rooms. He'd only gone to please her.

Unaccountably, he grew a bit melancholy at the notion of never again carrying on a conversation with her. She was the first woman he'd ever encountered whose company he had actually enjoyed.

Until that fateful night at Granfield Manor, assisting her had brought him great satisfaction. He had liked to believe he was the brightest star in her galaxy. Even though she probably said that to every man with whom she communicated.

He would miss the laughter, too. He'd not experienced so much mirth since childhood.

"Kind of you to remember about Virgil," he mumbled.

"I'm looking forward to reading it. You haven't forgotten you promised me a copy? I shall be happy to pay you for it."

His brows lowered with disdain. "You will *not* pay for it. It's the least I could do since I couldn't find the Chaucer for you."

"I have one last avenue of investigation."

"Mr. Whitebread?"

She nodded. "You did send a letter to him, did you not?"

He nodded. "I did. If I have a response, I shall bring it to you." He had sent the communication to the collector four days earlier. It was possible he could have a reply already.

A melancholy look came over her face as she nodded and returned her attention to the scenery outside their window. They were now following along the meandering River Avon. He had been right. They would be back in Bath by four o'clock.

It bothered him that his mention of not finding

the Chaucer had cast a pall over their coach. It also bothered him that he could no longer help her, but she had made her decision.

When the spire of Bath Abbey finally came into view, he cleared his throat. "I suppose you'll be happy to see those familiar walls of Number 17 Royal Crescent."

"It is true, I love my home, but the failure of our quest will result in Coutts taking possession of it."

"But what of your fiancé? Is he not one of the richest men in the kingdom?"

She whirled toward him, her eyes wide with shock. "What in the world are you talking about? I have no fiancé!"

Now his eyes widened. "But he told me. . ."

"Who told you?"

"Maxwell Longford! He came to Green Park Road expressly to tell me that you had agreed to become his wife."

"When was this?"

"Shortly before we left on our journey."

"Oh, dear."

The way she said *oh, dear* it sounded as if she'd just remembered that she *might* have agreed to marry the pompous baboon. Melvin would never understand the workings of a woman's brain. How could one forget that she had promised to spend the rest of her life with a particular man? His brows lowered. "What do you mean by *oh, dear*?"

She shrugged. "I may have agreed to such a request without realizing exactly what I was agreeing to."

Why did her explanation—weak as it was—make him happy? It was nothing to him if she married Maxwell Longford, but he was awfully glad she wasn't. He'd never been able to picture her settling down with the officious man. Melvin also took pleasure in vindicating the greed he'd falsely attributed to her.

Before he could ask her to explain herself, the coach pulled up in front of his house on Green Park Road, and he was forced to take his leave from her. He exited the coach, then turned back. "You might consider explaining yourself to Long*mouth*."

"You mean Longford, do you not?"

He smirked. "Terribly sorry for offending your betrothed, madam."

She yanked an apple from her basket and hurled it at him as the coachman flicked the ribbons, and the carriage jerked forward.

He was unable to duck before the apple bounced off his forehead. The woman had wounded him! He rubbed his head. There was going to be a knot.

And she would never see the results of her angry display.

He stood on the pavement and watched her carriage rattle toward the Royal Crescent.

How in the devil did a woman manage *not* to know if she was betrothed?

$\mathcal{C}$hapter 14

Catherine rushed into her house, trembling. What was she to do? Apparently Mr. Longford was spreading news of their so-called betrothal over Bath. Was she the last to know?

As soon as Mr. Steffington had told her, she instantly realized she must have nodded in the affirmative whilst Mr. Longford was droning on when just the two of them were supposedly engaged in conversation, but which was nothing more than soliloquy. Regrettably, Mr. Long*mouth* was rather incapable of conversing. Had it been at the Assembly Rooms that he'd posed so momentous a proposal? Or perhaps it had been that day they rode in Sydney Gardens.

But she had made a concentrated effort to listen to him that day at Sydney Gardens. She froze in midstride as she went to the sideboard to examine the post that had accumulated while she was away. The reason she had tried to make so pointed an effort to listen to Mr. Longford that day they went to Sydney Gardens was because of little innuendos he'd let drop at the Assembly Rooms the night before. Innuendos about how singularly she honored him.

Oh, dear. She could hardly tell the man she rarely listened to a word he uttered because he was the most boring person she'd ever encountered.

She hated to humiliate him by letting it be known she'd never had any intention of marrying him. (Which was the truth, of course.) She would rather beggar herself than spend the rest of her days with that blithering braggart. She didn't care how rich the fool was.

A letter in her sister's familiar hand was at the top of the stack. As she thumbed through the correspondence beneath it, she sadly acknowledged the rest of them were duns from tradesmen.

"Welcome home, madam." Simpson was emerging from the basement stairs.

"Thank you, Simpson. It's good to be home."

"Mr. Longford called for you each day of your absence, and as you instructed, I told him that you had taken ill and weren't seeing anyone."

"Excellent. Did I have any other callers?"

"Felicity was here this afternoon."

"And you told her I was sick?"

"I did. She penned a quick note which I neglected to put with the post." He extracted it from his waistcoat pocket. "Here it is."

As Simpson carried her valise upstairs, she unfolded Felicity's brief missive.

Dearest Catherine,

I do pray that you're well tomorrow night for Glee will be passing through Bath and plans to go to the Assembly Rooms. She particularly requested to see you.

You should have seen the Steffington twins' sister's come-out. (I don't mean that the sister was a twin, but she is sister to the twins!) She was most lovely. A pity you—and the smart twin—had to miss it.

Catherine had never been able to conceal anything from either of the former Pembroke sisters, her lifelong friends Felicity and Glee. It was obvious from this note that Felicity knew Catherine had gone off with Mr. Steffington. She would have surmised, too, that they were attempting to locate the Chaucer manuscript.

Catherine sighed. Four more days wasted. It had now been more than a week since she had received the terse letter from Coutts. There was one slim prospect remaining, but she held little hope for its success.

In the library she was pleased to find a fire burning. It was an expensive practice she had yet to abolish, though she knew she should economize. As she settled on the green settee and somberly stared at the flames, she grew melancholy. In the fourteen months since Mr. Bexley had died, she had never allowed herself to feel lonely. But now she felt more alone then she ever had.

Only recently had she stopped thinking of this room as Mr. Bexley's. Now, instead of thinking of it as hers, its very walls seemed to echo with Mr. Steffington's presence. She could almost hear his earnest dialogue. Not only had this chamber perfectly suited the tall, broodingly dark scholar, without him it seemed a most lonesome place. His absence was almost palpable.

She had to keep telling herself their estrangement was for the best. She needed to become a self-sufficient woman. Never again would she be dependent upon a man.

It was looking like a certainty that she was going to have to become the aging aunt in her brother's overcrowded house. Not only would she be buried there for the rest of her life, but her little sister, too, would be denied the opportunities to be presented, to make a good match. Catherine had planned to bring her out next spring.

She would never be able to solve the dilemma about Mr. Longford as long as she was in this chamber that almost seemed to breathe Mr. Steffington's name. This library was entirely too sad without him. She wished it weren't the case, but she missed him.

From the coziest room in the house, she dragged herself away and trudged up the stairs to her bedchamber. What to do about the odious Mr. Long*mouth*? How well the twins' moniker for Mr. Longford suited him!

Even though it was an expense she couldn't afford, she rang for the parlor maid to build a fire in her chamber. Four days of chilled air made the room practically glacial.

She began to pace the carpeted floor in an effort to keep warm until the fire heated the room. Mr. Longford was sure to call upon her the following day. Since no one else would be around, that would be the perfect time for her to explain about the misunderstanding. But how was she to do that? She could hardly say, *I'm sorry, but I'd rather listen to* Faust *in German than listen to your drivel, Mr. Longford.* (And she was not conversant in that Teutonic language.)

It might be better if she resorted to a little white lie. That was it! She'd tell him her hearing was deficient. She was terribly sorry if she had mistakenly agreed to marry him when she'd thought she was merely admitting that his companionship was agreeable. All right. So it was more than a little white lie. It was a big, whopping falsehood.

Really, she was flattered that he'd determined he would like to spend the rest of his life with her—an untitled woman. The man was so enamored of peers that she'd always thought when the time came for him to marry, he would settle for the ugliest girl in the kingdom—if her father answered to Lord.

Though it was early, she decided to go to bed. The long carriage ride had been exhausting, and she hadn't slept well the night before. She'd been steeped in remorse because of her iciness to Mr. Steffington at the completion of their dinner.

The man was far better off without her inflicting chaos into his heretofore orderly life.

Divesting herself of her wrinkled traveling costume, she donned a warm winter night shift and climbed upon her bed, confident that when Mr. Longford called the following day, she could clear up this terrible misunderstanding—without bruising his pride too badly.

She would even give him leave to tell people *he* had called off the betrothal. She cared not if that tainted her in other men's eyes. It wasn't as if she were interested in ever marrying again.

On second thought, she realized he would not wish to have it known he had broken a betrothal. A man who cared so acutely what others thought of him would not want it known that he'd broken an engagement. Gentlemen were honor bound to abide by their proposals.

She lay there in her dark room that was illuminated only by the fire in the grate. She wished she had closed the curtains around her bed, but she was too tired and too cold to get up now.

Memories of hers and Airy's bedchamber at Granfield Manor flooded her. She remembered him closing her bed curtains, then thought of the narrow opening where she'd been able to glimpse him—the shirtless Adonis who had nearly stolen away her breath.

Even after they had argued later that night— after her ill-judged trip to Lord Seacrest's library— she had felt warm and safe in that cozy bedchamber.

Because Airy was there.

She'd not experienced such a feeling since she'd been a little girl who believed her father could slay every dragon in the kingdom.

After he'd come home the night before to an empty house, Melvin turned in for a good night's sleep, then he rose early and took his horse to Sydney Gardens for a morning canter. Following a solitary breakfast, he went to the library while his siblings still slept.

It amazed him that being idle never bothered his brother. Melvin Steffington did not like not having a purpose. Now that he was no longer helping Mrs. Bexley, he needed to initiate queries regarding employment in private libraries. Dr. Mather would be helpful in that regard.

He was in the middle of penning a letter to his old mentor when Elvin strolled into the library. "Welcome home, old chap."

Melvin looked up at his brother, who was nattily dressed. "Is this not exceptionally early for you to be up and shaved and dressed?" Melvin's glance darted to the clock upon the mantle. "It's not quite noon."

"I thought that now that Annie's out, I'd take

her around to call on Mrs. Bexley."

"How did you know Mrs. Bexley had returned to Bath?"

"Just because I wasn't here when you returned, dear boy, did not mean I didn't learn that you'd come home. I checked your bed every night you were gone." He came to sit near his twin. "How did the journey go? Did you find the Chaucer?"

Melvin shook his head remorsefully. "Things couldn't have been worse."

Elvin's brows lowered. "How so?"

"We not only had no success, but Mrs. Bexley has terminated my services."

"She didn't!"

"She did, though I had suggested that she might wish to do so."

"The poor woman's all alone in the world. She needed you. That wasn't very gallant of you! "

Melvin nodded. "She has remarked upon my lack of gallantry." He shrugged. "I cannot help it. I was born without the Graces. You hoarded all of them in the womb."

"Why, pray tell, did you suggest she turn you out?"

"I didn't actually suggest she turn me out. I just said that if my opinions were to be ignored, and she was desirous of endangering our lives, then perhaps she would be better off without me."

"Whoa! What's this about endangering your lives?"

Melvin told his brother about Mrs. Bexley's nocturnal trip to Lord Seacrest's library.

Elvin's eyes narrowed. "That was a damned stupid thing to do!"

"Unfortunately, that's what I told her, and she

accused me of thinking her stupid merely because she was a female."

"What did you say to that?"

"I angrily retorted that her stupidity had nothing to do with her gender."

Elvin's roar of laughter filled the room.

"That was the first time she hurled something at me."

"There were others?" Elvin's brow lifted.

Melvin pushed his dark hair from his brow. "Take a look at that!" There was a sizeable knot on his forehead.

"Good lord! What did she throw at you?"

"This was from an apple."

"It's a good thing she's neither big nor strong. She could have cracked your head open!"

"Enough talk about my stupendously failed mission. Tell me all about Annie's come-out."

A smile transformed Elvin's face. "Know she's me sister and all that, but she really was the prettiest girl there. And she never lacked for a dancing partner. Not once. I wish you could have seen her."

Melvin had no regrets. At least not about missing a night at the Assembly Rooms. Even to see sweet Annie be the belle of the ball, he would rather not go there.

He thought about regrets regarding his and Mrs. Bexley's mission. Yes, he had regrets aplenty on that score. He felt guilty for not assisting the poor widow—no matter how vexing she could be.

But this dissolution of their partnership was in accordance with her wishes. She had made it abundantly clear that he lacked gallantry. And she seemed to delight in throwing objects at him. She was likely sitting there at Number 17 Royal

Crescent right now thanking her lucky stars that Melvin Steffington was out of her life.

"I say, Mel, would you rather I not visit the Widow Bexley?"

"I wish her no rancor. Go ahead. You can still be friends with the lady." His brows lowered. "But you must be sure not to let Annie in on the secret of our journey. We must protect Mrs. Bexley's good name, and as sweet natured as Annie is, I'm not sure an eighteen-year-old girl can be trusted with secrets."

"Daresay you're right." Elvin stood. "Annie's dressing as we speak. Lizzy's pouting. She thinks she ought to be able to do everything her sister does."

"She actually wants to pay morning calls?" Melvin ranked morning calls only slightly more favorably than dancing at the Assembly Rooms.

"You know what social beings girls are."

That was rather the pity of it. Melvin actually knew very little about girls. Or women. "I daresay astutely gauging females is another of those traits you stole in the womb."

Frowning, Elvin mumbled. "While you were stealing all the intelligence."

"*Touché.*" Melvin was far too truthful to claim false modesty.

From the doorway, Elvin turned back. "I take it you'd rather not call on Mrs. Bexley."

"I doubt she'd want to see me."

After Elvin left, Melvin pondered whether his brother was smitten with Mrs. Bexley. Should he warn Elvin that she was somewhat betrothed to that damned Long*mouth*? How could a woman not know if she was betrothed or not? No wonder he would never understand their sex. There was nothing logical about them.

As Catherine dressed in a clean dress, thankful to no longer have to wear her wrinkled traveling clothes, she thought of Mr. Longford. While she was not particularly looking forward to meeting with him to break their mysterious betrothal, she would be inordinately pleased to have the meeting behind her.

She wished she'd never been civil to him in the first place. If only she'd learned to hone a bit harder an edge, she wouldn't have to be having this confrontation today. (Not to mention that she wouldn't have had to endure his insufferable companionship.)

Once she was dressed she started for the coziest room, then stopped herself. She no longer had any desire to walk into her library for she missed Mr. Steffington's presence too keenly.

As she stood in the corridor in front of her bedchamber, a knock sounded upon her front door. Simpson opened it. She had told him she was available to callers today.

It hadn't occurred to her that the other Steffington twin would be paying her a morning call. And this time with his sister! It was only then she remembered he'd brought her out while she and Melvin Steffington were away.

She met them in the drawing room, where Simpson had taken them. "How good of you to call, Sir Elvin." She offered her hand for him to kiss, then turned toward a rather pretty girl. It was quite remarkable how one could look so much like her supremely masculine brothers yet still be feminine and lovely. "You must be Annie Steffington. I am so sorry I was unable to attend your debut into Society, but now that I see you, I know it had to have been stupendously successful. Did you dance every set?"

The girl's black eyes—so much like Airy's—sparkled. "I did have that good fortune."

The two females sat at the silken settee, and Sir Elvin took a seat in an arm chair across from them.

"I suppose I should tell you," Sir Elvin said, "only me brother and I call her Annie."

The girl looked at Catherine, nodding.

"How silly of me," Catherine said. "I suppose your given name is Ann."

"Yes."

Even though the girl's coloring was the same as her twin brothers, and she was slender as they were lean, she was not tall like them, as Catherine had expected her to be. She was a bit taller than Catherine but still no more than average height. "You must tell me, Miss Steffington, were you filled with trepidation upon entering those lofty chambers of the Upper Assembly Rooms? Afraid no one would wish to stand up with you?"

The young lady offered Catherine a lovely smile. "Indeed I was! Do you mean to tell me all the girls have the same fears that plagued me?"

"All I expect, save those who are vastly conceited."

Sir Elvin cleared his throat. Was that a Steffington family trait after all and not peculiar to Melvin Steffington? "I am happy to see you're up and about after your illness, Mrs. Bexley. Allow me to say you look like one in the bloom of good health now."

"Thank you, Sir Elvin. Thank you, too, for

bringing your lovely sister here." A pity he had selected this day to pay a morning call. For she knew Mr. Longford would be turning up at any moment.

A knock sounded upon her drawing room door, then Simpson entered, announcing that Mr. Longford was calling.

As Mr. Longford strolled into the chamber, she thought she had probably never seen so expertly tied a cravat nor such fine leather boots. No doubt, Mr. Longford patronized only the finest tailors and boot makers. As well as carriage makers.

He came to offer her a lovely nosegay of some purple flower she'd never before seen.

"Thank you. They're beautiful. How thoughtful of you."

"I am so delighted to see the bloom back in your cheeks. Your illness was frightfully worrisome."

"You are too kind." Her gaze went to Sir Elvin's sister. "Have you met Miss Steffington?"

Mr. Longford moved closer to the young lady and bowed. "Your servant, Miss Steffington. I had the opportunity to observe you at the Assembly Rooms two nights ago. You certainly did not want for dance partners."

"And it was her first dance at the Assembly Rooms," Catherine added.

"You looked as if you've been dancing your whole life." Mr. Longford spun around to face Sir Elvin. "Which twin are you?"

Sir Elvin smirked. "Can you not guess?"

Mr. Longford's eyes narrowed. "Melvin?"

Sir Elvin shook his head. "No. I left Melvin in the library."

"I take note that until recently, Mr. Melvin Steffington has been on the reclusive side."

"Yes," Sir Elvin said. "We are vastly different."

In mid nod, Mr. Longford whipped around to face Catherine again. "Pray, Mrs. Bexley, I just remembered an errand I wish my coachman to perform. Allow me to go tell him, then return to you."

Before she could respond, he was flying from the chamber.

He returned five minutes later, took a seat in a chair next to Sir Elvin, and made himself agreeable to Miss Steffington. "As I was saying to Miss Steffington, you look like one born to dance. It's the same with the woman to whom my brother is betrothed. You've no doubt heard of Lord Finchton?" he asked the young lady.

She looked perplexed. "I'm not sure that I have."

"He's quite exalted and happens to be a particular cousin to Miss Turner-Fortenbury, my brother's fiancée."

Miss Steffington looked suitably impressed.

Then the gentleman directed his attention at Catherine. "And you, too, my dear Mrs. Bexley, are an outstanding dancer."

"And Mrs. Bexley's uncle is the Earl of Mountback," added Sir Elvin, whose amused gaze spun to Catherine.

"Is he not your mother's brother?" Mr. Longford asked.

Catherine nodded. "Yes. His father, the fourth earl, was my grandfather." It always made her a bit uncomfortable to discuss her mother's family's rank. Perhaps the discomfort had arisen when she realized her father's lack of rank made him unattractive to many in Mama's family in spite of his many attributes, which unfortunately did not include wealth.

At first Catherine had been most solicitous of Miss Steffington, but as time dragged by she found herself wishing Sir Elvin and Miss Steffington would leave so she could clear up matters with Mr. Longford. She therefore quit addressing comments to the sweet young lady.

It was obvious to Catherine that Mr. Longford also wished to be alone with her because he too began to exclude the Steffingtons from his remarks.

But Sir Elvin was oblivious to any snub and seemed content to spend the afternoon at Number 17 Royal Crescent. "I say, Mrs. Bexley," he said, "did you know that the Blankenships will be in Bath tomorrow? We're all to meet at the Assembly Rooms. Will you feel up to going?"

She smiled. "Nothing could keep me away. I haven't seen Glee in an age."

"Delightful creature," Sir Elvin said. "Did you know she and Blanks are expecting Child Number Two?"

"Yes, Felicity told me."

"Blankenship needs a son," Mr. Longford said. "All men need a son."

"But think how much fun it will be for them to think of more mirthful female names to go with little Joy Blankenship," Catherine said.

"Perhaps she could be known as Happy," Miss Steffington added, smiling broadly.

"Daresay it's time we got a little Gregory or Richard or some such proper name," Sir Elvin said. "At least those Pembrokes haven't foisted those mirthful names on the male side of the family."

"I suppose, being a baronet," Mr. Longford said to Sir Elvin, "you've got the responsibility for continuing your family's long, prestigious line upon your shoulders."

Sir Elvin held up a palm. "Whoa! I'm in no hurry to get meself shackled."

Mr. Longford's eyes narrowed as he turned back to Catherine. "Is Melvin Steffington still assisting you on that mysterious matter you think would bore me?"

"Not any longer," she said.

His demeanor brightened. Surely he wasn't jealous of Mr. Steffington! What an utterly ridiculous notion.

Catherine found herself looking at the clock upon the mantle. The four of them had been together for more than an hour, and none of them showed signs of wrapping up the visit. What was she to do?

After he finished his correspondence, Melvin decided to walk to the lending library. He had ordered a new translation of Marcus Aurelius and wanted to see if it had come in. Though Elvin would not deem him properly attired, Melvin thought he looked perfectly acceptable for a stroll along the streets of Bath.

It wasn't as if he would see anyone he knew. He knew so few. The ones he'd been friends with had married and set up nurseries far away from this enchanting town.

Donning his beaver hat, he departed the house on Green Park Road and began to walk toward the town center to his favorite of the city's lending libraries. As he walked, he found himself wondering how Elvin and Annie were getting along with Mrs. Bexley. He hadn't expected them to be gone this long.

He wondered if Mrs. Bexley was happy that he'd not come. In spite of their differences of opinion, he thought she did not dislike him. (Except when she threw things at him.) Would she feel badly if she saw the goose egg she'd put on his forehead? His experiences with her told him she would be remorseful. The woman was possessed of a tender heart.

The pity of her entertaining callers was that she wasn't free to continue looking for the *Canterbury Tales*. It was a shame she was such a mutton head. Could she not see she really needed a man? Too much rested on her dainty shoulders. Melvin would have been happy to take away some of her burdens.

But of course he couldn't deal with a hard-headed woman who made nonsensical decisions of which he would never approve.

There were so many patrons at the public house on Pierepont Street, they were spilling from the doorway. It seemed to him a bit early in the day for tipping the old bumpers.

It was while he was passing the crowded, noisy public house that he became aware that someone was trying to get his attention.

"Sir! Sir! Could you please lend me a 'and?" A grizzly fellow with white whiskers, portly frame, and servant's garb approached him. "It's the lady. She needs yer 'elp. She's fallen, and there's a prodigious amount of blood."

"Where?"

"Just into this lane." The man pointed toward an alley as the two men started in that direction.

Melvin was too concerned about the bloody woman to question why she would be down a dark alley. He was too concerned to notice the portly man had dropped behind him.

It wasn't until a rope slipped around his neck from the rear that Melvin realized what a stupid thing he'd done. As the rope pulled tighter, he tried to yank it away. It was cutting off his windpipe. What the deuce?

The man shoved Melvin into the brick wall and spoke to him in a guttural voice. "This is a warning, Mr. Steffington. If you continue searching for the Chaucer, you'll be killed." The man twisted at the rope once more as he slammed Melvin's head into the bricks.

Until everything became black.

$\mathcal{C}$hapter 15

Mr. Longford had launched into one of his colossally boring stories about the groom to the Duke of Bedford complimenting him on his four perfectly matched black horses. Catherine really wished Sir Elvin and his sweet sister would leave so she could disavow Mr. Longford of the misunderstanding about their betrothal.

Her attention was drawn away from the Soliloquyist by a rapid pounding upon her staircase. Even Mr. Longford stopped in mid-sentence, his eyes rounded, his gaze—like the rest of those in the chamber—darting to the doorway.

The door flew open, and a winded Simpson said, "Sir Elvin! A servant from your house has come to fetch you. Your brother's met with some terrible calamity."

Miss Steffington screamed and leapt to her feet, as did her brother. It was only then that Catherine realized she too had screamed. She watched in terror as Miss Steffington clutched her brother's arm and cried out, "Is he . . . alive?"

Simpson nodded. "He's been taken back to your house."

Catherine felt as if she could drop to her knees and offer a prayer of thanks.

Sir Elvin spun to her. "We'll bid you a good day." Then he raced from the room.

She hurried after him. "Pray, allow me to come.

Perhaps I can be of some meager assistance. I spent a great deal of time in my husband's sickroom."

"Oh, please come," a tearful Annie Steffington said, tossing a beseeching gaze to her brother.

He nodded and began to speed down the corridor. "We must hurry."

All them, including Mr. Longford, flew down the stairs, and a Steffington servant met them in the entry hall.

"What's happened to my brother?" Sir Elvin demanded.

"We don't really know, sir. He's not gained consciousness."

"Come," Sir Elvin said. "Jackson, ride in the coach with us."

She bid farewell to Mr. Longford before climbing into the carriage. He stood there looking rather forlorn, but he most definitely was *not* her concern.

Once the Steffington coach was rushing back to Green Park Road, Sir Elvin asked his footman for a more detailed accounting of what had happened to his twin.

"Lord Henderson said 'e was riding along in his coach when he noticed a crowd gathered around an injured man, and he stopped when he recognized the injured man was one of the Steffington twins. His lordship had him placed in his carriage and brought him to Green Park Road."

"I shall be indebted to Lord Henderson," Sir Elvin said. "What is the nature of my brother's injuries?" Sir Elvin inquired.

The footman shrugged. "'e was bleeding from the head."

Miss Steffington winced.

"Does anyone know how he was injured?" Catherine asked.

"Since 'e was found in an alleyway, Lord Henderson believed he'd been attacked and robbed."

"But Melvin never carries large sums of money." Sir Elvin gasped. "Dear God! The thief must have taken my poor brother for me!"

As soon as they reached Green Park Road, Sir Elvin threw open the coach door, raced up the steps, and entered the house, Catherine and Miss Steffington directly behind him. Catherine's slow pace was at odds with her racing heartbeat. Terrified that Airy had died, she was once again incapable of stanching the tears that beaded in her eyes. *Please let him be alive.*

She wasn't the only one so affected. Even tall, strapping Sir Elvin was fighting back tears as he attempted to communicate with the first servant to greet them. At that same moment, an incredibly pretty young lady of Quality raced from behind a closed door, then fell into Sir Elvin's arms and wept uncontrollably.

Oh, my God, he's died.

"What's happened, Lizzy?" Sir Elvin's deep voice cracked with emotion.

"There's such a lot of blood."

Sir Elvin's face blanched, then he surged toward the room from which Lizzy had just come.

It seemed to Catherine her heart stopped beating, yet she was compelled to go after him. She had to see if there was something she could do. As she entered the chamber, the first thing she saw was Airy's long legs stretched out on a silken sofa, splotches of fresh blood on his buff colored breeches. Her pulse pounding prodigiously, she forced her gaze to ever so slowly move to his face, and she could see the source of the blood wasn't his face—though it was a profusion of blood. She was almost certain he had suffered some kind of blow to the side of his head. Had he perhaps fallen from a horse?

Was he alive? She could drop to her knees and pray fervently that his life be spared, but if there was any way she could help, that must be her first priority.

Sir Elvin just stood beside the sofa, staring down at the twin to whom he was so close. It was a heartbreaking sight. She moved up to Airy and began to feel for a pulse. As her thumb pressed into his flesh, he began to stir. Her gaze connected to Sir Elvin's for a fraction of a moment, both of them buoyed with hope.

"Pray, Miss Steffington," Catherine said to Annie, "can you procure some cloths so that I can try to clean away the blood?"

A moment later Catherine was removing the blood which had begun to dry on his face. His lids began to lift, and her heart soared. The next thing she knew he was looking at her, a puzzled look on his face.

It happened that her right hand was gently stroking his brow as his eyes came fully open and connected with hers. For a long moment their gazes locked and the two of them seemed to blend together like a curious liquid. He swallowed, his hand slowly moving to his neck and coiling around it. "You look like an angel."

"Thank God you're all right!" Sir Elvin exclaimed. "What in the bloody hell happened to you?"

Mr. Steffington's gaze flicked to his brother, but it was a moment before he could articulate. "It was. . .I was called to help a maiden in distress, but it was a ruse to get me in the alley..."

"So you *were* robbed!" Sir Elvin nodded. "I knew it. They mistook you for me."

Melvin Steffington shook his head. "Not they. He. . ." His voice lacked stridency, and his words came slowly. He had started to say something else, then stopped and shifted his gaze back to Catherine.

"What did the beast do to you?" Catherine asked. "There's a terrible knot on your forehead and a gash on the side of your head."

"He somehow came up behind me and as quick as a cat roped my neck." His hand went to neck.

Without saying a word, she began to untie his cravat. Were she a maiden, she would have been prevented from disrobing a man's upper torso, but she did not give a tuppence about propriety at that moment. Once she removed the linen that was caked with dried blood and little tufts of hemp, she saw that the flesh of his neck had been rubbed red. "Thank God you're neck's not blue."

He tried to smile. "Thank God he didn't succeed in strangling me."

"And thank God Lord Henderson happened by when he did," Sir Elvin said.

Airy looked puzzled.

"He came by the scene of your injury and brought you home in his coach. Daresay, your blood's all over his seats. I shall offer to have them replaced."

Airy's voice was already gathering strength. "If I hadn't been taken by surprise from the back, I could have beaten him. He told me . . ." He stopped, eying Catherine intently, then shook his head. "As to the lump on my forehead, you caused that, madam."

She detected a teasing gleam in his eye. Then she realized this was no teasing matter. "Surely you don't mean I caused that bruise . . . oh no, the apple!" She was mortified. "Can you ever forgive me? I feel like the worst sort of criminal. Oh, Airy, I'm ever so sorry."

Sir Elvin cocked a brow. "Airy? I take it, that's short for Aristotle?"

Catherine nodded shyly. "Aristotle's much too formal." She had thought to add *for friendly traveling companions* but thought better of it in front of the Steffington maidens.

The baronet also must have realized her need to avoid speaking of their recent journey for he changed the subject. "Did you know your attacker?"

Airy shook his head.

Catherine kept looking at the oozing gash on the side of his head. "How did you get this?" she asked as she gently blotted at it.

"He. . .slammed me against the wall. I think it was the wall of the public house. It's bloody embarrassing that I wasn't better able to defend myself."

"So you're saying this ruffian lured you into the alley with the made-up story of a woman in distress, then dropped back behind you and slung the rope around your neck?" Sir Elvin asked.

Melvin Steffington nodded. "I wasn't able to defend myself because I had to use my hands to keep the rope from tightening more around my neck."

Annie moved closer to the sofa. "I'm going to send for a surgeon."

Airy sat up. "No, I'm fine."

"I'd feel better about it, old chap." Sir Elvin nodded at Annie, and she started to move from the chamber.

"How did it feel when you sat up?" Catherine asked, her voice soft.

"I said I'm fine," he grumbled, his eyes narrow as his gaze flicked from her to his twin. "Don't send for a surgeon."

Annie's eyes locked with Sir Elvin's, and he sadly shook his head.

Catherine had continued to softly blot at his oozing wound. "It is bleeding less. I don't believe it will have to be sewn up."

At the mention of sewing her brother's flesh, Lizzy promptly fainted.

Her heart was not in tonight's festivities. If she weren't looking forward to seeing Glee, she would not have budged from her home.

She was so blue-deviled about Airy's injury. It had been difficult to leave him earlier that afternoon. He had proven to her he'd not suffered any dangerous effects from his beating, but for some reason she continued to worry about him. Even in those days when she'd know Mr. Bexley was not long for this world, she'd never experienced a feeling of raw, painful dread such as she had experienced that day over Airy's injury.

And that wasn't the first time she'd been so inordinately worried about that Steffington twin. Her thoughts flashed back to his trip to Cheddar and how her worry over his well-being had made her almost senseless.

She could hardly have a motherly fixation on him. They were the same age. So why in the devil did she worry over him like that?

Just before departing for the Assembly Rooms she took one long glance into her looking glass. She rather liked the way she looked in saffron but hoped others wouldn't think her too monochromatic because of her yellowish hair.

Ten minutes later she was strolling into the Assembly Rooms. She had always been more comfortable coming into these balls after they had gotten underway instead of being early and sitting around like a wallflower watching critically as each person entered the chilly chamber. For her part, she'd rather wait until the chamber had warmed up with the heat of hundreds of dancing bodies.

The first thing she saw upon entering the ballroom was Glee waltzing with her husband. Catherine stopped in mid-stride to gawk at the remarkable couple. Tiny Glee with her thick coppery hair was stunning yet entirely different from her elegant blonde sister, Felicity. As pretty as Glee was, though, it was impossible not to stare at her husband. Gregory Blankenship was acknowledged to be the most handsome man to ever have graced this watering city.

As Catherine watched him she realized many of his physical attributes were ones possessed also by the Steffington twins. All of them were tall, rather lean with broad shoulders, and in possession of very dark hair. Blanks' hair was so thick as to almost be bushy while the Steffingtons' dark hair was as straight as a paintbrush.

Felicity came up to Catherine as she stood there. "Are they not a lovely couple?"

Catherine nodded. "A family trait, I should think. Is that not what everyone says when you dance with your husband?"

Felicity's smile accentuated her deep dimples. "I cannot help it. I do believe my dear Thomas is the most handsome man in the kingdom."

"And your sister would likely fight you over the right to say that particular honor should be bestowed upon her husband."

"If I'd been two years younger, I'm sure I'd have fallen for Blanks myself, but I always thought of him as a little brother."

The music stopped at the termination of the set, and Mr. and Mrs. Gregory Blankenship crossed the dance floor to greet Catherine.

"Oh, Caffy, it's so good to see that you've thrown off that horrid mourning garb." Glee had persisted in referring to Catherine by her childhood name. "I do hope you'll meet a perfect mate and marry again."

Catherine adamantly shook her head. "I have no desire to remarry."

Blanks kissed her hand, bowed, and took off for the card room.

"Of course you'd say that. By his debauched ways, your Mr. Bexley poisoned you against all members of his sex." Glee's voice softened. "You must believe there are other good men out there. I know Blanks' first concern is always for my well-being."

He loves her more than he loves himself. That's the kind of husband Papa had been to Mama. Catherine had thought that breed had died with her father. But as she stood there, and Thomas

Moreland came up to Felicity, Catherine realized these sisters had found that rare wonder: a loving, devoted husband.

Because Catherine had enjoyed so happy a childhood, she felt doomed to a lonely, loveless adulthood. Expecting happiness at both ends of her life would demonstrate an unbecoming sense of greed. She'd tasted happiness once; now it was time for others.

Catherine's gaze flicked to Glee's stomach. "Pray, where are you hiding that baby?"

Glee shrugged. "I am worried about my poor son. Every time I try to feed him, I end up casting up my accounts. Blanks is beside himself with worry. Over me, as usual."

"A son?"

"I do hope for a boy this time."

"Dearest," Felicity said to her sister, "you shouldn't set yourself up for disappointment. You know you and Blanks will both be deliriously happy just to have a healthy babe."

Glee giggled. "You sound exactly like Blanks. And, of course, you're right. We'll love a he, she, or it. As long as it's ours."

A deep, gnawing pang strummed through Catherine. She was jealous of Glee and Felicity. Not that Catherine ever wished to have to put up with a husband again, but a babe of her own? What woman wouldn't want one?

If she'd been melancholy at the start of the evening, she was downright blue-deviled now.

She and Glee settled down on one of the red damask settees and started babbling like dear old friends who had long been separated. When Catherine saw the diminutive Mr. Longford come cockily strolling toward her, her blue-devils deepened.

Why had she ever been civil to him? He was like a barnacle she couldn't dislodge.

She needed to have a face-to-face conversation with him—one in which she listened to every syllable he uttered—and clear up this gross misunderstanding. Perhaps she could suggest the two of them go out to the Octagon. While it was not an intimate place, it was a great deal quieter than the ballroom. She vowed that tonight she would terminate this so-called betrothal to Mr. Long*mouth*.

He came and greeted each of them, then asked if he could sit beside her. Because it was the middle of a country dance, he was prevented from asking her to stand up with him.

He squeezed beside her on the settee. "Allow me to say how becoming you look in yellow, my dear Mrs. Bexley."

She was thankful for confirmation that she had not looked like a banana.

As her head bobbed from Glee at her left to Mr. Longford at her right, from the corner of her eye she saw a dark-haired man who towered over others in the room move toward her. She would know him in a million. Even if he did have an identical twin.

From the distance of twenty-five feet she felt his black eyes boring into her own. Her heart began to hammer more with each step closer he came. Like one witnessing a disaster, she was powerless to remove her gaze from him.

He came to stand in front of her, blocking her view of the dancers who were leaving the floor. His hair almost covered the worst of his injuries from earlier in the day, but nothing could conceal the bruises on his face.

"I should be honored if you will stand up with me the next set," he said.

$\mathscr{C}$hapter 16

Why was it every time Melvin danced with her the musicians struck up a waltz? Not that he objected. He'd come here tonight expressly to speak with Mrs. Bexley, and the waltz afforded them that opportunity.

After he'd asked her to dance, she'd placed her hand in his and strolled onto the dance floor. "Are you sure you're up to dancing?" she asked, concern in her voice.

He didn't like to be treated like a bloody child. "I told you earlier, I'm recovered." Except for his bruised pride. How could he have let a man at least twenty years his senior get the better of him? If he ever again saw that blighter, he'd take great pleasure in slamming *his* head into a brick wall until *he* blacked out.

"You never did tell us how much he stole from you."

He had no intentions of telling her or anyone about the guttural threat uttered to him by his attacker. A woman like Mrs. Bexley who lived alone did not need the burden of worrying about reprobates like that man. Melvin would make sure she was never harmed.

That was another reason he had come tonight.

He felt guilty for not being completely honest with his brother, but Elvin worried too much. If Elvin knew of the attackers' threats, he would do everything in his power to keep Melvin from seeking the Chaucer.

Today's threat only served to make Melvin more determined than ever to find it. He had to know who was behind the threats. How could someone have learned that he was searching for the manuscript? Only three people knew: himself, Mrs. Bexley, and Elvin—all of whom could be depended upon not to betray such a confidence.

His dance step slowed as he shrugged. "I couldn't say."

"It's horrifying that a big man such as you should be attacked in broad daylight walking down a busy street in Bath. I'd always thought this city to be perfectly safe."

"Daresay the fellow just took a dislike to me."

"There are small men who can be most jealous of height in their perceived rivals."

Small men like Longford? "This man was not of our class."

"Oh."

His step slowed, and he looked down into her face. He was unaffected by the feel of her or the light lavender scent of her. "So, Mrs. Bexley, are you still betrothed?"

"I told you I wasn't precisely betrothed."

A cynical smile crossed his face, and his brows elevated. "Precisely?"

"I may have misunderstood his question. At any rate, I've no intention of marrying Mr. Longford. Or any man."

"You realize that if you were to marry him you'd be free of financial worries for the rest of your life?"

"At too dear a cost, I'm afraid."

He chuckled. "Whoever does marry the man

has my sympathy."

"As soon as I have the opportunity to speak with Mr. Longford I plan to clear up his misunderstanding about a purported betrothal. I had hoped to do so this afternoon, but then we learned of your misfortune."

He would never forget that spiritual moment when he'd gained consciousness and looked up into her lovely, concerned face. For several seconds he was in another world, one inhabited by sweet smelling angels with Mrs. Bexley's face. "It was very kind of you to come to Green Park Road to offer your services as a nurse. My sisters are useless in situations like that."

"Kindness had nothing to do with it. I was incredibly worried about you. We did not know the extent of your injuries, and I think we all feared the worst. I prayed all the way to Green Park Road."

"I'm deeply appreciative."

"I suppose you came here tonight so you could see how successful your sister's launch into Society has been?"

He really should take more notice of Annie. "Actually I came here to speak to you."

"You've heard from Mr. Whitebread?" She peered into his face, smiling brightly.

"Yes, I've brought the letter so you can see it."

"It's probably another false hope, but it happens to be all I've got."

Even though it was by her own choice she was going this journey alone, he didn't like it.

And he wouldn't have it.

"You never did tell me where he lives," she said.

"He's in Wiltshire."

"How gratifying. That's close."

"Close, but still an arduous journey."

When the music began to taper off, they crossed the dance floor, going opposite Longford's direction and exiting into the Octagon where a number of people were quietly strolling and talking. He moved to stand beneath a wall sconce so the light would be better for her to read, then he extracted Whitebread's letter from his breast pocket. She took it, unfolded it, and began to read.

My Dear Mr. Steffington,

I must tell you how serendipitous getting your letter was. Only the day before I had been in communication with Dr. Mather regarding prospective employment of a curator for my book collections, and he had recommended you.

Conceive of my happiness when I received your letter the very next day! I will be in residence at Stipley Hall until after Christmas and welcome you. I beg that during your visit you allow time for us to discuss the duties here at Stipley.

Cordially,
Whitebread

"I will leave early tomorrow morning," she said.

What if the man who'd beaten him should make good on his threat? Only next time, it could mean Mrs. Bexley's life. "I can't let you. That letter was not written to you. How will you explain yourself?"

She put hands to hips and glared at him. "You have nothing to say regarding my search for the Chaucer."

"You have made that abundantly clear; nevertheless, I cannot allow you to go off like that.

It could be entirely too dangerous."

A flicker of emotion lanced across her face. "So what are you suggesting?"

"You need me."

Those spectacular eyes of hers regarded him curiously, but she said not a word.

"It goes against my nature to quit a project before it's reached a successful completion."

They stood there eying one another like two circling bantams. Finally she nodded ever so slightly. "My rented coach will call for you at Green Park Road. Six tomorrow morning."

It had been difficult for her to conceal her elation when Airy had told her he was back on their *project*. When she returned to the ballroom, her step was lighter. It was as if a heavy cloak of gloom had suddenly been swept from her shoulders. She could face anything now that she and Airy had returned to a hopefully amicable partnership. She vowed to herself that in the future she would seek his opinions and try to abide by them. No more barreling into potential disasters. Hadn't she originally engaged him because of his superior intelligence and sound judgment? She must respect that sound judgment. He had never once disappointed.

With her new-found radiance, she felt invincible. What better time to snuff Mr. Longford's unfounded hopes?

As soon as she reached their scarlet settee back in the ballroom, she smiled upon Mr. Longford. "I beg that you will come with me to the Octagon. There's a matter I wish to discuss with you."

Smiling widely, he leapt to his feet, offered her

his crooked arm, and the pair of them strolled from the ballroom.

"I am ever so glad to have the opportunity to have you almost to myself, my dear Catherine."

She spun toward him and glared. "You are not permitted to call me by my first name."

"But, my dearest, you've done me the goodness of consenting to become my wife."

She drew in a deep breath. "I beg your forgiveness. It was never my intention to consent to such a proposal. If I did so, it was because I misunderstood what you were saying. My hearing is most faulty. I daresay it's because as a child I was forever sick with the earache." That part was true; the part about her faulty hearing was a necessary lie.

"I don't see how I could be so mistaken. You clearly smiled at me and nodded when I told you I have been in love with you since you came out all those years ago and that I wished to ask for your hand in marriage."

Oh dear. "I am deeply appreciative, but I must point out that a crowded ballroom is *not* the best place from which to ask for a woman's hand in marriage. It was far too noisy for me to clearly hear the words you were saying."

Had she just told him that his esteemed carriage maker to the crown was a fraud, his face could not have fallen any lower.

Then he brightened. "Can you hear me now?"

Uh oh. "I hear you very well."

"Then I will repeat my offer. Even though I had once hoped to marry a woman whose name is preceded by *lady*, I find I shall have to settle for one whose mother's name is preceded by lady." He took her hand. "There you have it. No other woman will do for me. You're the one I want to share my name and all my wealth. As my wife, you'll never want for anything the rest of your life."

"I cannot tell you how honored I am, but I must decline. I have no intention of ever marrying again."

"You can't be that loyal to Bexley! He was never worthy of you."

Should she allow him to believe that loyalty to Mr. Bexley prevented her from remarrying? That would be the easiest explanation. But it was so false. One falsehood was quite enough for one night.

She could hardly tell him the truth—that Mr. Bexley exemplified all that was wrong with his gender. She had vowed that she would never sully her husband's memory. "If you must know," she finally said, "I found that I excessively disliked being married."

Eyes rounded, he nodded. "If you were my wife, I would never patronize Mrs. Baddele's."

She had never been more humiliated. *So everyone in Bath had known about Mr. Bexley's attachment to Cyprians.* "Mr. Longford! I am mortified that you would bring up such a scandalous topic in the presence of a lady." She turned on her heel and left.

She would have gone straight home if it weren't for Glee, but good manners compelled her to take leave of her dear old friend. As soon as they exchanged farewells and promised to write to one another, Catherine returned to Number 17 Royal Crescent.

There, she dispatched Simpson to make arrangements for hiring a coach on the morrow.

Not sure how long the journey to Mr. Whitebread's would take, she packed her valise before readying for bed.

Why was it the night before leaving town she could never sleep? There were more spokes than normal wheeling around the hub of her brain. She thought of how soundly she had put down Mr. Longford. Looking back on it, she realized it had been fortuitous that he had offended her because it made it easier for her to rebuke him. She sincerely hoped she had seen the last of him.

She thought about the Chaucer and prayed that Mr. Whitebread would be the key to finding it. If the trip to his Stipley Hall did not prove helpful, she would lose everything. The thought of such destitution made her melancholy.

But it was difficult to be too melancholy now that she and Airy would be together again. His offer to help her was almost as good as actually reclaiming the Chaucer. With his aid, she had confidence that they would be successful. It wasn't just his intelligence that inspired confidence. Everything about him, from his wise counsel to his perceptive humor, gave her a security unlike anything she had experienced in her entire adulthood.

Not for the first time, a spark of jealousy spiked when she thought of the fortunate woman who would one day capture his heart. For Mr. Melvin Steffington was a man like her Papa had been. He would not only be a loyal husband but he would also be one who would command any woman's respect.

She was happy too that he still wished to assist her. She had feared that she'd alienated him with her careless dismissal of him at Granfield Manor following her own foolish actions. As she lay there in her bed thinking about him, a smile stretched across her face.

Before she'd learned of his injury that afternoon, she had not realized how very dear he was to her. She would never forget the fear that nearly incapacitated her in the wake of Simpson's announcement. She recalled the terror that sickened her when she'd witnessed his prone body on that sofa, blood splotches on his breeches. She had been afraid to look at this face, afraid to see death upon those features that had come to mean so much to her.

When his eyes had fluttered open, her hopeful heart lifted, and when he finally spoke and she heard the familiar voice she'd come to love, joy had sung through every vein in her body. She had thought nothing on earth could surpass that happiness.

Until tonight. When he insisted upon rejoining her in the quest to find her Chaucer, the elation she'd felt was ten times more than the effects of the finest French champagne.

Melvin Steffington was the only man in the kingdom she looked forward to spending time with—which was admitting that he was the only man she wanted to be with.

Ever.

Her heartbeat exploded. What was she thinking? She began to tremble. Nothing could quell her racing pulse. Had she fallen in love with Melvin Steffington?

Oh, dear God. She had.

$\mathcal{C}$hapter 17

"You didn't sleep well, did you?" Airy peered at her from across the coach the following morning.

How could she have slept well? What a shocking experience it was for a woman—a woman like her, who'd sworn off men for the rest of her days—to realize she had fallen in love. With that realization had also come the conviction that Melvin Steffington did not deserve to be thrown into the pit with the other unsatisfactory members of his sex.

He was a fine man. A pity he couldn't—in this instance—be more like his brother, who had shown interest in her womanly attributes. Was Airy blind to them? Or did he not find her attractive?

Thoughts of him had made sleep impossible. She'd felt a dizzying excitement over the prospect of traveling with him the next day. Being with him was comfortable while at the same time exhilarating. She had become closer to him than she'd ever been to any man.

She peered into his dark eyes, her heart fluttering. He may not be in love with her, but the very fact that he could tell she hadn't slept last night spoke to his deep connection with her. "I never seem able to sleep the night before a trip. I'm always afraid I'll forget something important. What about you? How did you sleep?"

"Very well."

A pity. That meant he'd not given a thought to her. "At the risk of sounding like a doxy, I do recall your propensity to immediately drop off to sleep."

He grinned. "No one could ever think you a doxy. Neither my brother nor I would ever let it be known that you and I have so intimately traveled together."

Intimately traveled together—the contemplation of which accounted for all those sleepless hours and the present reality giving her a great sense of well-being.

The twins were every inch gentlemen. "I am gratified to have the assistance of a man whom I so implicitly trust."

His face twitched into a mischievous gleam. "Speaking of having a man to assist you, I must ask if you are still affianced to Long*mouth*."

Her expression matched his in levity. "I was able to clear up that misunderstanding last night."

"Thus, a heavier load upon my shoulders to keep Mrs. Bexley from the Poor House."

She tucked the rug around her and stuffed her gloved hands into her fox muff in an effort to warm herself. The fierce cold winds outside rocked the coach from side to side. She prayed her motion sickness would not inflict itself ruthlessly upon her.

"I know of no more capable man than you, but you mustn't feel so deep an obligation. Remember, before we became so well acquainted, I was already facing my potential destitution."

He winced. "I understand what it's like to crave independence. No adult wants to be an appendage to a sibling, no matter how agreeable that sibling is."

"And when that sibling is married and has a house full of children, the attraction of being dependent upon him is even more unwelcome."

"I will do everything in my power to restore the Chaucer to you." There was no mirth in his voice this time.

"And if we should fail, you must not blame yourself."

"I've never been able to tolerate failure."

She gave a little laugh. "I cannot believe you've ever failed at any endeavor."

He appeared to ponder this. She studied his pensive face. Its solid masculine bone structure and aquiline nose bespoke his keen intelligence. "I once omitted a word when reciting Hamlet's soliloquy."

She was incapable of stifling a laugh. "How trying it must be for you to have to put up with me. I'm not only *not* a bluestocking, but I'm also exceedingly prone to making poor decisions." Like her nocturnal jaunt into Lord Seacrest's library.

Or her marriage to Mr. Bexley.

The marriage to Mr. Bexley she better understood now. Now that she physically and mentally experienced the joy of falling in love. With Airy.

She had assumed the mild attraction she'd initially felt toward Mr. Bexley must be love because he was the only man who had ever produced any kind of reaction in her. Without any basis of comparison, how was she to have known that what she'd felt for Mr. Bexley wasn't love? Now she realized what she'd felt for Mr. Bexley had been fool's gold.

How was she to have known love could be so very much more encompassing? She had not then known that the very sight of The One could send pulses racing and heart hammering. She had not then known that the very contemplation of The One could produce a physical yearning to be in his company. She had not then known that when she was with The One it was as if there was no one else in the universe, save the two of them.

Now there was an even greater urgency to find the Chaucer. If they did not find it, she might never see him again. He was likely to take a position with Mr. Whitebread, and she would be doomed to her brother's home in the gloomy North Country.

The very notion of never seeing him suffused her with despair.

He brushed off her statement about her ineptness. "You're not stupid. Not at all, and I beg your forgiveness for saying you acted stupidly." He shrugged. "You may not always exercise sound judgment, though."

"You could have omitted that last sentence," she said, a smile betraying her lack of anger.

"We may have our differences, but you're the only woman I've ever been comfortable with. It's much like being with Lizzy or Annie."

"Just what every woman wishes to hear."

He looked puzzled.

"Unmarried women do not desire that unmarried men perceive them to be sisters." That was as close as she could ever come to flirting.

"Oh, I don't precisely think of you as a sister. I meant. . . I'm as comfortable with you as I am with my sisters, though I truly don't think of you as a sister."

Just hearing those words tumble from his lips sent her pulse thumping. "I'm comfortable with you, too." During her sleepless night she had decided that she would never declare her feelings to him. Unless he were to make the first move—which was not likely.

He was nowhere near making that first move. If only they had more time. Time to cultivate this growing affection for one another to its natural conclusion.

The very contemplation of a *natural conclusion* felt like falling from a great height.

The words in Mr. Whitebread's letter continued to imprint themselves upon her mind. "It sounds as if Mr. Whitebread has already decided he wishes to engage you."

"I daresay Dr. Mather was excessively generous in his praise of me. He's very kind in that regard."

She completely understood how Airy's Oxford mentor would be prone to praise his shining star of a student. "I wonder when you would have to begin your employment with him—provided the two of you can come to agreeable terms." The idea of him being buried at Stipley Hall was palpably painful.

"I hadn't thought that far ahead."

"You might also wish to give thought as to what kind of compensation you'll require."

"I never thought of that either."

"You see, Mr. Steffington, our minds complement one another. I am practical, and you are far more cerebral. One, I think, needs the other."

"I suppose two heads are better than one. That's what Elvin always says."

Her meaning had been completely lost on the

unromantic man.

"I hadn't thought about financial settlements. Since the post would come with lodgings and food, I should think the salary would not be great."

"You also need to be compensated for the deprivation of having to live away from your affectionate brother and the others who love you."

He looked quizzically at her. "Love? I assure you, it's not a word Elvin and I would ever utter to one another." He shrugged. "Though I daresay it describes how we feel. Men don't express feelings."

"That explains why you're not enamored of poetry."

"Perhaps. I like things to be logical. As you know, I was almost a mathematician."

"And there's nothing logical whatsoever about falling in love."

"I know nothing of falling in love."

She fervently wished she could change that. If only there was more time. "I do hope that's an emotion you will one day experience."

He gave a little chuckle. "If the poets are to be believed, falling in love's typically accompanied by pain. I would do well to steer clear of such a thing."

It was too painful to think of him living under Mr. Whitebread's roof. How could something mental cause her breath to shorten or her heart to beat in a most erratic fashion? This awakening to new love made her feel like a schoolgirl.

Then there was the opposite swing of the pendulum: from joy to gloom. The *probability* was that much pain was in store for her. The probability was not great that he would return her affection. And the probability of them living happily together forever was so remote as to be miniscule. "You may be right about the pain that accompanies love."

He flashed a sympathetic look at her. No doubt he—like everyone else, except Felicity and Glee—thought she was mourning the death of a much-loved husband.

She had best change the conversation. "Did you get the opportunity to speak with Blanks last night?"

"I did. He has significantly tamed, but then it was always Lord Sedgewick who was his catalyst."

"In uncaging the beast?"

He chuckled. "You might put it that way."

Thinking of Lord Sedgewick and Blanks brought a smile to her face. Now that they were married, they were as tame as aging felines.

When would Sir Elvin be wanting to follow suit? She could understand where his future decision to wed would impact Airy. It was only normal that Airy would wish to carve out an independent life of his own away from his brother.

And her.

A deep chill penetrated every centimeter of her body, yet it was oddly comforting to be ensconced with him in this small coach as cold winds whipped throughout the countryside.

"What do you know of Mr. Whitebread?" she asked.

"Not much. I seem to recall something about him inheriting sugar plantations."

"I daresay that's as good as owning coal mines."

He nodded.

"You got his direction from Appleton?"

"I did—before we went north to Granfield Manor."

"How does Appleton know Mr. Whitebread?"

"Appleton knows everyone—and he has an extremely competent, well-organized secretary who can instantly retrieve any kind of information the rest of us would never deem important."

"Things like the direction of those with whom his employer corresponds?"

"I'm not clear that Appleton actually corresponds with the fellow. It may be that Whitebread was acquainted with Appleton's late father."

"The father from whom Appleton inherited the efficient secretary?"

Airy's black eyes glittered. "Exactly."

They rode on in silence, each of them peering from the coach window. It was a blustery day which made her glad to be inside a coach. On days like this she sympathized with the poor coachmen who were exposed to the worst weather conditions. At least it wasn't raining.

She looked up at Airy. "I see you didn't bring your Euripides today."

A mischievous glint in his eyes, he touched the knot on his forehead. "I shouldn't want to inflame my traveling companion again."

Her first instinct was to hurl something at him for his unmerciful teasing, then as she observed the bruise she'd inflicted upon his brow, she was filled with remorse. "Oh, Airy, I am so sorry I threw that apple at you. Please forgive me." She hadn't meant to call him Airy to his face. The name had—at least to her—become synonymous with intimacy.

And there was also the fact he hadn't liked her to use it.

"If I held any rancor," he said, "be assured I wouldn't be sitting here."

She smiled at him, pleased that he'd not objected to her use of the nickname.

He shrugged. "My former nurse would tell you one admonishment is all I ever needed."

She started giggling.

"May I ask what you find so amusing?"

"I was picturing you as a little boy being punished. I daresay it took your brother more than once to learn proper behavior."

"I was always nurse's pet."

"Because you were no doubt a model child."

"I doubt that. I wasn't everyone's favorite. An heir generally commands more respect than a second son. This even applies to one's mother."

"I daresay that's life's compensation. He gets the title, you get the brains—not to say your brother has no brains."

He nodded knowingly. "You sound exactly like Elvin. We were recently discussing something similar. I accused him of stealing the Graces in the womb, and he acknowledged that I had hoarded the intelligence."

They both laughed.

"The weather has turned very cold."

She nodded. "It must be the coldest day of the season."

"We are on winter's doorstep."

As they rode on in a comfortable silence, the winds howling beyond the thin coach walls, she felt oddly secure. And incredibly content.

This was one of those days she never wanted to come to an end.

* * *

At nightfall, they stopped at The Crow's Nest Inn which was within ten miles of Stipley Hall. "We can call on Mr. Whitebread the first thing tomorrow morning," Melvin said as he helped her from the coach. "I'll send a messenger with a letter to announce our arrival."

"Will you say you just happened to be in the area and thought to call on him?"

"I don't like to start off with a lie." He would be glad to be inside. It was bloody cold and had begun to rain. By morning, the ground would be covered with frost.

To enter the inn's worn timber door, Melvin had to duck down because he was too tall. They went directly upstairs and down a long, L-shaped corridor until they came to her chambers where a fire was already blazing in the brick hearth of her large parlor. He took her valise into the adjacent bedchamber and set it down.

"I forgot to ask," she said from the doorway. "Are we Mr. and Miss Smith again?"

"Yes, we are." His strode back into the parlor, his gaze flicking to a table near the fire. "Our tea should be here any minute. Excuse me while I sit here and scribble a letter to Mr. Whitebread." He sat at the table and began to write.

"I shall be glad of a hot cup of tea. It's beastly cold." She went to stand in front of the fire. "The fire must have just been built."

He nodded. "I know. The room's still cold."

She peered solemnly at him. "Thank you for respecting my irrational fears and stopping when darkness fell."

He looked up from his writing, his eyes locking with hers, a grin pinching the lean planes of his cheek. "I have no desire to ignite Madam's fury."

"I just may throw something at you. Something that's not too hard." Her gaze went first to the knot above his brow then to the cut on his scalp which was partially covered with his hair. "How's your other wound? When I returned home last night I started thinking about you becoming concussed, and I grew worried about you."

She was as bad as Elvin. But her concern was rather endearing. "I told you yesterday I was fine." He felt her gaze on him as he continued to draft the note.

"Does your head not hurt? I beg that you be honest with me."

"I've a bit of a headache. Daresay it could have been worse."

There was a knock at the door, and a serving maid with a tea tray came into the parlor. After she set, up Melvin produced his quickly written letter, along with a crown. "I would be ever so grateful if you could see that this is delivered to Stipley Hall tonight."

Her youthful face lit up. "I'll send me brother straight away. Thank you ever so much."

Mrs. Bexley poured the tea, and he came and sat across the table from her.

She took a dainty sip. "Hot tea is just the thing on a bitterly cold evening like this."

He was glad they had stopped here. The coach had gotten very cold. "Chamber's warming, too."

She nodded. "When you wrote to Mr. Whitebread initially, did you mention my name?"

"Of course not! If he's such a committed book collector, he'd be bound to associate the name Bexley with *Canterbury Tales*."

"And if he were behind the theft. . . "

"He'd hide any sign of the Chaucer from us."

"So how will you introduce me tomorrow?"

"Who says I'm taking you? There's no reason you can't await me here."

She pouted. Even her pout displayed her dimples. "Oh, Airy, you know I must go with you."

Good lord! That was the second time today she'd called him Airy. And she'd had nary a drop of wine. "Now see here, Mrs. Bexley, you can't be calling me by that ridiculous name."

That lower lip of hers worked once more into a provocative pout. "It's just the two of us. I promise not to use it around others."

"Give me your word?"

Her lashes lowered. "Yes, of course."

"Why do you think you have to go with me tomorrow? Do you not trust me?"

"I've told you before, I trust you more than I've ever trusted any man."

Why did her words make him feel as if he'd just grown by two feet? Once more he vowed to do everything in his power to restore the Chaucer to her. "I pray I'm worthy of your confidence."

"To answer your question, I must go tomorrow. I promise not to go around snooping into closed cupboards or anything like that. It's not that I don't have supreme confidence in you. But there are some things at which a woman's. . . perception is needed."

"What do you mean by that?"

"I believe I would be able to tell if the man is dishonest with you."

"I mean no disrespect, but that's impossible."

"It is not impossible. Allow me to rephrase. There is a high *probability* that I will be able to determine if he's lying."

"It's back to women's intuition, is it?"

"Perhaps. You just don't understand it because it's not logical."

Before he could respond, their dinner was delivered by the same young serving girl who couldn't be a day older than Lizzy. He wondered if she was the daughter of the inn's proprietor—or perhaps his granddaughter. Since the huge tray was as much as she could manage, he leapt up and helped her set the food upon the table.

And a lot of food it was for just the two of them. There were three good-sized veal cutlets, a macaroni pie, a loaf of bread with good country butter, pig's feet jelly and an assortment of sweets.

When they finished setting the table, the girl reached into a huge pocket on her apron and produced a bottle of wine which she proceeded to decork.

When it was just him and Mrs. Bexley again, she met his gaze with a sheepish grin. "Will you allow me to imbibe wine?"

His eyes flashed with mirth. "I am not your master."

"I shall promise not to drape myself over your person." She began to pour wine for both of them.

His heart thumped erratically when she mentioned *drape myself over your person.*

"Shall we toast?" she asked, holding up her glass.

He nodded, and their glasses clinked. "To our success," she said.

After the toast, their gazes locked. "Go on, Mrs. Bexley, I know you wish to eat your apple tart first."

She let out a little giggle. "I'm not accustomed

to anyone taking notice of my eating patterns."

He shrugged.

For the next ten minutes or more they ate in relative silence. They had each drunk a small glass of wine when he refilled their glasses.

She was buttering a slender slice of bread as he stabbed the last cutlet, put it on his plate, and began to eat it.

"You haven't told me if I'm to be permitted to accompany you to Mr. Whitebread's tomorrow."

"Since I am somewhat in your employ, I shall have to yield to your wishes."

"And how will I be introduced?"

He'd lied already to Lord Seacrest and had no desire to continue such deceptions with Mr. Whitebread. He found himself wondering if Lord Seacrest had somehow found out that he and Mrs. Bexley were attempting to find the stolen Chaucer. Was he the one who ordered the attack on Melvin?

Even though Melvin had taken an instant dislike to Lord Seacrest, he'd felt relatively certain the man was not in possession of the Chaucer. Could he have been wrong?

"Are you certain you've never before met Mr. Whitebread? Is there any possibility he could recognize you either as Mrs. Bexley or Miss Hamilton?"

Her mouth dropped open. "I am flattered that you recall my maiden name."

"Actually, it was Elvin who reminded me of it."

"Then I'm impressed that you remembered it if you'd heard it just once."

He ate the last bite of meat. "A good memory can also be a curse."

Having finished eating several minutes earlier,

she eyed him as he cleaned his plate. "So. . .?"

"I suppose the easiest way to explain your presence in the morning is to lie."

"Will I be your wife again?"

The sound of *your wife* rolling off her tongue struck an oddly satisfying note. Not that he had any desire to wed. It was just. . . He was powerless to understand these peculiar feelings. Their eyes met, and he shook his head. "I cannot have a wife since I plan to give serious consideration to accepting a position at Stipley Hall."

Her face fell.

"You shall have to be my sister."

When he finished eating, they moved to the sofa. It was not even seven yet. Far too early for bed. He proposed a game of two-handed whist, and she was agreeable.

He cleared his throat. "It goes against my nature to approach something without a plan, but I think tomorrow we're basically just trying to determine if he has the Chaucer."

She nodded. "As you said the last time, if he's so passionate a collector, he would quite naturally want to display the library's most valuable acquisition."

He cleared his throat again. "You must start making plans. What will you do if he doesn't have the Chaucer? It pains me to say it, but I do believe he's our last hope."

"I think so too," she said, her quivering voice sounding youthful.

He had best try to get her mind off her desperate situation. At least for now. He refilled their wine glasses and began to deal the cards,

"Does Sir Elvin know where we are?"

Guilt surged through him. "Yes, I left a note." He'd intrinsically known that had he told his brother about the prospective journey, Elvin would not have approved so soon after Melvin had sustained his injury.

If his brother had an inkling about the threats, he would do everything in his power to keep Melvin in Bath.

During their play the next couple of hours, his chief concern was to see that her thoughts were happy ones. They laughed a lot. And he kept refilling their wine glasses.

"Could we have more?" she asked, her voice childlike.

He thought of the last time when she had drunk too much wine and had felt badly the next day. Most of all, he remembered the pleasure he'd felt when she'd snuggled against him. He found himself wishing she would do that again.

Good lord! What was he thinking? Melvin never entertained such thoughts about women. Perhaps he had drunk too much. He vowed that at the end of this hand, he would go to his own bedchamber.

He actually let her win the last hand because he liked to see a smile upon her face. Then he rose. "I do believe I'm getting tired."

She rose too and walked with him to the door. When he reached the door he turned to her. Her sweet lavender scent wafted to him. There was delicacy about the petite blond, who was also remarkably pretty. A feeling like nothing he'd ever experienced flooded him with the force of a tidal wave. He wanted to kiss her. Her pretty little face was turned up to his. She was not even a foot away from him.

As if he were being controlled by an external

force, he lowered his head and gently settled his lips over hers. To his surprise, she did not push him away. Her arms came fully around him, prolonging the kiss.

She was once again that sweet-smelling angel he had awakened to the previous day, and he felt as if he were being swept up into the heavens with her.

Then he realized what he was doing. He was in the lady's bedchamber! And he was taking advantage of her sweetness. He pulled away. "Forgive me." Then he swung open her door and stormed to his own bedchamber.

$\mathcal{C}$hapter 18

She solemnly watched the door close. Nothing had ever been more difficult than suppressing her need to race after him and beg to lose herself in his embrace. Her back to the door, she slid all the way down until her bottom settled on the wooden floor, fissures of delight continuing to explode inside her.

She had no idea how long she sat on the smooth wooden planks, teary and smiling and happier than she had ever been. She tried to recall what might have precipitated Airy's nearly debilitating kiss.

When he'd begun to take his leave of her, she had felt a strong compulsion to walk with him to the door. And when he'd turned to her, she may have moved close to him (because of her reluctance to have him go). If he had taken her nearness as an invitation to kiss, so be it. Perhaps unconsciously it was, though the idea of kissing him had not crossed her mind.

And now it was all she could think of.

Surely he would not have kissed her had there not been an attraction. Whether he knew it or not. She was eternally gratified that he must share some of the deep affection she held for him. That affection had grown by small increments. First, he had effortlessly commanded her respect with his intelligence, manliness, and humility. His character conveyed a nobility that was lacking in the other men of her acquaintance.

During the days that had followed—days in which they'd shared nearly every minute—she'd grown so comfortable with him that when a separation was necessary, she felt as if she were missing a vital appendage.

Then there was the laughter—more than she'd ever shared with another person. It was as if they were bound together by some mystical force.

She could not discount the physical attraction, either. The very sight of his tall, lean broad-shouldered body sent her pulses racing. She could never tire of his dark, handsome features, the masculine bone structure, the distinctive indentation in his square chin.

Of all the men in the world Airy was the only one for her.

Eventually her heartbeat returned to something close to normal and she managed to dress for bed and climb atop the big four poster. It would be another sleepless night. Thoughts of Airy wound through her brain like endlessly skeining varied colors of yarn.

Intrinsically, she knew tonight's was most likely his first kiss. (Though it most certainly was *not* the kiss of a clumsy novice.) Her knowledge of him told her he would be exceedingly confused over this action of his. Being methodical, pragmatic, and logical, he would have to contemplate The Kiss for a considerable period of time before he could either renew such an action or—something he might never do—discuss it.

So she would wait for him to do one of those things.

At present he was likely admonishing himself.

Being the gentleman that he was, he would believe his conduct most unbecoming. If only she could assure him such conduct was as welcome and natural as sunshine.

But she must wait.

Her thoughts flitted ahead to the next morning and how she should greet him. Above all, she must not be stiff for he would think her repulsed by his wondrous kiss. She most decidedly could not very well use any of the wide range of endearments he brought to mind. *My love. My darling. Sweetheart.* She sighed.

She must convey to him through her conduct that she was not displeased with him. A pity she could not convey more. The fact was that even if both of them admitted to falling in love, neither of them was in a position to act upon it since neither of them had the means to set up a home together.

Which made it more imperative than ever that they find the Chaucer.

What must Mrs. Bexley think of him? Not even someone as ill mannered as Long*mouth* would have forced a kiss upon a lady. What had gotten into him? Melvin Steffington never acted rashly. Melvin Steffington never acted less than a gentleman. And Melvin Steffington had never before kissed a lady—nor had he ever before desired to kiss a lady.

He must blame it on the wine.

He peeled off his clothing, doused the light, and climbed upon his bed, but he was far too exhilarated to sleep. Would Mrs. Bexley think him a depraved sex lunatic? It *was* just a kiss, he consoled himself. His brother frequently stole kisses from ladies of good birth. And Elvin most certainly was *not* a sex lunatic. (Though he most heartily endorsed the conjugal union.)

It was as if the brothers' traits had somehow gotten mixed up. Melvin found himself more and more acting like his twin. As he lay there in the darkness, the only light coming from the fire in his warm chamber, his thoughts went to that other night when he had entertained such uncharacteristic thoughts.

That last night at Granfield Manor—the night she had been so out of charity with him she had thrown a cushion at him—he had lain on the floor pallet picturing Mrs. Bexley undressing. He'd been shocked over and ashamed of his errant thoughts.

Now he was shocked and ashamed of his errant actions.

Would she throw something at him in the morning? Would she be so angry she'd call off their quest and sever all ties to him? He couldn't allow that to happen. A compulsion to restore the Chaucer to her would guide all of his actions for the next four days—when Coutts planned to take ownership of her home.

His concern for her extended beyond his desire to find the Chaucer. He feared for her life. Those harsh words uttered by his attacker in Bath made him sick for her. Melvin knew that whoever sought the stolen manuscript was marked for death.

He had to protect her these next four days.

After that—if they were not successful—she would be under the protection of her brother in the North Country.

Why did the notion of her absence make him

so low? He shouldn't like not to ever see her
again. He'd meant it when he'd told her he was
closer to her than he'd ever been to a woman. He
would even go so far as to acknowledge that he
cared for her as a friend. Like Blanks. Or
Appleton. Of course, it was entirely different. He
certainly didn't want to kiss Blanks or Appleton.

Because of his deep concern for her, he decided
to do everything in his power to keep her from
turning him out. At least until the Coutts deadline
had passed. He would start in the morning by
acting as if the kiss had never occurred.

A pity his body could not act as if nothing had
happened. While he lay there thinking of her, he
was powerless not to remember the kiss and how
much he had enjoyed it. When her arms had
come around him, he'd actually groaned with a
needy pleasure. Feeling her in his arms was every
bit as thrilling as the kiss. The very memory
caused his breath to grow short.

Now Melvin better understood his twin's strong
attraction to females.

Lying in the dark, listening to the brutal winds
outside his windows, he could not purge from his
mind thoughts of The Kiss. He had never expected
kissing to be so pleasurable. And even though he
knew it was not the gentlemanly thing to do, he
thought he would like to kiss her again.

Once they were seated in the coach the
following morning and heading for Stipley Hall,
she congratulated herself on how smoothly
breakfast had gone. She had knocked upon his
door and invited him to her parlor for the day's
first meal. By so doing, their first contact (since
The Kiss) had not been face to face, eye to eye.

She'd felt that would have been uncomfortable for him. Her ploy also served to allow him to know she was neither angry with him nor desirous of terminating their relationship because of The Kiss.

Throughout breakfast they had conversed in a normal fashion—mostly upon the weather. *Beastly cold. Wicked winds. Thank goodness no rain.*

Now she was wrapped in the rug, wearing her heavy merino cloak, warmest gloves, furry muff, and she was still chilled. But she did not have a care. For sitting there with Airy was where she wanted to be more than anywhere. Especially since The Kiss.

Just peering at his brooding good looks gave her a heady sense of possession. He had desired to kiss her. That knowledge allowed her to believe she possessed at least a piece of his heart.

Whether he knew it or not.

Her happiness was tinged with melancholy. She knew neither he nor she could ever act upon a mutual attraction until they found the Chaucer. And if they did not. . . all her hopes and dreams would be destroyed.

"I have decided what I shall do when Mr. Whitebread wishes to speak to you about the position," she said.

He raised a brow in query.

"I shall ask for his housekeeper to give me a tour of Stipley Hall."

"I should think that would be most agreeable to you."

"You know me too well, Airy."

So intimate a comment obviously made him uncomfortable. His attention turned to the view from his coach window.

In three-quarters of an hour, they reached Stipley. Airy had been right. She found grand country homes very agreeable and never tired of touring them. As their coach came down the long drive to Stipley, she observed it from her window.

They drove through the fine deer park in front of Stipley. Evenly spaced rows of beech trees lined the drive, and off in the distance, rolling hills outlined against the gray horizon. Stipley must encompass many hundreds of acres.

"I must say, though Mr. Whitebread is no aristocrat, this house looks as if it was built for a grand old titled family," she said.

"I believe you're right. I think it was Appleton's secretary who told me one of the early, extremely wealthy Whitebreads purchased the house from the estate of Lord Something or Other."

She smiled. "Come, Mr. Steffington. I am sure you will be able to retrieve from that brain of yours the name of the peers who formerly owned the house." His memory was, after all, quite remarkable.

A lopsided grin on his face, he regarded her. "Very well. I believe it was built by the Lords of Penwick, the last of whom died without issue and whose title went extinct."

"To the satisfaction of the Whitebreads, I should say."

Though it dated to the same era as Burghley House, Stipley wasn't as large or as grand as that great Elizabethan palace. Stipley was constructed of gray stone, and had a bit of the look of a fortress about it, owing to its corner towers. She suspected it featured a central open courtyard which so many houses of the era had.

He peered at the house as they drew close to its entry. "It's very fine."

She hated to think that this might become Airy's new home.

The coach stopped, and a moment later, their coachman was assisting them from the carriage. The poor fellow's face was bright red from the stinging winds.

A footman in purple livery swung open the huge, iron-hinged timber door.

"Please announce Dr. Steffington and his sister have arrived," Airy said to the tall, youthful servant.

He nodded. "If ye will just 'ave a seat on the bench, I'll tell me master." He began climbing the stairs, his long legs taking two steps at a time.

She was ever so glad he had not offered to take her cloak, for the massive entry hall was only slightly warmer than it was outside on this blustery day.

Her first impression was that she was sitting in an old country church. It must be the ecclesiastical-looking, stained-glass windows pointing to gothic arches that evoked a religious sanctuary. The scenes depicted on them— armored men on horseback—were in no way religious.

Her gaze elevated to the wide staircase. Its wood—oak, she thought—had turned nearly black from age. The lower stairs terminated at stone floors, many of the squares smoothly indented from centuries of footsteps.

Furnishings in the entry hall were minimal: the long, armed wooden bench upon which they sat and a chunky wooden sideboard. She suspected the sideboard had reposed on that same spot since the house was built.

As the footman descended the stairs, she thought the livery a bit incongruous with a home that had so many medieval flourishes. It mimicked the fashions of the last quarter of the past century—including the era's powdered wigs.

"My master will be down in a few moments," he told them as he crossed the corridor where they sat.

Within ten minutes, Mr. Whitebread slowly descended the wide staircase, his gnarly hand carefully gripping the banister with each step. Though his identity had not been confirmed, she would wager her last guinea he was the owner of this ancient house. One of the reasons for her certainty was the high quality of his clothing. Even if the cut of his coat was a bit outdated, it had obviously been cut by the finest tailors.

One glance at him and she thought perhaps his name should be White Head, for his hair was snow white. She judged Mr. Whitebread to be nearing eighty. For some illogical reason, she had thought he would have been a younger man. Like Lord Seacrest.

"Dr. Steffington?" he said when he reached the foot of the stairs and looked at Airy.

Already standing, Airy shook the man's hand. "Yes, and this is my sister, Miss Steffington."

Catherine stepped forward and dipped into a curtsey. "I do hope you don't mind that I insisted upon tagging along with my brother. Once Melvin told me yours was one of the finest libraries in the kingdom, I just had to see it, but I promise to get out of your way when you and my brother get down to your important discussions."

"I don't mind at all," Mr. Whitebread said. "It's

always a pleasure for me to show my library to others."

"Do you think I could impose upon your housekeeper later to give me a tour of Stipley?" she asked.

"I am sure she will be delighted to. Our public days are on Thursdays, so your tour today will be just you and Mrs. Denson." He turned back to Airy. "Now if you two will just come down the corridor I shall lead the way to the library."

"How old is your home?" she asked, slowing so as to not get ahead of him. His wobbly gait was typical of one who was well along in years.

"This section's the oldest and dates to the sixteenth century. The home was built by the Farrington family—the Lords of Penwick. It was my family's good fortune that the title went extinct for lack of heirs." The old man sadly shook his head, and he spoke somberly. "Now, alas, the Whitebreads shall die out, too."

She felt awfully sorry for him. Should she comment on this? Had he never married? She wondered what would become of this fine old home when he died.

"I hope you don't think it unpardonable," he said, "that I am not an architectural purist. I hired Robert Adam to design a grand, classical library which I'm afraid is rather at odds with the architecture of the rest of Stipley."

"I have always found much to admire in Mr. Adam's works," Airy said.

She had not known that Airy's interests extended to architecture. But of course he was enamored of all things classical. And Adam's neoclassical works would be sure to please him.

At the end of the west wing they came to a set

of double doors. He had been right. These elegant gilt and white doors with gold knobs were vastly out of place in this Elizabethan home that nodded to England's past rather than to the Greeks.

Once he swung open one of the gilded doors, she forgot about the incongruity. She was so dazzled by the elegance of the massive library, it was impossible for her to suppress her amazement. "Oh, it is so magnificent."

Eyes she had thought tired a few moments earlier now twinkled like those of a man half his age. "I am happy, Miss Steffington, over your reaction."

She stood frozen in the doorway, her gaze sweeping from an elegant marble chimneypiece at one end of the elongated chamber to its twin on the opposite wall some fifty feet away. Tall white and gilt bookcases with fan-shaped crowns and gilt fluting were stuffed with high quality leather volumes and set into walls painted in a vibrant light blue.

The attraction in this room was obviously books, more books than she had ever before seen in one chamber.

She looked up at their host. "How many volumes have you?"

"In all, there are some thirty thousand titles, but only about forty percent are in this chamber."

Now it was Airy's turn to make appreciative noises. "I can certainly see why you need someone to oversee such a collection."

She wished he wouldn't bring up that dreaded topic. "Pray, Mr. Whitebread," she said, "what is your most prized acquisition?"

He began walking toward a glass case. "I am proud to say I have Shakespeare's first five plays in their first printings."

Her heartbeat thumped when she saw the special case. Then it thudded when she realized the glass-fronted case did *not* contain the Chaucer.

Airy's eyes widened. "How long did it take you to collect those?"

From Airy's state of marvel, she deduced that these only rarely—and individually—came upon the market.

Mr. Whitebread regarded Airy, affection in his countenance. "I started searching them out when Mr. Adam began to design the library back in 1777. It was six years before I was able to acquire the first. Numbers two through five I'd managed to get one at a time over a three-year period, but I had the devil of a time finding that first one. And I don't need to tell you, Mr. Steffington, I had to pay a king's ransom for the bloody thing."

Their host's gaze flicked to Catherine. "I beg your forgiveness for my unpardonable word choice."

She shook off his apology.

"My library was sadly neglected during the years I helped care for my late wife, whose health was rather delicate in her later years."

Catherine was touched that caring for his wife had taken precedence over his well-known collection.

He spent the next forty minutes happily showing them his most valuable works. His voice became more strident, his step quicker with the excitement of having guests to view his library. She suspected that visitors enlivened his lonely life.

She found out rather a lot about the childless

widower—including the fact he could neither be behind a theft nor consider the purchase of stolen goods. He came across as being a remarkably honest and likeable man.

When she could tell he wished to speak to Airy about the proposed duties of Stipley's librarian (his late librarian had died two months previously), she asked if she could trouble the housekeeper for a tour of Stipley.

Soon she was effecting great interest in everything the elderly housekeeper was telling her about the massive Elizabethan home, while each minute her thoughts were on Airy. She feared he was agreeing to come live at Stipley.

Under normal conditions she would have had no difficulty expressing her interest in a fine old home like Stipley. But now she was too low. Learning that Mr. Whitebread did not possess the Chaucer made her feel as if she were standing upon a collapsing bridge.

Her melancholy thoughts went to the interview that was presently taking place between Mr. Whitebread and Airy. Now that Airy knew finding the manuscript was hopeless, he was likely making arrangements to come into Mr. Whitebread's employ in the near future.

Her future looked as bleak as the day's skies.

By the time her tour of Stipley Hall was completed, Airy was already waiting for her, seated back on the bench near the front door and ready to return to Bath.

They entered their carriage beneath darkened skies that perfectly matched her gloom. She and Airy were both silent as the coach started back.

"As long as it doesn't rain," he said after the coach started rattling away, "we should be able to make Bath by around seven tonight. Will that be agreeable to you?"

"Yes, of course." She wasn't such a complete ninny that she feared highwaymen at five o'clock.

Sometime later she penetrated the silence. "You agree with me that Mr. Whitebread is not in possession of the Chaucer?"

He nodded morosely. "I'm confident that he does not have it."

They were more than an hour into their somber journey before he voiced what was on both their minds. "It pains me to admit defeat."

She peered into his solemn eyes and nodded. "You did all you could. I am in your debt."

"I failed."

She shook her head. "No, you did not. It's through no fault of yours that I have been robbed. I owe my destitution to my own carelessness."

"It's not your fault a thief made the decision to steal your manuscript. One way or another, he would have succeeded."

"I suppose leaving my door unlocked was better than having armed men bursting into my house while I was in residence."

He attempted to offer consolation. "There you have it."

A small part of her had held out hope that he would have a trump card to play now that all other avenues had come to dead ends. But it was not to be. He was a scholar, not a conjuror.

She drew her breath. No matter how painful it was to acknowledge, she must be happy over his prospective employment. "When does Mr. Whitebread want you to start?"

He favored her with a devilish grin. "What makes you so certain I suited him?

"I never had a single doubt. Who wouldn't want a competent man like you?"

"I do not deserve your praise. I was hardly competent with your problem." His voice lowered as he mumbled. "I told him I couldn't start until sometime after my present commission ended on the 22nd."

Her eyes misted. "I appreciate your loyalty, but I think we both know it's hopeless."

"I won't give up until the eleventh hour. I shall write to Dr. Mather straight away and ask him to be on the alert."

"Mr. Christie, I know, would alert me if he learns of the Chaucer coming on the market."

He frowned. "A pity we have so little time."

"I keep feeling we're overlooking something," he said a moment later. "How can it be the most valuable manuscript in the English language is stolen, and none of the prominent collectors have learned of its availability?"

She shrugged. "I will own, it is most perplexing. It's almost as if the thief never intended to put it on the market."

"Which doesn't make sense. Is not a collector's greatest joy in exhibition?"

"Yes, of course. Pride does not exist in a vacuum."

They both went silent again, the mood as gloomy as a wake.

As darkness began to fall, she said, "I beg that you talk to me to keep me from thinking scary thoughts."

He gave a hardy, masculine chuckle. "What should you like to discuss?"

"Do you think you shall be happy at Stipley Hall?"

He chuckled. "You are given to using words that would never cross my mind."

"What kind of words?"

"Words like happy and love. I don't think in those terms. I prefer things that can be empirically proven."

"Then I feel very sorry for you. Life is empty without the promise of love and happiness."

A moment later, his voice went somber. "I'm sorry you may have to go live with your brother."

That wasn't nearly as agonizing at the prospect of future without him.

$\mathcal{C}$hapter 19

Her first full day back in Bath was one of the gloomiest in her life. No letter from Mr. Christie greeted her. Tomorrow was the 22nd. If she had not satisfied Coutts that she could pay the monies owed by midnight, she would lose her home.

She was powerless to keep her life from edging into a lonely oblivion.

It was too late to even expect answers from either Mr. Christie or Dr. Mather, if she and Airy dispatched letters today. Somehow, though, she believed neither of those men had knowledge of who might have taken her Chaucer or where it was now located. She kept remembering Airy's statement the previous afternoon. It made no sense that the most valuable book in the English language had been stolen, and no one had heard about it, and no one had tried to sell it, no one was prominently displaying it.

She had come to believe that a crazed collector was behind the theft, a man so obsessed that he wanted it, even knowing that he could never claim ownership. Which did not make sense.

Everything she and Airy knew about a collector's need to display his prized acquisitions was being discounted.

As she dressed for the day, a deep melancholy stole over her. There was nothing more either she or Airy could do now.

Simpson knocked upon her door. "Madam, you have several callers who have arrived at once."

She stopped tying her satin sash. "Pray, Simpson, what are their names?"

"Sir Elvin Steffington came first with two young ladies and his twin, and just as the baronet extended his card, Mr. Longford arrived with the largest bouquet of flowers I've ever seen."

Upon learning that Mr. Longford was calling, she could not suppress a groan. She almost wanted to collapse into tears. Had Mr. Longford not understood that her rejection of him was irrevocable?

Though she would have preferred to spend her day trying to determine if there was something she had overlooked regarding the Chaucer, she knew her situation was hopeless. Being around others—except for Mr. Longford—should help improve her blue devils. She was happy the Steffingtons had brought the youngest member of the family for Catherine had taken an instant liking to Miss Lizzy Steffington the day Airy was attacked. Her heartbeat drummed. Was it because that lovely young lady bore a resemblance to the man Catherine loved?

She couldn't bear to think that after tomorrow, she would never see him again. Grief surged through her. Perhaps long after she was at her brother's the day would come when memories of Airy's lanky body and pensive face would no longer send her pulses rocketing. But the way she felt at present, she could not imagine that day ever coming.

A peek into her looking glass assured her she was dressed appropriately for a morning call in her dainty sprigged muslin, a pink sash tied beneath her bosom.

Melvin was the only silent person in Mrs. Bexley's drawing room. That was a common occurrence for him, especially when in mixed company, but today there was even more of a reason for his silence. That damned Long*mouth* was there. Melvin glared at the long-winded, self-important, braggart. The damned man was still attempting to press his attentions on the poor widow who had so desperately tried to douse Longford's unfounded hopes.

The windbag had presented Mrs. Bexley with a bouquet that was demmed near as tall as she was. Most crass of him. Such a "gift" did not demonstrate good taste, though Elvin had assured him Long*mouth*, as obnoxious as he was, had impeccable taste in clothing, and Melvin had been able to ascertain for himself the man's eye for fine horseflesh. "I daresay one with pockets that deep can purchase good taste," Elvin had said. That had to explain it.

To put Melvin in an even grumpier disposition, his twin was making a cake of himself over Mrs. Bexley. "You must, my dear Mrs. Bexley, allow me to take you driving in Sydney Gardens," Elvin said. (This came not long after he plopped himself down on the sofa right next to her.)

Long*mouth's* eyes had been reduced to slits as he watched Elvin. "Now, pray, which twin are you?"

He was forever asking that question of the twins. When the one being questioned was Melvin, Long*mouth* continued to glare. But if Sir Elvin responded, a smile transformed the old toad-eater's face.

"I am Sir Elvin."

True to his stripes, Long*mouth* offered Elvin a broad smile. "I remember fondly our days at Eton. You were quite the cricket player."

"Actually my brother was the better player." Elvin nodded in Melvin's direction, but Long*mouth* obviously did not deem a mere Mister worthy of a glance.

Mrs. Bexley smiled at Elvin. "Lord Sedgewick told me everyone wanted *both* Steffington twins on their teams. He said you were very fine players."

"Sometimes our brothers will allow us to play with them," Lizzy interjected. "When we're in the country."

"And when they are exceedingly bored," Annie added with a little laugh.

"Sir Elvin," Mrs. Bexley said, "you must introduce Mr. Longford to your youngest sister."

Elvin glanced at Long*mouth*. "She's certainly not old enough to be out yet, but she and Mrs. Bexley have taken a liking to one another, so I told her she could come with us today. Mr. Longford, may I present to you my youngest sister, Miss Elizabeth Steffington."

"There is a striking family resemblance among all of you." Toadie got to his feet and crossed the room to bow in front of Lizzy. "I am pleased to make your acquaintance, Miss Steffington."

Melvin was proud of how gracefully Lizzy inclined her head and wasn't excessively talkative—which she was at home. She was acting like the perfect lady.

Long*mouth* continued to stand. "Actually, Mrs. Bexley, I can only stay here for a moment. I had to assure myself on your health. I understand you were sick the past two days, but you look very fine today."

"Thank you." From the expression on her face, Melvin could tell she wished that particular caller to perdition.

Long*mouth's* gaze swept to Elvin. "I shall have to compete with you, Sir Elvin, to win Mrs. Bexley's companionship for a ride to the Sydney Gardens."

Curiously, she had not answered in the affirmative to either man. Melvin knew where her thoughts were today. Tomorrow was the 22nd. It was a wonder she allowed any of them in her home. She must be devastated.

If only there were something he could do.

"I must hurry home to meet with my solicitor this afternoon," Long*mouth* said. "Please, my dear Mrs. Bexley, tell me you are up to coming to the Assembly Rooms tonight."

"I don't know how I shall feel tonight." She looked incredibly tired—though not unbecoming. In fact, Melvin thought the little roses on her frock matched her mouth. He supposed she looked awfully pretty. If he knew about such things. Which he really didn't.

Elvin settled his hand over hers. "You mustn't overdo. You have so delicate a constitution."

For a fraction of a second, Melvin considered crashing his fist into his brother's face. What did Elvin know of Mrs. Bexley's constitution, Melvin wanted to know! Melvin was the one who understood her better than anyone in this chamber. He wouldn't be surprised if he didn't understand her better even than her *dear Mr. Bexley*.

Furthermore, Elvin knew just as well as Melvin

that she had not been ill. He was the only other person who knew exactly what she'd been doing the previous two days. It was obvious he was up to his old rakish ways, trying to seduce a lady. And Melvin would not stand for it!

Added to Melvin's uncharitable thoughts toward his brother, he wondered what right Elvin had to put his hand on Mrs. Bexley's? That was entirely too intimate.

As Long*mouth* took his leave, Melvin managed to mumble some kind of a farewell. His gaze kept darting to his brother's hand, which continued to rest atop Mrs. Bexley's.

Melvin was out of charity with his brother. And he was even more out of charity with Long*mouth*. The longer he sat there, the more inflamed he became.

Suddenly, he stood. "I have just recalled a prior appointment. I shall walk back to Green Park Road."

Worry flashed across Elvin's face. "Will you be all right? I can send you in the coach."

"It's but a short walk." Melvin eyed Mrs. Bexley. "If I can be of any service to you—any service at all—you must send for me."

Her downcast lashes lifted, her smoky gaze connecting with his. And she nodded solemnly.

Melvin had decided he would go to Long*mouth's* and bluntly tell him his attentions were *not* wanted by Mrs. Bexley. She had enough on her mind without having to be pestered by the most intolerable bore in the kingdom.

Melvin was in so foul a temper, his long legs chewed up great stretches of Bath pavement in a short span of time. If Long*mouth* had gone straight home, and since he was being conveyed in a fine coach with prized horses, he would have gotten home ten to fifteen minutes before Melvin rounded the corner of Longmouth's street. His fine coach was in front of his residence, the coachman sitting on the box and another man climbing up to sit beside him.

The coachman flicked the ribbons, and the carriage started to roll toward Melvin. As it drew nearer, Melvin got a better view of the man sitting next to Long*mouth's* coachman. From a distance, Melvin realized there was something familiar about that man. As they sped past him, he got a clear glimpse of the man who was chattering away to the driver.

It was his attacker.

In a matter of seconds, Melvin understood everything, including the whereabouts of the Chaucer.

He must rush to Mrs. Bexley.

$\mathcal{C}$hapter 20

He must warn Mrs. Bexley! If that cut-throat
had succeeded in disabling a big fellow like
Melvin, he could kill a delicate creature like her.
Melvin sprinted uphill toward the Royal
Crescent—not without attracting attention. One
ruddy potato cart driver—his eyes wide as he
watched Melvin—came to a complete halt and
turned to watch the frantic man racing through
the streets of Bath.

The farther Melvin went, the more winded he
became. He remembered the last time he'd grown
this short of breath. That had been when he
carried Mrs. Bexley up the seemingly never-
ending staircase at Lord Seacrest's. This wasn't
nearly as steep, but the distance was much
greater. No matter how desperately his lungs
begged for rest, he would not allow himself to stop
until he reached her home.

He was still some distance away, not even close
enough to observe the grassy park in front of the
Royal Crescent. When the neoclassical semicircle
of stately residences finally came into view, he
was mildly disappointed that his brother's coach
was no longer in front of Number 17. It was
looking as if Elvin might have to be called upon to
be of significant service to Mrs. Bexley in the next
four and twenty hours.

Once the numerals of Number 17 came into

view, his pace—by necessity—slowed, but he still walked briskly. He mounted the steps and knocked upon her door.

When Simpson opened it, Melvin was too winded to speak coherently. "I need. ." Gasp.

"Allow me to show you to the library, Mr. Steffington. I shall tell Mrs. Bexley you are here."

How in the deuce could Simpson tell which twin he was? Outside of his family, only Mrs. Bexley and Blanks had ever been capable of identifying him.

Simpson started for the stairway, then turned back. "You do not require me to show you to the library, do you?"

Already on his way to the cozy chamber, Melvin offered Simpson a smile and a decisive shake of his head.

He went to sit upon the sofa in front of the library's fire. More than any room in the kingdom, he felt at home within these walls on the sofa covered with green fabric selected by Mrs. Bexley. Now why would he remember a useless piece of information like that? It wasn't as if fabric held any allure for him.

Another perplexing matter was how he could like being here so much even though it had belonged to her *dear Mr. Bexley*—a man for whom Melvin had no affection.

His memories skimmed to those days he and Mrs. Bexley had sat here at the desk facing one another and how content he'd been, how comforting had been their joint silence, how being close to her always wrapped him in a deep contentment.

The library door flew open, and she breezed into the room. "You've found out something about the Chaucer!" A rosy glow that was absent an hour earlier now tinged her cheeks, and her pretty eyes twinkled with what appeared to be happiness.

Why was it impossible for either of them to hide something from the other? "I believe I know who took the Chaucer."

She gasped, her lashes never flickering as she watched him. "Who?" she finally managed.

"I believe it was Longford." This once, he had no desire to use the man's playful moniker. There was nothing funny about what that man had done to Mrs. Bexley.

"You can't possibly be serious. Mr. Longford isn't even interested in books, and I don't think he reads. I don't mean to say he *can't* read. He just doesn't avail himself of the practice."

"Daresay he's too busy going around buying horses," he mumbled.

Her eyes widened. "You think he purchased it because he enjoys owning objects that he perceives have extraordinary value?"

"He did not purchase it."

A puzzled look on her face, she asked. "Then what? Surely you're not accusing him of stealing?"

"Men that wealthy send others to do their evil deeds. I know this first hand."

She dropped onto the sofa beside him, her shocked gaze never leaving his. "What do you know firsthand?"

"You remember when I was beaten a few days ago?"

She nodded solemnly.

"I have reason to believe my attacker was in the employ of Longford."

Her brows arched. "Go on."

"I saw him leave Longford's house this afternoon as I was returning to Green Park Road from you house."

"How can you possibly connect the beating—as dreadful as it was—to the theft of a Chaucer?"

"There's something else, something I didn't tell anyone about my attack."

Her eyes rounded. "What?"

"I was threatened. He told me it would be dangerous for me if I continued to seek the Chaucer."

"Why did you not tell me this?" she demanded, anger in her voice.

"I thought if either you or my brother knew of the threat, you'd do anything in your power to prevent me from continuing to seek the manuscript."

"That's true! Your life is more precious that any manuscript!"

"I appreciate the sentiment."

Their gazed locked. Her eyes were moist, then as if revealing her fragile emotions embarrassed her, she shook her head and attempted to speak in a more strident voice. "I don't understand any of it. Why would Mr. Longford wish to steal from me? He claims to, I believe. . ." She finished on a whisper, "love me."

"Let me ask you this. Had he attempted to court you before you married?"

An even more puzzled look crossed her face. "Yes, he did. How could you know such a thing?"

"I didn't know; I guessed."

She shook her head. "I fail to understand your meaning, Mr. Steffington."

"The only way I can make sense of this is to

theorize."

"And?"

"And it's my belief that Longford has been in love with you all these years. I believe that to ensure you would accept his proposal of marriage once your mourning was over, he wished to see you penniless."

"You're saying he had the Chaucer stolen for one purpose only: to make me destitute enough to wish to marry him?"

"I am."

"That's preposterous! Diabolical!"

"I'll say it's diabolical! Especially when he sent his evil-doer to bash my head against a brick wall."

She winced. "I can't bear it! You could have been killed!" Her eyes narrowed, and she glared at him. "I shall never forgive you for withholding such information from me. Pray, Airy, why did you continue to help me, knowing you could be killed?"

"I told you. I don't like not to complete something I start."

Her hands flew to her face. "The man's evil!"

"Longford?"

"Yes! I'm sure he must have also perceived you as a rival for my affections."

"That's ridiculous."

"The day you were attacked Mr. Longford briefly left my drawing room, and I've just remembered he did so as soon as he ascertained which twin was in the chamber with us that day. I believe he knew you were alone, and he went out to his coachman and instructed his servants to see you harmed and threatened."

"You have just demonstrated remarkable

deductive thinking."

"Thank you." She sat there peering into the fire, shaking her head for several moments. "What will we do now?"

"You, madam, are to do nothing. That's why I came first to you. I have no way of knowing if that vile man might harm you if you continue to seek the Chaucer. You must stay here until I return."

"Return from where?" she asked in a shaky voice.

"I'm going to Longford's, and I'm going to demand he hand over the Chaucer, or I shall report him to the magistrates."

Stiffening, she put hands to hips. "You will do no such thing! You've already been threatened once."

"I'm not afraid of a man who employs others to do his dirty deeds."

"I don't care what you're afraid of!" She huffed. "And I *used* to think you intelligent! Can you not understand that your life is far more important than that manuscript?"

"You are too kind." What a wonderful woman she was to feel so favorably toward him when they'd been strangers just a fortnight ago. Of course, she could not possibly be serious. No one in her right mind would consent to a life of destitution to preserve the life of a reticent scholar. Well, a deeply moral person would. And he didn't mean to disparage Mrs. Bexley. She was undoubtedly a deeply moral person.

He fleetingly thought of their kiss and of her arms closing around him in a most affectionate manner, and his heartbeat skittered. The very memory of that exceedingly pleasant experience emboldened him. "I have no fears for my life."

She abruptly stood, put her hands to her hips, and glared at him. "I shall confront Mr. Longford myself. I'm sure he won't harm me."

Melvin bolted up. "You are not to leave this house until I have secured the Chaucer!" He'd never before spoken so harshly to a member of the delicate sex. It made him feel beastly. At the same time he remembered how angry she's made him that night she had sneaked into Lord Seacrest's library. The woman's head must be made of granite. "Did you not once agree *not* to embark on a trail over which I did not approve? Was that not one of the terms we agreed to when I came back to assist you?"

She directed at him that juvenile pout that reminded him so much of Lizzy. "I may have agreed to such meekness, but that was before I knew your life had been in jeopardy."

The woman was inordinately worried about him. "Surely you don't think I'm afraid of that diminutive toad-eater? Why, I'm more than a foot taller than him."

Her demeanor softened. "Will you do one thing for me?"

The pity of it was, for some inexplicable reason, he would do anything for her. "Of course."

"All I ask is that you promise me you won't go to that odious man's house without your brother. If Sir Elvin is with you, I shan't worry."

"Very well, madam. I shall not go there without my brother."

Their eyes met, and the intensity of her gaze gave him a feeling of incredible well-being. "I know you're an honorable man," she said, her voice barely above a whisper. "You really do give me your word?"

He had no choice but to get his brother to accompany him. "You have my word."

A somber nod was her only reply.

$\mathcal{C}$hapter 21

"Suskins?" Melvin directed himself to their Green Park Road butler. "Where's my brother?"

"I couldn't say, Mr. Steffington. Perhaps Miss Ann or Miss Elizabeth knows. I believe they were last with him."

Disappointed, Melvin directed a nod at the butler, then raced up the stairs to the drawing room. His sisters enjoyed sitting about there reading and sewing and busying themselves at things that young ladies liked to do.

He threw open the drawing room door to behold the quiet domestic sight of his pretty sisters embroidering and chattering away. "Where's Elvin?" he asked.

While both of his sisters met his gaze, neither of them spoke for a moment. Finally, Lizzy cleared her throat as if she were about to pronounce something of great import. "Though Elvin did not confirm it, I believe he's taken Mrs. Pratt for a spin about Sydney Gardens."

Good God, how could Elvin allow his innocent sisters to know about a woman like the infamous Mrs. Pratt?

Eyeing her sister from beneath lowered brows, Annie gasped. "You are not to speak of such ladies!"

Beastly scandalous of his brother to flaunt his relationship with *that* sort of woman so openly. In fact, Melvin was seized by a desire to plow his fist into his brother's nose. How dare he take a woman like Mrs. Pratt to the very same place that he wanted to escort a paragon like Mrs. Bexley! And what if Elvin placed his greedy hand on Mrs. Pratt's so soon after contact with Mrs. Bexley's? It was unthinkable. No two women could be more opposite.

Anger boiled within him. How could Elvin even think of a woman like Mrs. Pratt after being in Mrs. Bexley's company? Shameless, that's what it was.

He had a very good mind not to allow Elvin to accompany him to Longford's.

But he *had* given Mrs. Bexley his word. And Melvin had never gone back on his word in his seven and twenty years.

Mumbling under his breath, he took leave of his sisters, hurried back down the stairs, and went to the mews to get his horse. Even though the walk to Sydney Gardens wasn't all that far, the gardens themselves covered many acres. He should be able to catch up with Elvin much faster if he were on horseback.

Twenty minutes had passed by the time the groom had saddled his horse and Melvin had clopped along Pulteney Bridge which was heavily thronged with window shoppers. When he reached the gardens, he looked for his brother's phaeton, but he saw no sign of it. What if Lizzy only had the impression he was going to the park? What if Elvin were actually. . . well, Melvin was very happy Lizzy hadn't suspected her brother might be conducting so scandalous an assignation.

And it wasn't even night!

A pity Melvin had no inkling where the opera dancer lived.

Appleton! No question could ever be posed about that sort of woman which Appleton could not answer.

Fortunately Appleton was home—availing himself of catching up on his now-yellowed newspapers from the Capital—and handily directed Melvin to Mrs. Pratt's establishment.

"Never known you to fancy a bit 'o crumpet," Appleton said as Melvin was taking his leave.

"I certainly don't." Melvin went off mumbling crossly again.

As he rode to Churchill Street, Melvin was most anxious. He didn't like the idea of disturbing his brother if, indeed, Elvin were. . . ahem, *dallying* with Mrs. Pratt. What would he be able to say to the woman's servant to ensure his brother . . . forgo his crumpet?

Appleton had told him he should be able to distinguish Mrs. Pratt's home from the others on the staid street by its scarlet draperies. His gaze on those very scarlet curtains, Melvin wondered what her neighbors thought about having such a . . . colorful woman residing next to them.

As he knocked upon her door he wondered what manner of man would be employed by that manner of woman. Melvin supposed the chap who answered her door would be very large. A burly man, to be sure. The men who had answered the door at Mrs. Baddele's were always big fellows.

But none were as large as Mrs. Pratt's man. A more sinister-looking fellow Melvin had never seen. His blondish hair was streaked with gray, and one of his front teeth was missing. Added to this, he must stand six-feet, six. A real giant with a deep voice. "Yes?" Then the giant cocked his head and lowered his brows as his glance flicked to the stairs. "How can ye be in two places in once?"

The giant obviously mistook Melvin for the twin who was *dallying* upstairs. "I have reason to believe my twin brother is here."

The giant's eyes shifted. Obviously, his mistress had given orders that she and her visitor were not to be disturbed.

"I've come on an urgent matter and demand that you tell my brother I'm in grave need of his help."

It was as if the giant were a marble statue. Not even his lashes moved a hair. He just stood there glaring at Melvin.

Melvin drew in his breath and came striding into the house as if he were master here, hoping like the devil that the giant didn't knock him down. To his complete surprise, the servant stood aside and allowed Melvin to pass.

Not that Melvin had a clue what he should do now.

He, therefore, stood at the bottom of the wooden stairs and shouted at the top of his lungs. "El-l-l-l-v-i-i-n!" He repeated it several times before he heard the distinct sound of a door slamming. This was followed by a thumping sound. Like a man's footsteps coming from above.

He peered at the top of the stairs where his brother had planted his boots. Elvin looked most untidy as he glared down at his twin. "This better be good."

Catherine was in a daze after Airy left. How

incredible it seemed that Mr. Longford could possibly be the mastermind behind the theft of her Chaucer—all because he fancied himself desperately in love with her. It was the most utterly foolish thing she'd ever heard of. In the past decade she had been alone with him on exactly one occasion: that day two weeks ago when she'd consented to drive with him in Sydney Gardens.

How could he be such an imbecile he'd think poverty would drive her into his arms?

Even though her first inclination had been to doubt Airy, she knew he must be right. (Wasn't he always?) Now that she had learned the man who had beat him—the man who'd tried to keep him from searching further for the Chaucer—was in the employ of Mr. Longford, everything fell into place.

She had an overwhelming urge to spit in Mr. Longford's face. After she scratched out his eyes. That odious, disgusting, pompous, dishonest, conniving, thief!

Added to his unforgivable deeds, the man had ordered that her dear Airy be practically beaten to death! She would never forgive that kind of viciousness.

Her anger extended to Airy. The more she thought of him withholding from her the truth about his attack, the more livid she became. How could the headstrong, authoritarian, uncommonly sweet, dear man have so endangered himself just to find for her some musty old papers that just happened to be extraordinarily valuable? How could he not understand that she would pitch the one-of-a-kind manuscript into the ocean before she would allow him to be harmed because of it?

She quite honestly did not believe his obsession to reclaim her *Canterbury Tales* was to earn the fifteen percent commission. As surely as she would always be able to recognize him over his brother, she knew he was risking his life for her. So she would not lose her home. So she would not have to go live with her brother. So the vibrant life now burning inside her wouldn't be extinguished beneath the gray skies of Yorkshire.

It was impossible to keep her thoughts from the vision of him lying lifeless on that sofa after his beating. For one agonizing moment she had thought him dead.

What if the evil Mr. Longford decided he would as soon kill the Steffington twins than have it known he was the worst sort of thief? Her heartbeat thundered. Dear God, what could she do? The very idea affected her ten times more profoundly than carriage sickness.

Since Airy was the only man she had ever been able to count upon, she had no one to whom she could turn. But perhaps there was someone. . .

Melvin hadn't meant to actually slam Mrs. Pratt's door behind them as he and Elvin hurried from her house. "At least you're not tarnishing the family's good name by leaving your coach in front of such a residence," he said, half scolding the brother who was his senior by fourteen minutes. If people saw their coat of arms on the coach door, it could do irreparable harm to Annie's prospects.

"I will have you know that I am always conscious of comporting myself with an eye to how my behavior reflects upon our family. Especially with two sisters whom I must successfully launch." Elvin stopped, his gaze narrowing as he watched Melvin untether his mount and—reins in hand—continue to walk beside him. "What in the bloody hell, may I ask, is so important that you had to drive me from a fair lady's exceedingly compliant arms?"

"Calling that woman a lady! A mere hour after you left a real lady! How can you acquit yourself? One moment you're making a cake of yourself with a true lady, the next you're off . . . sticking your spoon in the communal batter!"

Glaring at his brother, Elvin halted. "You have no right to admonish my behavior! How dare you stand at the bottom of Mrs. Pratt's stairs hollering for me as if I was some wayward sheep."

"That's not why I came."

"Then why in the blazes *did* you come?"

"Because I know who stole the Chaucer, and Mrs. Bexley wouldn't allow me to claim it alone. She insisted you come with me."

Elvin's entire demeanor changed. Melvin would swear he was prancing about like a peacock! "I daresay the woman has the good sense to recognize my manliness," Elvin boasted.

Melvin was seized with a sudden rage toward his twin, a rage he was powerless to control. His hands fisted as he slung back his right arm and hurled it into Elvin's cheekbone. The force of the blow knocked his brother down.

As he stared down at Elvin sprawled on the pavement, blood trickling from a gash where his forehead struck a hitching post. Melvin was nearly overcome with remorse. "Forgive me. I don't know what got into me." He offered his brother his hand, and a silent Melvin got to his feet.

"I don't either. You haven't tried to hit me since we were twelve."

"I'm beastly sorry."

"So who is the thief?"

"Longford."

"The hell you say! It can't be him. He's rich enough to buy the damned thing for kindling."

"You're partially right. He did not want it for his own personal gratification or elucidation." Melvin silently handed his handkerchief to Elvin, who took it and began to blot the thread of blood sliding down his face.

Elvin cocked his brow. "Then for what?"

"I believe he's fancied himself desperately in love with Mrs. Bexley since the time of her come-out. When old Bexley died, he knew her only thing of value was the Chaucer. . ."

"So he thought if she were destitute, she'd look favorably upon the suit of a wealthy man!"

Melvin shrugged. "I believe that is what the deranged man must have thought."

"Do you have any evidence to corroborate your assumption?"

"I think so." He hated to tell Elvin that he'd withheld the truth from him. That was something he had never done in their seven and twenty years. "You remember about the bloke who beat me?"

Elvin's mouth gaped open. "You don't mean..."

"He's in the employ of Longford. And there's something I omitted to tell you." Melvin cleared his throat. "While the fellow was bashing my head into a brick wall, he told me he would do worse if I continued to seek the Chaucer."

"And you went on to Wiltshire with Mrs. Bexley knowing you could be killed?" Now Elvin was livid.

"But the poor woman. . . I'm all she has."

"And you happen to be the only twin brother I have! I don't fancy some guttersnipe slitting your throat. Even if you do knock me to the pavement for no reason."

"I'm awfully sorry. I know it's unforgivable."

"Perhaps that bashing to your head is to blame."

Melvin shrugged. "But now that I know what my attacker looks like, I won't fall into his trap again. In a fair fight, I know I could beat him."

"Men like that never play fair! He'd just as soon plunge a dagger into your back!" Sheer, naked hatred shone in Elvin's face.

Which is exactly the kind of anger Melvin hoped to channel when confronting Longford in a few moments. "Where is your coach, by the way?"

"I told my driver to wait over at the circus."

Melvin frowned. "The opposite direction from Longford's. Let's just walk to his house."

They strode briskly along the pavement. Melvin could not understand why he was so out of charity with his brother. "Now see here, Elvin, I just won't have you dancing attendance upon Mrs. Bexley—especially when conducting liaisons with women like Mrs. Pratt."

The puzzled look on Elvin's face cleared, then a sly smile spread. "Why do you not just admit it?"

"Admit what?" Melvin asked.

"That you want Mrs. Bexley for yourself."

Melvin gave a hardy harrumph. "That's nonsense."

"It is not. I am equally as certain of one other thing."

Melvin glared at his twin. "What are you so

almighty certain of?"

"You have fallen in love with Catherine Bexley."

Chapter 22

Melvin thought that was the most idiotic thing his brother had ever said. "Nurse must have dropped you on the head when you were a babe."

"You, my dear brother, may surpass me in mathematics and other scholarly pursuits, but I am the scholar when it comes to women."

"I never claimed expertise in that direction."

"I'll say! You don't even know when you've fallen in love."

"That's because I have *not* fallen in love. I think I should know it if I had."

Elvin's step slowed. "Allow me to inquire. . . have you ever kissed Mrs. Bexley?"

At the memory of that remarkable experience, Melvin's pulse stampeded, and his breath became labored. How dare his brother ask him something so personal! "I don't have to answer that."

Elvin began to laugh.

"What is so bloody amusing?"

"You, my dear brother. It's taken you seven and twenty years, but you've finally succumbed to the feminine charms." He held up both hands, palms facing his brother. "I give you my word, now that I know how you feel about the widow, I shall no longer pursue the delectable creature."

Melvin whirled at his twin, glaring. "I don't like you referring to her as if she's something edible."

"Forgive me." He started chuckling again,

shaking his head as if in dismay.

They silently continued in the direction of Longford's house.

Melvin kept thinking of his brother's claims. Of course he wasn't in love with Mrs. Bexley. But why in the blazes could he not rid his mind of her kisses? Why did he keep thinking of how much he'd like to kiss her again, keep remembering the pleasure of kissing her? Why did he long to return to those comforting days when he and she shared her library? Why in the blazes would he rather be with her than with anyone else?

Even if it were possible for him to be in love with Mrs. Bexley—which he couldn't be—he was in no position to act upon it. He had nothing to offer a wife.

He'd best direct his thought elsewhere.

"I say, Mel, should we not be armed when we go to confront Long*mouth*?"

"That runt?"

Elvin shrugged. "I suppose you're right. We could almost squash him with our boots."

"He deserves far worse."

"You're sure you saw his killer driving away?"

"The man may not actually be a killer."

"He might have killed you! Head injuries should never be taken lightly. And don't forget, he did threaten your life. I say the man's a killer."

Melvin may as well humor his twin. "So we'll refer to him as a killer."

"What if he shows up? What if he's armed?"

It then occurred to Melvin that Elvin was sounding more like him than he did. Melvin was the one who never did anything, never went anywhere without a plan. Until today. He was in such a rage of hatred toward Longford he wasn't thinking with his usual clarity. Melvin's pragmatism had vanished along with his self control. He still felt bloody remorseful for slamming his fist into Elvin's face.

For likely the first time in his life, Melvin had no plan. He had not considered that the "killer" could show up during the confrontation—possibly with murderous intent. He had not thought of arming himself. He hadn't even planned what he would say to Longford. Melvin gave his brother a puzzled look. "I don't know what's wrong with me. I hadn't thought of anything except landing a facer on that swine."

Elvin nodded. "Women can do that to you. They can shake the contents of your brain like a game of pick-up-sticks."

Melvin couldn't understand why his brother persisted in accusing him of being in love with Mrs. Bexley. "I wish you'd stop saying that! I am not in love with Mrs. Bexley."

"Keep telling yourself that, old boy."

Melvin supposed that because he enjoyed Mrs. Bexley's companionship it might appear that he had a romantic interest in her.

He would leave the romantic bits to Elvin—as long as he didn't pursue Mrs. Bexley. Melvin could not deny that he was inordinately relieved to learn his twin would no longer try to court Mrs. Bexley.

Just past the next block they would come to Longford's. While Melvin was not remotely frightened of the vile toad, his pulse unaccountably quickened. He had always hated confrontation. Even with Elvin. Arguments upset him.

Part of him, though, rejoiced at the prospect of

flattening Longford's face and recovering the Chaucer. "Surely you don't think we need to arm ourselves?"

Elvin shrugged. "Not unless he sics the killer on us."

Melvin stopped and peered at his twin. "I shouldn't like to jeopardize you. Perhaps we ought to go back to Green Park Road and procure some kind of weapon."

"I'll take my chances with the runt. The sooner we confront him, the more likely we'll finish before the killer returns."

They rounded the corner, and Longford's fine neoclassical house came into view. It was the largest house on the street, covering half the block. All three stories featured identical Palladian windows—ten across for a total of thirty sparkling windows. Melvin took a deep breath and hurried up the steps to knock upon Longford's front door.

Walking toward Green Park Road *from* the Royal Crescent was a great deal easier than walking uphill *toward* the Royal Crescent. It bothered Catherine that she practically had to bypass Mr. Longford's house, which lay between hers and Green Park Road. She hated to think that Airy could be there—and possibly be in danger—and she wasn't in a position yet to be of service to him.

Thankfully, the uncommonly brisk walk was almost all downhill, and she arrived at the Steffington home in just ten minutes.

When she reached their door, she rapped with extreme impatience.

The stiff butler opened it and gave her an innocuous look.

"Pray, I must see the Steffington sisters at once."

He lazily perused her. "And you are?"

"Mrs. Bexley."

Catherine heard a clopping upon the stairs behind him. Just beyond the butler's shoulder, she could see Lizzy racing down the staircase. "Oh, Mrs. Bexley! I thought that was you. Do come in."

The elder Miss Steffington was well behind Lizzy, moving with far more grace.

Catherine stepped into the foyer, her gaze shifting from Lizzy to the butler, then back to Lizzy. "Pray, Miss Steffington, I've come on a matter of some urgency and beg a private word."

Annie spoke up. "Show her into the morning room, Lizzy."

A moment later the three of them stood in an intimate circle just inside the closed door of the morning room. "Pray, Mrs. Bexley," Annie said, her brows lowered, "What is this grave matter which brings you here today?"

"First, do you know if . . . Mr. Steffington was able to collect Sir Elvin in the past half hour?"

The sisters exchanged wide-eyed stares, then Annie cleared her throat. "I can tell you with certainty that Melvin came here looking for Elvin, and we directed him to where we had reason to believe our other brother was."

"I do hope he found Sir Elvin."

"Why are you so frantic?" Annie asked.

So much for Catherine's ability to conceal her emotions. "It's a long, muddled story, but I fear one or both of your brothers may be in danger, and it's all my fault."

Lizzy cried out. "Does this have something to

do with Melvin's beating the other day?"

Catherine nodded.

"See, Annie, I told you it was *not* an unpremeditated act of violence!"

"Perhaps you'd better explain," Annie said to Catherine.

Catherine quickly sketched the details of the stolen Chaucer, the threat against Melvin, and credited Melvin with solving the crime. "Now," she concluded, "he's gone to confront Mr. Longford. I'm ever so worried about him. He gave me his word he wouldn't go without Sir Elvin."

Annie nodded. "Thank goodness! Two are much stronger—and safer—than one."

Lizzy's brows elevated. "What if that odious attacker shows up? Why, he could kill both our brothers!"

Catherine was powerless to stop her voice from cracking. "I should die if anything happened to him. He's more precious than a hundred Chaucers."

Both sisters eyed her sympathetically. "You refer to Melvin?" Annie inquired.

. Catherine, her eyes moist, met Annie's gaze and gave a somber nod.

"Well," Lizzy said, "they won't dare harm our brothers whilst we're there."

"She's right. No one would dare harm three innocent females." Annie began to stride for the door.

"I agree, but before we leave, I must send a message." Catherine eyed the little French desk. "May I?"

"Of course," both sisters said at once.

Catherine scratched out a note. "Pray, have you a servant who can deliver this to Winston

Hall?"

A smile lifted Annie's face. "Yes, of course."

Longford looked from one twin to the other, a puzzled look on his face. "How nice of you gentlemen to pay me a call. Forgive me for not recognizing which of you is Sir Elvin."

Glaring, Elvin moved toward the desk Longford stood behind. "I'm Sir Elvin."

Apparently alarmed by Elvin's stiff demeanor, Longford asked, "Is something the matter?"

Now Melvin rounded the desk and rammed himself into the thief. The top of Longford's head did not reach Melvin's shoulder. "I've come to collect Mrs. Bexley's Chaucer."

The half smile disappeared from Longford's face. His eyes widened with something akin to fright. "I have no idea what you're talking about."

Elvin directed an icy stare at Longford and spoke dryly. "My brother s not stupid."

Longford's nervous gaze flicked to Melvin. His face had gone white, and a vein throbbed at his temple. "Your intelligence is well known." The shakiness in his voice betrayed his guilt.

"Then don't expect me to believe you innocent. We can report you to the magistrate and have you arrested, but we only want the Chaucer." Melvin gripped the top of Longford's arms and easily lifted the man until their eyes were level with each other. "What you did to Mrs. Bexley is unpardonable." Melvin's guttural voice was thick with malice.

Then for the second time in the same day, something within Melvin snapped, and he hurled Longford with all his might. The man's body struck against the desk, and he cried out. Slowly, and not without wincing in pain, he turned toward Melvin, his eyes narrowed to slits, his sputtering voice weighed down with hatred. "I should have had Stockton kill you!"

That comment enraged Elvin, who whipped around the opposite side of the desk from where his twin stood. Now the sniveling Longford was wedged between the two angry twins. "How dare you threaten my brother!"

Melvin forced himself to count slowly to ten to keep the rage from obliterating his words. "You have as good as confessed to the theft by acknowledging your association with the loathsome Stockton."

Now color rose like flames in Longford's face, and his voice trembled with only barely controlled fury. "What makes you think I could possibly have stolen the manuscript?"

Melvin's eyes glittered. "How did you know it was a manuscript? All Chaucers in the world are printed—save two manuscripts. I'd say your choice of words gives away your culpability."

"Why would I stoop to common theft? I am wealthy enough to purchase anything my heart desires."

Melvin lunged toward Longford and sneered. "You cannot purchase Mrs. Bexley." Saying that made him feel as if he were the lady's champion. He'd feel even better if he could crash a fist into the bounder's face, but he was trying to act civilized.

Longford's eyes rounded.

"You meant to force her into marrying you by rendering her penniless," Melvin continued. Just thinking of the motivation behind Longford's theft enraged Melvin.

Longford cackled. "That's preposterous."

Melvin's gaze swung to Elvin. "Why don't you run along now and fetch the magistrate? I'm sure Mrs. Bexley will be happy to also give a statement about the theft."

"Wait!" Longford pleaded.

Both Steffington twins eyed him.

Footsteps shuffled beyond the closed door of Longford's library, then the door banged open. The unshaven, unkempt man standing there looked even more menacing today than he had the day he'd attacked Melvin in that alley.

Now he pointed a musket at them.

"It's loaded and ready to use, Guv'nah. Just give me the word."

Chapter 23

Melvin knew the man Longford referred to as Stockton could not kill both twins with one musket ball. While he did not fancy stopping a musket ball himself, he wasn't about to let his brother be the one to take it. He peered at Elvin, hoping like the devil he would start talking. If Stockton's gaze would shift to Elvin, Melvin might be able to disarm him.

What had he to lose?

"Which of ye twins is the one I met in the alley?" Stockton's bushy, reddish brows lowered, a cocky smirk deforming his mouth. Melvin had failed to notice the first time that the ruddy man was missing two of his front teeth.

"Don't answer!" Elvin said.

As Stockton's gaze darted to Elvin, Melvin pounced upon him. Stockton whirled toward him but not soon enough to prevent Melvin from knocking him off his feet. As he fell backward—with Melvin sprawling on top of him—the musket discharged.

What the bloody hell? Accompanying the near-deafening sound of the musket firing, Melvin could swear he heard the sound of multiple females screaming out.

Just before he landed on Stockton's barrel chest, Melvin's gaze connected with the doorway. Through the smoke that now filled the air, Mrs.

Bexley stood in the doorway like an angel rising from clouds. Good lord, this was the second time Melvin had thought her an angel.

"Oh, my poor Airy!" she cried, hurling herself toward him. "You're far more precious than a thousand priceless manuscripts."

Good lord, no one had ever said anything that flattering to him before. While he might fancy the idea of holding her in his arms once more, he wasn't about to let Stockton have the opportunity to hurt her.

It was then that he noticed two other things. Well, three actually. She gripped an umbrella in her hands even though there wasn't a cloud in the sky. And Lizzy was on one side of her, Annie on the other. All three of them clutched umbrellas. Had it started to rain?

As Mrs. Bexley flew toward him, she batted her umbrella against Stockton's scruffy face! "How dare you try to harm Mr. Steffington!"

Stockton snatched at her skirts, and she came tumbling down on top the pair of them. As she landed, Stockton's meaty hands encircled her neck. "Ya want me to take care of this woman, Guv-nah?"

"God, no!" Longford yelled. "That's the woman I intend to marry!"

Stockton's hands uncoiled. The poor angel was gasping for breath! "I. . .am . . .not ever going to marry you." Her gaze drilled at Longford.

"But you must," Longford said. "I've loved you for more than nine years. I've compared every woman against you, but no other one will ever do."

"Even had you not stolen my Chaucer, I could never marry you."

Longford stood there solemnly gazing at her. "Is there . . .someone else?"

Still eyeing Longford, she nodded.

Longford's gaze arrowed to Melvin. "You've fallen in love with a penniless man?"

"I refuse to discuss the personal details of my life with you, Mr. Longford." She still clutched at her umbrella.

It then occurred to Melvin that she and his sisters had converged upon Longford's house intending to protect him and his twin with their umbrellas!

Laughing, Melvin snatched Mrs. Bexley's umbrella and drove its sharp tip between Stockton's ribs. "That's for trying to harm this lady!"

Stockton uttered the most appalling words.

Melvin drew back on the umbrella, then jabbed it into him again. Harder this time. "How dare you use such coarse language in the presence of a very fine lady—and my two maiden sisters!"

Though Stockton tried to get up, he was unable to do so because Melvin straddled his chest. His immobility made him even angrier. The angrier he became, the more foul his language.

"I say Elvin," Melvin said, "we can't have the ladies exposed to such indelicate language."

"Then perhaps you should quit provoking him," Elvin suggested.

"I had thought instead that you could remove the ladies from this room."

Elvin's brows lowered. "And leave you here with these two pieces of excrement?"

Longford's hands fisted. "How dare you!"

Melvin chose to ignore the runt. Directing his attention at the man beneath him, Melvin said, "I know you stole a manuscript from Number 17 Royal Crescent."

"I don't know what yer talking about."

"You have two choices," Melvin said. "You can cooperate with me in order to restore the manuscript to its rightful owner, or you can rot in prison."

"Is you saying that if I 'elp you find that book, no guilt would attach to me?"

"Exactly. All we want is the book." Melvin looked at Longford. The poor fellow's humiliation was complete. "I have no desire to blacken your employer's name. We only want the book back."

Stockton's gaze locked with Longford's.

Longford nodded. "All right. I have the manuscript." He was too ashamed to meet Mrs. Bexley's gaze. He removed a key from his pocket, strode to a built-in cabinet, and unlocked its door.

Mrs. Bexley's breath hitched.

There in the lower cabinet was the oversized holograph.

"Elvin," Melvin said, "may I suggest you claim that for Mrs. Bexley?"

Elvin nodded.

Footsteps pounded on the corridor, then Thomas Moreland's large body filled the doorway, his wife, Felicity, standing behind him. "Need help?" Moreland asked.

Mrs. Bexley stood. "Thank you so much for coming. Can you help tie up that vile man beneath Mr. Steffington?"

"I say," Elvin said, "it was good of you to come, Moreland."

Melvin glared at Mrs. Bexley. "I will have you know I'm perfectly capable of fighting my own battles. I don't need assistance from three helpless females toting umbrellas! And you didn't have to send for Moreland to rescue me." How did he know she was the one who sent for Moreland? Because the connection to her was so deep he had come to understand the workings of her mind.

Then he nodded at the former nabob. "Though it was good of you to come."

Moreland nodded as he took a length of rope his wife had fetched.

Mrs. Bexley stared back at Melvin, something like malice on her pretty face. "It was not your battle! It was mine, and you've risked yourself too many times for my benefit." Her gaze flicked to Felicity's. "Thanks ever so much for allowing you husband to come, dearest." Then, tearing up, Mrs. Bexley rushed from the house.

Perplexed, Melvin met his twin's gaze and shrugged.

"Go after her, you idiot!"

Now Melvin was more perplexed than ever. Why was his brother calling him an idiot? He thought he'd executed his duties for Mrs. Bexley most admirably. It was he, after all, who had figured out who was responsible for the Chaucer theft.

Elvin frowned at him. "Even Longford could see she's in love with you!"

Dear God, could they think Mrs. Bexley was in love with him? Why, she could capture the heart of any man in the kingdom. She was . . . well, she was beautiful. And for a female, she was intelligent. She had a wonderful sense of humor. Being with her was always pleasant.

His heartbeat hammered. Could any other

woman's kisses ever bring the pleasure hers did? He would very much like to kiss her again.

But she couldn't possibly have a romantic interest in him.

Even if she did say she'd rather have him than *a thousand priceless manuscripts*. It only this minute occurred to him that her declaration had made him feel . . . like his heart was taking on the consistency of melted butter.

But, really, she couldn't have a romantic interest in him.

As soon as she sold the Chaucer, she would be a very wealthy woman. She could move within some fairly exalted circles. Surely she would have no interest in a dull stick like him.

"At least go talk to her," Elvin said.

Moreland had begun to bind Stockton's hands, and once he knotted the rope, Melvin got off Stockton's chest. "I gave this man my word that if the manuscript was recovered—and my brother is now holding the recovered holograph—he could be free."

Moreland nodded. "I shall release him after you've gone, then. He's rather out of charity with you at present."

Melvin eyed his brother. "What would I talk to her about?"

Elvin rolled his eyes.

Annie stepped up to Felicity and whispered, but not in so low a voice that Melvin couldn't make out the gist of her words, which sounded like, "I believe Mrs. Bexley's fallen in love with Melvin."

And Felicity had said, "That's the smart one, right?"

To which Annie responded with a nod.

Why did all these people think a paragon like Mrs. Bexley could fancy herself in love with him?

In all other matters, Melvin had always let probabilities dictate to him. Surely if all these people perceived that Mrs. Bexley was in love with him...His pulse pounded so rapidly it reverberated into his eardrums. Could the probability be that they were right?

Illogically, he felt as if his heart melted. Her words kept coming back to him. He was more precious than a thousand priceless manuscripts. By God, that's exactly how he felt about her!

And the more he thought of her, the more he longed to kiss her.

He cleared his throat and tossed an embarrassed glance at his twin. "I might just go . . . make sure she's . . . unharmed."

Elvin, Annie, and Felicity all exchanged amused glances.

$\mathcal{C}$hapter 24

Simpson showed him into Mrs. Bexley's library. For some unaccountable reason, his heartbeat escalated. As he moved into the chamber, she stood and faced him. The fire to her back, she was framed in its glow, and once more he thought her as angelic as she'd looked the day of his beating when he'd opened his eyes and beheld the perfection of her concerned gaze.

"I didn't bring the Chaucer," he announced with a shrug.

He thought perhaps she was disappointed when she said, "Then why have you come?"

"I wanted to see if you were all right. You fled in an awful hurry. Then I remembered that fiend trying to choke the life from you. . ." He could have murdered Stockton with his bare hands. Melvin gulped. "I was worried about you."

She held out her arms and twirled. "As you can see, I'm as good as new."

Physically, she might be as good as new, but he could tell something was bothering her. All the way here he'd practiced the words he would use when he saw her, but now that they were face to face, his mind had been wiped clean like a school child's slate.

"Won't you sit down, Mr. Steffington?" She indicated the green sofa.

He strode to it, and she sat next to him. "I liked

it better when you called me Airy," he mumbled.
Now why in the devil had he blurted out
something so nonsensical?

"But I thought you disliked it."

"I thought I did, but I find that I was
mistaken."

Her eyes danced. "Truly, Airy?"

"When it's just you and me, that is." He eyed
her. No more than one foot separated them. He
found himself desiring to close the gap because
he was possessed of an almost overwhelming urge
to haul her into his arms. What in the devil had
come over him?

His gaze switched to the fire. "My brother and
Moreland will bring the Chaucer before long. I've
instructed my brother to give Coutts whatever is
owed on this property. You can pay him back
after you sell the manuscript."

"That's very kind of Sir Elvin."

"Coutts won't bully him as they're trying to do
with you. That's you problem, Mrs. Bexley."

"What's my problem?"

"You need a man to look after you."

She sighed. "I thought I'd found an excellent
candidate for the role, but it seems he's not
interested in me that way."

"What way might you be talking about?"

"It's really too embarrassing to discuss. That's
why I fled from that odious Mr. Longford's."

He gave her a sympathetic look. "How could
someone as perfect as you ever have anything to
be embarrassed over?"

"Oh, Airy, that is so sweet of you to say! But
you—more than any man in the kingdom—know
of my abundant shortcomings."

More than any man in the kingdom? Funny

she should put it that way because he felt as if he did understand her better than any other man in the kingdom possibly could. "Thank you for acknowledging that . . . peculiar bond which unites us, but I assure you I know of no shortcomings—other than your propensity to act rashly before calculating the consequences."

Her lengthy lashes lowered. "How kind of you to say that."

He cleared his throat. "So with the recovery of the Chaucer, you will be a wealthy woman. Will you be spending more time in the Capital?" He could see her dancing with the *ton* at Almack's, being courted by aristocrats, and even remarrying. All of those prospects made him feel low. He would miss her.

"And with your fifteen percent, you won't have to go work at Stipley Hall unless that is what you truly want to do. As a man of some means, what would you enjoy most, Airy?"

He thought about it for a moment. "Nothing could bring me more pleasure than spending my days in a cozy library exactly like this one, reading and writing to my heart's content."

"I used to always think of this as Mr. Bexley's library—which made me reluctant to come here." She smiled at him. "But now I think of it as ours."

Melvin's brows lowered. "Yours and your late husband's?"

She shook her head. "No. Mine and yours. I didn't know it during those days you and I poured over those old newspapers, but since then I've longed to recapture those peaceful days of contentment."

"It's exactly the same with me!" Then he cleared his throat. "Does it not bother you that you no longer think of this chamber as your *dear Mr. Bexley's*?"

She was so silent, he feared he had upset her. "Forgive me," he said. "I didn't mean to bring up so somber a topic."

"I. . . think there's something I should tell you, but you must give me your word to tell no one."

"I give you my word."

"Mr. Bexley wasn't very dear at all."

He whirled toward her. "What can you mean?"

"Surely you know he preferred to spend his time at Mrs. Baddele's—never with me."

His eyes rounded. "Forgive me for saying it, but your *dear Mr. Bexley* was a profligate fool."

"Oh, I couldn't agree with you more."

Stunned by her revelation, he was silent for a moment. "You truly deserve to have a husband who cherishes you." He remembered her confession to Longford about loving a penniless man. "I shouldn't like to see you throw yourself away—again—on an unworthy man."

In that instant, he felt like something exploded inside of him. Dear God, could she. . . surely a woman of such perfection would not want a dull stick like him. "Pray, Mrs. Bexley. . ."

"Do you think, when it is just you and me, you could call me Catherine?"

His heartbeat accelerated. "As I was saying. . . ahem, Catherine, I don't like the idea of you throwing yourself away on an unworthy man."

"What does it matter to you?"

He turned to the dear woman. He could never tire of that lovely face. "Since that first day when my refusal caused you to cry, I seem to have appointed myself to look after you."

Her voice softened. "No one's ever treated me

with more concern."

He moved closer to her and murmured. "Would you mind if I kissed you again?" He felt if he didn't kiss her right then he would go mad from the want of it.

She answered by molding her torso to his, encircling him with her arms, and lifting her face to his.

He settled his lips over hers, softly at first, then hungrily, all thoughts rushing from his head. Only one thing mattered at that moment: the intense pleasure this delicate, adorable, loving creature was giving him.

Before he did something that might shame him, he summoned the will to stop, but he could not stop holding her against him.

Though he had no experience on which to base his assumptions, he thought perhaps she enjoyed kissing him as much as he enjoyed kissing her. Which meant there was a probability that he just might be that penniless man she fancied herself in love with. The very idea of her being in love with him made him extraordinarily happy.

"Airy? Do you think there's a probability that you could. . .ever settle down with a woman like me?"

"You know I'm a dull old stick?"

"You are not! You're the most unselfish, courageous, brilliant man I've ever known."

He couldn't help himself. He kissed her again.

"I would say there's a very high probability that I could grow old with a woman exactly like you," he murmured between nibbling kisses.

&pilogue

Six months later. . .

All of her dearest friends had returned to Bath and were to gather here at the Assembly Rooms tonight. It was the first time since she and Airy had married that they would see Glee and Blanks. Not that Catherine had seen them yet. In fact, she hadn't even seen Airy since they walked in the door half an hour previously. He'd gone off to the card room to see his brother.

She had brought Annie as well as her own sister, whom she would be presenting in London soon—now that she was a lady of means. The girls were both the same age, got on famously, and were both looking for the ideal suitor. Her fondest hope was that each of them could find a true love as wonderful as Airy.

The very thought of how complete her life was now that she'd united with the finest man in all of England caused her insides to flutter. Each time Airy's amused gaze met hers, she fluttered anew. The connection between them was extraordinary. Not that her dear husband was able to articulate his feelings about how close they were. Incapable of speaking of his love for her, he *showed* his love with his frequent displays of concern, with his desire to be with her above all others, with the physical intimacy that neither of them ever tired of.

She felt as if she'd never lived before Airy slipped that gold band upon her finger that magical day at Bath Cathedral.

Glee, on the arm of her handsome Blanks, breezed up to where Catherine sat. Promptly getting to her feet, Catherine and Glee hugged, and Glee began to gush about how happy she was that two of her favorite people had married. Then she turned to Blanks. "Do go find Mr. Steffington."

Blanks dutifully left the two ladies alone to continue their conversation. "I always knew Melvin would make someone a wonderful husband, but I cannot imagine him ever actually proposing marriage. It seemed *that* part of his personality was never properly formed."

Catherine giggled. "That is so true. I'm still not precisely certain how it came to pass that we were able to convey to one another our desire to marry, to never be parted. I would have to say it was a proposal by a committee of two."

"I love that!" Glee's head looked to the left, then right. "Is it true what Felicity told me about Longford?"

"I don't like to speak of it, but it is true." Now that time had passed and so much happiness had been bestowed upon her, she held no rancor, only pity for the misguided man.

"He should be in prison!"

"He's paying for his crime in other ways. He's so humiliated, he's left Bath and will never show his face in London, either. I feel sorry for him." Then Catherine smiled at Glee. "I must congratulate you on producing a little Blanks."

Glee's lashes lowered. "I had help." Then she

looked up and smiled. "I know he's mine, but baby Gregory is the most perfect little boy, though I can't express that opinion in front of Felicity. She thinks their three sons are all perfection."

Catherine placed a hand over the almost imperceptible swell of her midsection. "I do hope ours is son."

Glee's eyes widened. "I had no idea you were breeding. . . I thought- -"

"You thought I was incapable because my first marriage produced no children." She too had thought she would never bear a child, and now she was excited enough about the impending event to shout it from the spire of Bath Cathedral.

"It truly won't matter if it's a girl or boy. You and Melvin will adore either one."

"Surprisingly, Melvin's wonderful with girls and boys both. He's never shy with what he calls little people." As she spoke, she saw Melvin moving toward her, his eyes never leaving her.

He bid good evening to Glee, then addressed Catherine. "I've come to claim Mrs. Steffington for the waltz."

She adored to hear herself addressed as Mrs. Steffington.

On the dance floor, he asked, peering down at her with concern, "Are you certain it won't disturb the babe for you to dance?"

"I am certain."

He squeezed her hand.

"I've been thinking, Airy."

"Heaven help me. . ."

"Do you realize your new book will be out the same month next summer as our babe?"

"It's not really my book. I just translated it from the original Greek."

"It will have your name on it, and I shall be inordinately proud of my brilliant husband."

"I pray you never speak like that to others."

"Only to those whose last name is Steffington. Your siblings are as proud of you as I am."

"I was just thinking about the first time we danced together in this very chamber. That afternoon—in our library—you had asked me to come that night. Why?"

"I didn't understand it, but I knew you were the only one I ever wanted to dance with."

"It's the same with me. You're the only one I ever want to be with. Ever."

He may not have used the word *love*, but he didn't have to. No woman could be loved more, nor could any woman love more than she loved her Airy.

The End

Author's Biography

A former journalist who, in her own words, has "a fascination with dead Englishwomen," Cheryl Bolen is the award-winning author of more than a dozen historical romance novels set in Regency England, including *Marriage of Inconvenience, My Lord Wicked*, and *A Duke Deceived*. Her books have received numerous awards, such as the 2011 International Digital Award for Best Historical Novel and the 2006 Holt Medallion for Best Historical. She was also a 2006 finalist in the Daphne du Maurier for Best Historical Mystery. Her works have been translated into eleven languages and have been Amazon.com bestsellers. Bolen has contributed to *Writers Digest* and *Romance Writers Report* as well as to the Regency era–themed newsletters *The Regency Plume, The Regency Reader*, and *The Quizzing Glass*. The mother of two grown sons, she lives with her professor husband in Texas.

Made in the USA
San Bernardino, CA
26 January 2014